KING OF SORROW
James Fouché

www.jamesfouche.com
@james_fouche

Cover design by Paul Yates-Round of
www.absurdgestureonline.com

The ineffaceable, sad birth-mark in the brow of man, is but the stamp of sorrow in the signers.

from "The Whale" by Herman Mellville

And the name of the dark forest was Sorrow; but of the vision that the good knight saw therein we may not speak nor tell.

from "Three men and a boat" by Jerome K Jerome

I have learned to love the darkness of sorrow, for it is there that I see the brightness of God's face.

Madame Guyon

INTRODUCTION

The air smelled fresh and flowery, almost sweet. The salty presence of the sea was faintly detectable in the air, lingering in the nose for a long time. It was a summery smell, a happy smell, the type memories were made of.

David closed his eyes and listened to the world. The sound of constant traffic, cars coming and going, the occasional car horn, and the discernible noise of rubber on tar was a constant therapeutic drone. Then there was the gentle chatter of birds, a cacophony of chirps and whistles so brilliantly orchestrated by nature that no musical genius could copy it.

Elizabeth smiled shyly when his eyes were on her.

Her eyes, hidden behind sunglasses, were peaceful. Looking at her, he still found it hard to believe that she was the mother of the two boys in the backseat behind them. It didn't seem possible. Yet, there they were. Two strapping lads, healthy and perfect.

"So, do you like driving?" David asked.

"You should let me drive more often."

"You drive the kids to school every day."

Elizabeth was still smiling. "That's *so* different."

David unclipped his seatbelt and looked at the boys. "It's not different, is it boys?" he asked, winking at them.

Both boys shook their heads from side to side and giggled, saying, "No, no, it's not."

A few years ago, when they had been tiny lumps of flesh, either of the boys would have barely fit into his hands. Now they were on the express train to manhood. They were his reason for living and his ambition for providing.

"See, it's not different at all. Besides, the king should drive his family around, don't you think?"

"But you always get to drive. Sit back and enjoy the scenery, your highness. You need this holiday more than we do. And put on your seatbelt."

He leaned back into the seat and prepared himself for the beach. Elizabeth was right. He really needed this holiday. The last eighteen months had been stressful beyond comparison. This was his time away from the office and he was sure to make the most of it.

If only he had planned the trip better, he would've been able to get accommodation on the beachfront. No driving. He disliked driving. But it was summer – the silly season. All the best spots were taken.

Elizabeth guided the Jaguar along the winding road, down the mountainside, towards the beachfront. It was a long and narrow road with colourful, aromatic shrubs growing wildly on either side, as was the norm in Cape Town when summer broke.

"Can you put this in the cubby?" she asked, holding out a CD cover. "It's rattling here in this side panel."

David took the CD cover from her, but fumbled with it, accidentally dropping it between her legs. She glanced down for a millisecond. At that precise moment, a Land Rover, which had been racing up the steep hill, veered into her lane. There was no time to react.

Before the silence ended, life had been complete. The world was turning as it should, ants scurrying around in the underbrush in search of food, birds flipping through the air, and the concept of tragedy and pain not part of his world.

There was the sound of tyres screeching, followed by a loud crash. On impact the Land Rover glanced away, scraped along the side of the Jaguar, and pushed it off the road. The car shuddered all over and David's door swung open. Elizabeth tried to regain control, but the steering wheel was unresponsive. The Jaguar skidded sideways across the road and burst through the demarcation barrier. David was flung from the car as it became airborne, ripped out of his seat, momentarily suspended in the air, looking up at the Jaguar in flight. He hit the ground hard and was rendered powerless. He saw the weight of the engine pulling the Jaguar's nose down, the earth curling over as it ploughed into the side of the hill, the tumbling mass of metal twisting and bouncing as it rolled down the steep slope, then slamming into a tree.

The last thing he remembered was the smell of fire, the screams.

CHAPTER 1

05:22.

Morning did not arrive abruptly with the blaring of an alarm clock. The element of surprise was nonexistent in this life. A highly defined sense of anticipation ruined every day for her. She lay there looking at the clock radio. It seemed to be standing on the bedside table with a smirk on its plastic face, taunting her. The glowing red numbers burned in the dark.

05:27.

05:28.

05:29.

She waited for the clock radio to start buzzing before switching off the alarm. 05:30. Time to rise. She had to get ready. She still had to shave today. It's been five days already. People were starting to notice.

Why was she dreading each day as if she knew something bad was waiting to happen? Why was there a lingering feeling of apprehension when she woke up each morning? She tried to recall her dreams of last night. It was just a little too overwhelming before coffee. She forced her eyes shut and gently massaged her temples.

In the bathroom, she hoisted a leg into the air with some difficulty and slung the other over the edge of the bath for support. She shaved her legs with soap and a blunt razor, using very little warm water to save electricity.

The bathroom was small. Even with shiny white tiles and shocking white paint thrown on by the landlord, the room could not appear bigger. A man would have difficulty urinating because the washbasin had been situated opposite the toilet, and one could only use the toilet sitting down. There was no place to stand. Next to the toilet was a bath that could accommodate either one's legs or upper torso, but not both simultaneously. That was it. That was the entire bathroom.

By 06:10 she was dressed in fairly comfortable clothing: comfortable suede slip-ons, blue jeans, black shirt. She looked like a million other people in those clothes. Like a waitress.

Dillon stammered out of the bedroom. His blonde hair stood in every direction and his face was puffed up with sleep. Though only six years old, he looked irritable. He rubbed lazily at one eye, clearing away the sleep, then yawned shamelessly.

She stood in the kitchen and watched him with a sense of pride. She'd bought those blue and beige pyjamas almost two weeks ago with some extra tip money. He looked so adorable, like a giant teddy bear. As Dillon made his way toward the toilet, she continued with breakfast.

She moved in a machine-like manner. She had done this numerous times without any deviation. This had become her norm. There had been no choice in the matter. This was her life and she now had to live it.

By the time Megan finally came out of the bedroom, the breakfast was ready. Monday morning breakfast consisted of warm Oats with syrup and a drop or two of lemon juice – when the fridge could afford to stock lemon juice. The kitchen table was also the open-plan working area so there was only space for two chairs.

Megan was the first at the table, with Dillon in hot pursuit.

"Morning," she whispered when they were within earshot.

"Morning," they greeted back in a unified voice.

"Sleep well?"

"Like a tree," Megan whispered back in a huffy voice. "Even with this snoring monster sleeping next to me." She pointed at her younger brother and made a loud snoring sound.

She was two years older than Dillon, but she was so much more mature already. Eight years old and already she was comfortable to take up certain responsibilities when her mother was working.

"No I don't. I'm too young," he said, then added, "You snore."

Both youngsters hoisted themselves unto the high chairs and assumed positions behind the steaming bowls, salivating without even realizing it. They said a quick rambled prayer and commenced eating while their mother watched over them. This little family was all she had. She spent so little time with them. She really wanted to make the most of these precious moments, but couldn't. The harder she tried to commit herself to her children, the harder the world pressed in on them. It felt as though there was a surprise around every corner. She found herself fighting back every second of every day. She was trying her best as a single parent, but everyone had a limit, especially mothers. She dreaded what the future would hold for them.

In many ways Megan looked exactly like her mother. She was a brunette, had shoulder-length hair, deep brown eyes and a confident demeanour. She was such a strong-willed girl and so disciplined. Looking at her daughter, she remembered exactly where and when she had lost her own once-confident attitude. It seemed like decades ago, a distant memory in a far-off place.

"Am I missing breakfast again?" Margie hissed from behind the two munching children.

"Morning gran!" Megan exclaimed.

Dillon tried to greet his grandmother but, instead, he spat out some form of acknowledgement in broken English, followed by bits of oats flying over the countertop.

"Morning," she said as she took out a bowl for Margie.

"Don't worry about me," Margie said and pushed her way into the small kitchen. She took the bowl from her daughter's hands and spooned a meagre helping of oats into it. "I might be old, but I'm not dead yet."

From granddaughter to grandmother, she found herself in the middle of an unrelenting life cycle wherein the young grew old, a familial timeline of sorts. She was constantly reminded about where she had come from and where she was going.

Looking at Margie, she saw the mounting of years on her mother's face. Age sometimes revealed itself in more ways than the eye could see. Sure, the wrinkles on Margie's forehead and her thinning hair were physical proof that she was no longer in her forties. Sure, she no longer jumped up and down when she was excited and she complained about gout when it was cold. However, age did something to the spirit, something that was invisible, something more sensed than seen. It was a subtle exchange projected in the silent interaction between humans.

Lately, though, she could see the invisible. When she looked into Margie's eyes, she could literally see her mother's age. She could make out the years and the heartache and the pain and the joys and the memories. They were right there on the surface of her soul, like stains on clothing or scars on flesh.

What worried her, was the fact that Megan and Dillon would one day sense time withering away in her, when Granny Margie was no longer around and they had their own children to compare with their ageing mother.

"How is the gout this morning?" she asked her mother.

"I'll live," Margie said, then changed the subject. "Why don't you finish with yourself. I'll clean up the kitchen and get the kids ready."

"Thanks."

She stepped out of the kitchen and looked at the three people in her life. Margie, Megan and Dillon. She instantly became overwhelmed by a complex blend of emotions. She felt contemplative, but knew that there would never be time for her to indulge in contemplation or reflection. This was it.

"Kerin," Margie said softly and took her daughter's hand in her own.

Kerin snapped out of her daze and looked at her mother.

"Are you alright?"

"Yes, mom," Kerin lied.

He was on an airplane again. He felt it before he remembered it. There was a buoyant quality to his surroundings, as if he was floating in the sea. And the earthy smell of peanuts. Someone always kept peanuts in their carry-on luggage. A thin film of perspiration had formed on his forehead and his hands felt clammy. The temperature stayed regulated and he felt a hint of claustrophobia.

He had dozed off mid-flight. Sleeping on a plane was new to him. But, the last three months the sheer monotony of flying from here to there had tired him out so much that he no longer cared. Soon it would be over.

The slight tilting to the one side, then the compensating tilt to the other side indicated that they were getting ready to land. He braced himself for the announcement.

"Well, folks, we will be landing in the next ten minutes," a gentle male voice said over the intercom system. "If you look out your windows you will see the clouds have cleared up. To your right you can see Table View beach. Cape Town is a cool eighteen degrees and the wind is blowing, so have your jackets handy. Please keep your seat in the upright position and put your seatbelts back on."

David loved that pilots and hostesses mentioned a successful flight prior to the actual landing, when the majority of airplane crashes occur on takeoff or landing.

As the wheels touched the ground and the plane shuddered, just for that one terrible second, he pictured himself in his army camouflage. He felt the weight of the long-range rifle in his hands, saw the figure on the other end of the scope. The image was burned into his mind. He had to blink a few times to clear it away. It had been many years and he still couldn't shake that mental picture, that ever-present flash of death.

His bag was the first on the runner. Rule of thumb: last on, first off. Though David was a patient man, he opted for a quick escape from airports to avoid family reunions.

He picked up his bag and fetched his car. The Land Rover was waiting in the airport parking area. It had been parked there yesterday, the parking arrangements made by someone from the office.

David arrived, swiped a card and went his way. That was what he did. He was a property investor and developer. People were paid to arrange things for him so that his time could be used doing what others dreamt of doing but weren't able to do.

The traffic from the airport to the CBD was lighter than usual and the city itself seemed quieter in the sense that there was hardly any traffic. He wondered whether the taxis were on strike again. However light the traffic proved to be, the streets were still packed with thousands of people on their way to and from work, like ants patrolling the border between monotony and mandatory.

It was already 09:30 on a Monday morning. He had a meeting at ten, and was making good time. He despised being late. After that he had three more meetings, keeping him busy until late that evening. That was how he lived this part of his life. David Harlem the businessman. Tailored suit and jacket, no tie. He disliked wearing ties. Land Rover at the airport. Smart phone in his pocket. No more.

For years David had struggled with the authority of his position. He struggled with the money he made and the power money had over the people around him. How many people could own three Land Rovers and keep them on stand-by across South Africa? Who could frequent five-star resorts or hotels anywhere in the world and not even bother to do the breakfast buffet? How many people could buy a farm just to get away from the city? How many people could have all this luxury and be prepared to give it all up in a second?

David knew his place in the bigger scheme of things. He was but a man, nothing more. Anonymous donations from his portfolio alone amounted to millions of Rands every year. A charitable man by nature, he often humbled himself to the extreme by buying someone a car or a house for no reason whatsoever. He had endured far too much in his life not to appreciate the frailty or senselessness of it all.

At times David despised his wealth, yet his good fortune knew no end. The more money he gave away, the more returns he made on investments, both personal and commercial. In his personal capacity, he was a millionaire a number of times over. In the business world, his company was a powerful entity. He had built Harlem Properties from scratch. There was something to be said about humble beginnings.

David had realized early on that he needed two things to penetrate the property business: a lot of debt and a stable cash flow to maintain the debt. When he joined the army, he invested in two small flats on a whim. He rented out both properties, offering up the lease agreements to the bank as surety. His state salary and the monthly rental was paid directly into the bond accounts. Four years later his army life ended and he used his small pension fund savings to settle the balance owing on the properties. Then the fun began.

He earned a decent salary as a guest house manager on an estate, free accommodation included. He pushed everything into the bond, forcing himself to live on the breadline for as long as he could. He lived on a staple diet of Pro-Vitas, rice and pastas. Soup nights: a bottle of ketch-up to two bottles of warm water, served with bread. The temptation was always there to spend haphazardly and to dine in luxury, but he had purpose and determination. He had a vision – and he persevered.

Within two years he had four properties, no debt. He had struck during one of SA's largest property booms. He was ready to get the ball rolling on Harlem Properties, so he left the guesthouse. The four tenants provided a steady cash flow and the growing value of the properties served as collateral. That gave him bargaining power.

He opened a small office and set up shop. First on board was Raymond Gallagher, a property whizz and David's mentor. Ray was a source of wisdom, teaching David all the ins and outs of the industry.

David set up a trust for Harlem Properties, registering each new property as a separate business entity with its own bank account. It began as an uncomplicated process, but ten years later the trust portfolio included two small shopping complexes, five factories and a number of residential properties. The maintenance and management of the buildings were contracted out to other companies. Eventually there was a need to form a board of directors, opening the company to independent investors.

The ball hadn't stopped rolling since. Harlem Properties now had more than 60 properties throughout SA. The books showed a healthy cash flow and debt record. Many properties still had active bond accounts which were in a constant state of flux as contributions were made. As majority shareholder and president of the trust, David was obligated to take out key-individual insurance policies which would settle all accounts at death. These policies were ceded to the corresponding financial institutions and updated annually. The insurance premiums were astronomical and necessary expenses.

David had no idea which properties formed part of Harlem Properties' portfolio. It was virtually impossible to keep track of the purchases and sales. The board decided which properties would stay or go. That's why he had chosen a diverse board of directors. All decisions were made in the best interest of the company. David concentrated on the development of vacant land, rezoning of residential properties and commercial interests.

But when Elizabeth died, everything changed. His involvement in the company became far less mandatory. He no longer made decisions. He was an absent source of advice, only called upon when needed. He travelled the world, sharing his experience with Third World countries. All the while his company continued to grow in his absence. And now he was back.

With all the successes in mind, David had decided that his time in the industry had reached its end. It was time to step down and to get out. His work had been the driving force to conquering his sorrows. He had successfully buried his past and it was time to reboot his life. It was time to take chances and to make mistakes and to learn and grow and love, all over again. It was time to live life, time to sell it all and start over.

The only cause for concern was the ripple effect that would occur within his company and the whirlwind that was to follow his decisions. These things never worked out well. Starting a company was like putting a train into gear and applying the power. One cart pulls or pushes all the other cars, one solitary engine moving a gigantic hunk of metal along the lines. It starts slow, crawling along the tracks for the first part, but then it gains momentum.

Finally it becomes an unstoppable mass sailing along the countryside when everyone else is fast asleep and the world is unaware of its progress. Only those maintaining it and those with a desire to get on or climb off has any interest in what happens. David knew all too well that a train doesn't just stop. There are repercussions. Selling the entire company was the only way to successfully step off the train and give it to someone else, but what about the rest of the people who had helped building the company? Human nature was an unpredictable thing. It had a boomerang effect.

When the elevator doors slid open on the fourth floor, William Botes was there to greet him. His face lit up with excitement as David stepped off the elevator.

William was still a young man, thirty-five next month. He was clever, enthusiastic, ambitious, and eager to please. He was also an adrenaline junkie, speed-cycling through his gym's spinning sessions at five in the morning and hiking Table Mountain on the weekends. His appearance was smooth and very elegant, and his well-built physique caused his expensive suit to appear a bit too small for him.

Ten years ago, David had encountered the young man at a meeting in Pretoria. At the time William had formed part of centre management at a small shopping complex Harlem Properties were optioning. David had taken such a liking to William's unbridled and inquisitive nature, that he had offered the man a job on the spot. Since then, he had found a worthy general in William. Early last year, after a unanimous vote of the board, he had appointed William the new CEO of Harlem Properties, giving him carte blanche to all operations of the company. In turn, David had peace of mind that his company would carry on without his presence required at the helm. Though the appointment of a new CEO had been a necessity, it had also been a mere formality. David had never esteemed corporate titles and rather opted for an open-table approach in the boardroom. He was still the President with majority rule over all the members. Ultimately he had the final say, but after the accident he had to distance himself from his own creation.

William greeted David with a firm handshake and an easy smile.

"Welcome back. You had your coffee?"

David nodded.

"Good to hear. Come."

William led the way.

"Is everyone here?"

"Everyone except Parker."

David tried to hide his irritation with Ashraf Parker's decision to ignore the meeting.

"His secretary said he was busy in South America somewhere."

Over the last couple of years, Parker had been a constant source of annoyance to the company and the other members of the board. However, Parker's vote on the board was so small that it really didn't matter whether he sat in on the meeting or not.

"But everyone else is here?"

"Yes. They're a little freaked out, though."

"Why's that?" David asked as he stepped into the office.

"You know, people talk."

"Talk?"

David walked up to the reception desk and gave Jocelynne his warmest smile.

"Morning, gorgeous! You missed me?"

Jocelynne angled her head upward so that she could see properly with her powerful bi-focals. When she recognized David, she threw her hands in the air. The fifty-something secretary loved her job a bit too much. She was always excessively made up with colours that didn't compliment her features, and she always wore clothing which seemed to over-accentuate her bust. She was also a mother of three, all of them already out the house and accomplished professionals in the world. She was, and would always be, a good woman, and that made today a particularly difficult day. For many years Jocelynne had welcomed him to the office. She was an integral component to Harlem Properties.

"Well, hello stranger," she called out in the husky voice of a chain-smoker.

"You going to join us this morning? To take minutes?"

"Wouldn't miss it for the world." She leaned forward in acknowledgement, revealing too much of her ever-expanding cup size.

David quietly shuddered, turned back to William, who raised his eyebrows in agreement, and started down one corridor.

"That's a special kind of woman," he whispered.

"Yet she had softened many a business deal in that reception area just by being herself," William contributed.

"That's why I hired her. You can't fake sincerity."

David stopped in the middle of the office and looked at the machine he had built from scratch. Harlem Properties consisted of eight smaller offices, four over-looking the traffic of the Cape Town CBD, a boardroom where most of the business meetings took place, and Jocelynne's reception area. It was not much to look at, but this was the nature of the beast. Besides the members of the board, the company only employed twenty-odd people, scarcely fluctuating by more than five people at any given moment, and required very little office space as most business was done off site. Once a property was invested in, all that was left was for the property to be maintained and managed properly. Even with a sizeable portfolio, there was very little groundwork for foot soldiers. Buying and selling decisions were always done by the members of the board. A small number of agents made up the marketing wing and received windowless offices for their efforts. Two ladies tended to administrative duties and a third lady named Wendy was the personal assistant to the members of the board, resembling a chairman in any normal company but not reporting to anyone other than David or William. Most of the legal and maintenance responsibilities were outsourced to independent companies or attorneys, who were eager to be in good standing with Harlem and his team.

"Talking, you say? What about?"

"You called a short-notice meeting, David. People talk merger. They talk expansion, restructuring. They talk sale."

"People will always talk, William. It's human nature."

Before William could respond, David's cell interrupted their conversation.

They made their way to the boardroom.

David prepared himself. This was the meeting of all meetings. It would be one of the shortest meetings Harlem Properties had ever had, yet it would be the most memorable. Everyone was there. They were all waiting for him, all anxious, confused, and speculative. Some people could be vigilant to the point of endangering themselves and others could be quietly vindictive. When facing a board of directors, co-ordinators and upper management, a clenched jaw and a disguised smirk could divide an empire and form factions. It was the duty of the king to take note, to rule his kingdom.

"You are but a man. You are but a man," he whispered softly.

The big rosewood doors parted in front of him as he ended the call with Linden Sendiwe on his phone. It felt as though he was parting the waters and stepping into the unknown. Today was the day.

Every chair around the large desk was filled, except for the one where Parker should have been seated. An array of suits lined the desk on either side, with the exception of two skirts with tight dress jackets, totalling a number of twelve individuals present at the meeting. On the desk stood two water jugs and glasses for drinking. Some of the people had notepads out and others had their phones or tablets out.

"Good morning, gentlemen." David glanced briefly at Annabeth Girland and Josie Vermeulen, offering them a warm smile. "And ladies," he added, and they smiled.

He was a pleasant man. Everyone respected him and he cautioned himself not to abuse that respect. Those who didn't respect him, envied him.

The minutes of the meeting opened when Jocelynne joined them, tablet in hand. So began what would be one of the last board meetings of the Harlem Properties Group. It was a brief announcement so perfectly executed that there was little room for discussion or objection. Everything was going as he had rehearsed it.

"You cannot do this!" a pitched voice exclaimed when he had finished.

"It's been done, Ray."

Raymond Gallagher looked at Damian Motlante for support, but he saw that he was on his own. His face was even more puffed up and his eyes were wide with alarm. At last Ray's eyes fell on William Botes and peered at him in a manner of judgement, as if the young CEO had been the reason for this meeting, but William didn't flinch. Ray's gray beard stubble appeared to turn whiter than normal as his face became red with rage.

"It's not a good time now. We are ... We ..." Ray looked around the room for help from his colleagues. He looked like someone who was drowning. He gasped for air.

David had anticipated a revolt or an objection, but Raymond Gallagher was hardly worth any concern. Ray was a good man who lived for business. His wife had died many years ago and the company was all he had. Though he was overly passionate about the motion to sell the company while at its peak, David knew that in time Ray would come to appreciate the decision. Besides, the settlement of the sale would be so lucrative that few people would be able to oppose it without raising suspicions.

"Ray, my good old friend," David said in a warm tone. "Someone once told me that the most important lesson in business is to be the first one to get in and the first one to get out, to time and to strategize your exit." He leaned forward for emphasis. "You told me that over a cup of coffee almost fifteen years ago. You remember that?"

"Dammit, Harlem! You're gonna give me another heart attack with this nonsense." Ray shook his head in disbelief. His concern for retirement had been made known to everyone around the table over the years, and everyone present realized that Ray now had a personal battle to fight: old age. "You can't sell. You can't." Ray appeared to be instantly exhausted, like an old hunter who had the wind taken out of him. "I want to see figures first. Get it to make sense on paper."

"The figures are already on your desks or in your mail boxes. The details of the acquisition and the finer details are all included in the paperwork. An internal audit will be done this month and so will a valuation on all assets and buildings. Our future contracts will need verification and a detailed listing of investments has to be drawn up. This information should be made available throughout the month as well."

For a long time no one said a word.

"Then so it is. It's been done," Ray said softly and rose up from his seat. He pushed his chair back into place, keeping his head bowed to avoid eye contact. His movements were slow and methodical. He was now a retired old man of sixty-seven, a senior citizen. "If you'll excuse me, I have some matters to tend to." Gracefully he vacated the room, leaving a sullen silence in his wake.

David leaned forward on the desk and sighed. It's been done.

CHAPTER 2

There had been virtually no sun for five days. On the odd occasion a bit of sun broke through, even then thick purple clouds would roam the outermost extremes of the landscape, rolling in at a sedated pace. For now, though, the rains had temporarily abated.

This suited Kerin just fine. Walking in the rain had become rather unpleasant. The taxis only moved between Oswald Pirow and Long Street, which meant she had to hike up the steep hill leading up to the apartment building where they lived. It took her 25 minutes uphill to get to work and 20 minutes downhill to get home again. Twenty-five minutes might be a breeze to some, but in pelting rains with no umbrella even five minutes was pushing it. She also couldn't get to work with wet hair again - she couldn't get sick now. She relied on tips.

The overcast appearance of her surroundings was made worse by post recessionary signs of hardship. Grass was just a bit longer than usual, paint was flaking where revamps were due, gutters were loose or noticeably clogged up with weeds.

But within this dilapidation life was still a relentless reality. No matter how pressing circumstances, food still had to find its way to the centre of the table at supper time. Life had to carry on.

Kerin found herself going from day to day and barely coping. She was divorced in an age where marriage was just a piece of paper. She was a single parent in a world where women had fought hard for their independence and their rights, but now seemed indecisive about what to do and where to do it.

Hers was not a conventional sadness which normally ended up being carried around for a while before dissipating when the mood changed. She also did not wear her sadness like a mask. No, this was an inner sadness, a bitter sadness. There was something behind those deep blue eyes. There lay a longing within her, lurking where it was difficult to see anything. Her wounds also lay hidden away from the rest of the world.

At work, she kicked into gear. She shut the world out of her mind and concentrated on her livelihood. If she brought her worries with her to work, her children would never eat and they would not have a place to live. She couldn't make those payments anymore.

Before long the orders were streaming in and she was spinning. She had been doing this for almost two years and still she couldn't cope with the sheer madness. Her bay only had four tables and they were turning slower than the others. She refrained from engaging in idle conversations with clients but she also had to try and up her tips. She had become immune to the alluring smell of fresh coffee and she despised her green uniform. It was an unflattering colour and it made her look even older. She hated her job. She hated her life. She hated her circumstances.

The tray tipped sideways in slow motion. She saw the two cups of coffee sliding to one side, the coffee and the milk streaming over the tray and mixing mid-air, the cups and plate shattering and the last jumbo cranberry muffin bouncing down the aisle amidst a hail of ceramic shards. *No money means no food*, she reminded herself. *No money, no food.*

For the last two weeks she had been working twelve-hour shifts every other day. Technically working that number of hours as a waitress wasn't legal, but she was desperate. At first she had begged the managers for more shifts, but they had been reluctant to give her more because she struggled with the tables. Whenever someone cancelled a shift, she had jumped on it before the other waiters, but then the managers had decided to allocate shifts in order to make it fair on everyone. And then, when Thumbile had her baby, Kerin stepped in and grabbed all her shifts. That meant doubles every other day. She had chosen to burn herself out just to make last month's rent. She couldn't accumulate any more debt.

She diligently waited on her tables, collected orders at the coffee bar and frequented the kitchen drop-off where dishes were placed, moving to and fro in a disciplined manner while trying hard not to notice the look of pity in the eyes of her colleagues. She didn't need their pity, because pity had no value. Her children needed money and security.

Tonight he stayed at the Cullinan Hotel. It would just be for Monday and Tuesday evening, then off to Johannesburg where he had to stay over a couple of days to finalize the sale and all the accompanying paperwork. He dreaded the trip to Gauteng. The place irritated him.

David poked the bedside clock. It was only minutes after eight and he was sitting on his bed, staring at the clock, waiting.

His meeting with Sendiwe had been a ruthless affair and he was spent. For years Linden Sendiwe and his Elixir Holdings had been trying to bully Harlem into nonexistence. As President and CEO of Elixir, Sendiwe had become known in the media as a shark, and justifiably so. The man's nature was to take and destroy; to rip companies apart and break down the competition whenever possible. However, Elixir Holdings was not just met with resistance in the marketplace, but had to face the competitive growth from an independent trader like Harlem. This had obviously left a bitter aftertaste in Sendiwe's mouth. Many times Elixir had lost contracts to Harlem Properties and every time Sendiwe had been visibly enraged by the fact that David was a fly that he simply could not swat. Sendiwe had openly tried every possible trick in the book to keep Harlem from attaining success. His monopolizing antics included bribes to service providers, contractors, distributors and developers, not to mention leaking bogus information to the media. Nothing worked. The more unethical Sendiwe became, the more profitable and naturally competitive David's became. His machine fed on Sendiwe's pride and his rage, and it became a successful machine.

Then everything changed. News of Harlem's decision to sell had reached Sendiwe's ears within the hour and before long his nemesis had urged a meeting. The shark had smelled blood and now he was hungry.

"I will kill it, Harlem," he had told David while toying with the food on his plate, the same way a shark would toy with a baby seal. "You know I will."

"That depends who I sell it to."

"I don't care who you sell your company to. If I can't have it, no one will have it."

That had been the end of the meeting. David had always responded well to threats and the meeting with Sendiwe had not been any different. He had simply smiled an all-knowing smile, then politely excused himself from the table. That had been the end to Sendiwe and his corrupted Elixir Holdings, or so David thought.

Now, alone in the Hotel suite, he still sat looking at the bedside clock. It wouldn't stop. Time simply kept ticking away. He felt like pressing the pause button on his life, but knew this was out of his hands. Besides, he was aware that power such as that would be intoxicating beyond his control. He also knew that he would be too tempted to go back in time and change the past. This, of course, would have consequences.

Unfortunately things were exactly the way they were meant to be. He never pretended to understand the mysterious ways of life. He never claimed to know why HIV, hunger and malaria killed so many people every year, or why violence was rampant in the streets, or why the Land Rover had been driving so fast that morning. David firmly believed that sometimes not knowing certain details to the intricacies which made up our existence was also for the better. He *had* to believe this, otherwise he would've gone insane.

David forced his mind to shut down. It was just too early to go to bed. How long could someone sleep before growing tired of being tired all the time? But what else would he possibly do? There was a beautiful bar downstairs, but he disliked alcohol. There was a piano on the small stage, but he couldn't play it. Then there was a very active city life where anything could happen, but that did not appeal to him tonight.

The reality was that these moments of silence were very precious to him, or that had always been the case. Normally his mind and body longed for the quiet and the peace, yet tonight he felt unrest. That feeling of muted disquiet had been born to him a couple of weeks ago, after he had decided to sell everything.

He opened the patio sliding door just enough to let the constant hum of traffic and the buzz of people waft up to where he stood overlooking the busy streets.

Cape Town was such a beautiful place, yet he loathed coming here. No matter how well he hid the memory, the site and the mention of Cape Town brought every awful thing back in a heartbeat.

He closed the sliding door and enjoyed the silence once again as he went back into the room.

There was just one complication to the concept of peace, a mandatory side-effect to being David Harlem, and that was the emotional weight of solitude. Evidently this obstacle could not be overcome by any amount of reasoning or personal debate. No matter how hard he tried to sugar-coat his private life, he had to admit that there was a vacant hole he could not fill. He was alone. He was completely and utterly alone, and he felt alone every damnable second he spent by himself. He missed Elizabeth and the kids. He was incomplete. And there was nothing he could do about it. The walls around him couldn't speak when everyone went home at the end of the day. The tables and chairs couldn't hold him when the day was over. The night couldn't swallow the loneliness and the moon could not lighten his load. It was his ever-present burden, his personal sorrow.

Tomorrow held only meetings with accountants and lawyers. It would be a taxing experience, finalizing the figures and contracts as far as the sale was concerned. *What happens then?* he wondered.

He could not answer this terrifying question, but something about what he was doing felt perfectly fine. He sensed a storm before the eventual calm, but it certainly felt right.

Sendiwe was fuming. For what seemed like an hour, he sat looking at the scraps on his plate. He wanted to jump up from his chair, kick the table over and punch a hole in the wall. He wanted blood. However, after years of saying the wrong thing at the wrong moment or doing the wrong thing in the wrong way, he had learned to hide his true feelings.

David had left him sitting at the table on his own. It took a lot of courage to leave Linden Sendiwe to pick up the bill. Money was clearly not the problem. It was the principle of the thing. No one ever left the table before him. He was power and ruthlessness personified, and he knew it. In fact, he flaunted it.

Then David Harlem came along and defied the natural order of things. He was supposed to be submissive, afraid, or even just appreciative of the fact that Sendiwe had called the meeting.

The big man rolled his neck in a slow circle, his eyes shut. His chiropractor had tried many times to remove the tension building up in his neck, but without success. Finally the pain had been described as a constant mounting pressure point caused by bad posture. He didn't care about his posture, his weight, his height or his incessant snoring. It meant nothing to him. He wanted the pain gone. That was how it worked. You pay and the pain goes away.

Unfortunately this pain remained and there was no amount of money that could remove it. The more he tried to find the cause of the cause, the more easily it became enflamed, and the more confused the doctors became. Just yesterday tests had been done to test the blood sedimentation rate and other such medical nonsense. The results were still pending, and he felt neither here nor there about it. What could doctors possibly tell him? They knew nothing of business. Their professions originated from biology, not commerce.

This was his time to shine and no neck problem was going to stand in his way. He wanted to conquer South Africa while he still had a chance. This country was ripe for the picking and it would be him picking it. For years he had watched his parents struggle, yet their view of apartheid had never changed. From government to government, they remained resolute and convinced that the white man owed them something. It burned him that they could be so set in their ways.

Sendiwe lived by one firm view: winning wasn't everything, but losing was nothing. He was here for the taking. This was not politics – it was business. Thin line between the two, perhaps, but he made no attempt to suppress his desire to own most of the commerce in South Africa. He wanted a cut of everything. This would become Sendiwe's South Africa.

He aspired to be many things, but had no interest in ever becoming a politician. These stately men with their bodyguards and their empty threats could never be taken seriously. He despised that they were throwing the country away instead of reaping its wealth properly. He despised that they would get drunk and resort to singing old tribal songs. This was no way to excel in life. Sendiwe just could not understand politicians and the games they played. He enjoyed coming right at someone and telling them how it would be. This would make him a terrible politician, because they lied for a living and he disliked lying. Not that he was incorruptible. He was well aware of his shortcomings and his ruthlessness, but he was not a liar. He was a bad man, and in the business where bad men played games, he was the best.

There was still time for him. He was young enough to accomplish much. He would make a kingdom of this country and then set it free. Free in the sense that the next warrior could rise up and take it from him. If history had taught him anything about his ancestors, it was the inevitable likelihood of brother turning against brother, and child turning against father. So he didn't bother with the formality of aspiring to leave a legacy. Leaving a fortune behind for a bunch of spoiled brats to deplete did not invoke much interest in accumulating it in the first place. And speaking of brats, he already had some. Three of them, with two different women. He was quite indifferent about the concept of spawn. Having children was simply a result, a consequence. It was like a reaction to the very mundane action of sex. He had distanced himself very early on as to avoid any paternal duties. Due to the benefits of being one of South Africa's wealthiest men, Sendiwe could buy the women houses to stay in without breaking a sweat. He could also pay for proper schooling for the children and he would eventually force them to continue with studies after school. It was the least he could do. Something useful, like becoming businessmen, or even doctors. Unfortunately that was the extent to his commitment as their biological father. For the rest of their wonderful journey, they would be on their own. The women were doing a good enough job without him.

The waiter began clearing the table, his hands skilfully collecting the plate and the empty wine glass in one smooth motion.

Sendiwe swiftly grabbed the young man's arm and pulled him down into a seated position next to him. With his other hand he picked up the butter knife and slipped it under the waiter's chin. Shock and horror filled the man's eyes.

"Did I tell you to clear my table?" Sendiwe asked in Zulu.

The waiter, a thin film of sweat starting around his temples, slowly moved his head from side to side and swallowed nervously.

"Then leave me be, qwe'qwe."

When Sendiwe removed the knife, the waiter toppled backward and scampered off.

He turned to see who might have seen them, but the place was fairly empty. Only the barman and another waiter was there. To the one side of the restaurant sat two men drinking coffee. They were the only other patrons in the hotel's restaurant. To everyone else these two men appeared to be patrons, but they were actually part of his entourage.

Sendiwe nodded at the two men. Immediately they abandoned their coffees and marched toward the table, moving in a manner that appeared carefully rehearsed and smooth.

"I am leaving. Give this to management for the inconvenience," he said to his bodyguards as he handed them a wad of R200 notes.

He rose up and left the restaurant. When he came outside, his car was already waiting. The car door was opened for him and he got inside.

"I feel naughty," he told the chauffeur. "Take me somewhere."

As the car pulled away, Sendiwe reached for the cell phone in his jacket pocket and dialled a number.

"It's your new friend," he said. "He did not take the bait. We'll have to think of something else."

Indecision was a terrible thing. It could tear someone apart for the longest time. He was not only indecisive. No, it was far more than struggling with indecision. He was wrapped up in a severe reluctance because the current situation carried great weight. This whole scenario went far beyond the point of just saying yes or no to any particular action. There were consequences he hadn't thought of before. Every action had an obligatory reaction. It was the way of the world. No matter what he decided to do now, misery was sure to follow. Lives would be wrecked and he would be the instigator, the Antagonist. It was unavoidable, hence his indecision.

The Antagonist clasped his hands over his eyes and sighed. He took a long breath and released it again. He could hear the knocking of his heart in his ears, faint and constant.

How had it gotten this far? He just wanted money. Was there ever anything else? Was there another form of motivation? Other than the basic demands of greed? He had the perfect woman. He had the perfect career and a decent income. But, with all of this, he simply wanted more. He wanted to retire early, sit on a beach somewhere and live the life of luxury without having to work for it. He wanted comfort and stability in uncertain times. He wanted to be unattached and independently wealthy. He wanted and needed more until his want could no longer be stilled. By then R 350 million had been embezzled from Harlem Properties, embezzled in ways that would not reflect on the accounts while deeds to assets were in transit or while any of the properties were actively undergoing development. How easily his desire had morphed into a curse was astounding even to him. As circumstances changed, he instinctively resorted to protecting that which he had taken. He felt like a thief protecting his secret stash, even though it saddened him that he had taken it in the first place.

There was such an inner conflict and this added to the confusion. There were only a small number of ways to cover up the act, one of which was eliminating all those involved and the other was eliminating all those who might discover what had been done. Unfortunately there was only one way to tell the truth, but he was not prepared to go to jail. R 350 million worth of jail time would surely not be a breeze. Also, his family would bear the ridicule of his stupidity and the sins of the father would bestow great sorrow on the children. So, the saying that evil begets evil had certainly been proven adequate by his actions.

With hindsight it now seemed like such a futile practice to indulge in thievery. At first it had seemed so simple and it had worked perfectly without anyone being aware of the great deceit. When he first endeavoured to obtain R10 million to buy a property, it had felt like lot of money and it had quickly dawned on him that no one would know about it. Then greed set in and he confided in the wrong people to help him shift large amounts around or to generate the documentation required to legitimize development on the property. Soon he was a slave to the hunger and those he had confided in were fuelling the hunger. Finally it started to unravel. Now, as the ripple effect had worsened the situation, everything was spiralling out of control and he was looking every which way for a life jacket.

The Antagonist sat in his car. It felt like an office to him. He was struggling with the plastic wrapping. Why did they have to make the packaging so damned complicated? It only cost 99 cents, so why make it such a schlep? It was a conspiracy. The cell phone companies were hiding something secret in there. He bit open the edge of the hard plastic until the two pieces parted slightly. He tugged at the two loose parts to broaden the gap until his fingers could reach inside. While keeping one side in his mouth and the other side in one hand, he jammed his hand inside to reach the tiny SIM card. When he pulled his hand free the plastic cut open the back of his hand. He stared at his hand in awe. Small drops of blood slowly seeped out from the lesion. All this trouble to make a call.

He removed the SIM card from his phone and put in the new one. He loaded the airtime by following the voice prompts and made the call. He was dreading this.

"We have a problem," he said into the phone, his voice a little frantic. "Harlem wants to sell the company and he already has a buyer." He listened to the voice on the other end of the line. "Well if he sells it, they'll notice. It's too soon. I needed a couple of months, at least." Another pause. "How the hell should I know? I told Sendiwe to make an offer on a couple of buildings, including the Opus, to cover up the loss, but Harlem rejected it."

Being a petty man, the Antagonist poked at the plastic wrapping a few times. He licked the blood seeping from his wound, almost gagging at the metallic taste. Vile repugnance had a taste, and this was it. Blood in the mouth was enough to take the life out of him. It was disgusting, dirty and delicious.

"No, Sendiwe doesn't know anything. I'm not all that thick. Besides, I already have another idea. We need to meet. Soon."

He finished the call and put the old SIM card back in. He felt uncertain about what to do, yet he was doing it. This really wasn't the type of situation where going with the flow was the appropriate recourse, but it was a first for him and he was doing it as best he could. Attempting to cover his tracks seemed like the right strike.

His family would have to go away while this whole thing resolved itself. He would be the first to admit that he was worthless – a back-stabbing thief. He was absolutely aware of his trespass, but he was still a husband and a father and a natural crook. Instinctively his mind ran wild at the thought of causing his family harm. He would do just about anything to keep them out of it – or so he convinced himself. He adamantly believed he would cross the law and challenge the world to keep the focus on him for the sake of his family. Yet, deep within himself, The Antagonist knew his motives were actually driven by greed. And that, he suddenly realized, was the core of the matter. His family was a distant second, if that. When Harlem had announced the sale, his panic had made him resolute and the deepest darkest side of his being rose up with conviction, prepared to disrupt and expunge all that would jeopardize his brilliant disguise. This was all new to him, but he was ready to defend. Worst-case scenario would result in him taking his own life and ending it there. So, he was not just an indecisive thief. He was very much suicidal.

For the first time since he'd parked the car, he looked out the window. He was at Blaauwberg beach, Table View. He had no recollection whatsoever of driving to Table View. He had been so deep in thought that he never even noticed where he was going. The car was parked in such a way that he found himself looking out at the sea. The clouds were so thick and menacing, the dominating presence of Table Mountain seemed to be smothered in the distance. He found it amusing that this early evening view reflected his mood. It was actually ideal. He sat there for many hours as his mind jumbled around ideas. It felt as though he was doing a mental Rubik's cube.

When a police car pulled up next to his car and an officer shone a flashlight into his eyes, he decided he'd had enough of the smell of fish and salt and indecision, so he offered the suspicious officer a generous smile and drove off in the dark.

Suddenly the day was at an end and she was overcome by exhaustion. Her jeans felt dirty, her legs were sore, her shoulders felt heavy and her mind was weak. The doors were locked and the cleaning began with a forced vigour.

She carefully folded the cloth once more and started from the other side. The wooden table was wide across, big enough for six people, with slide-in leather couches on both sides. The table had been varnished to an abnormal golden gleam and she could almost see her reflection in it. She moved in slow concentric circles. It was late and she was tired. Double shifts were not for the faint-hearted. At least tomorrow evening she would be able to let herself go. Tomorrow night was her time to unload her misery.

Kerin rinsed the cloth again. The water was not even lukewarm anymore. Her hands moved through the bits of chips and burger debris which floated around the bucket like flotsam and jetsam on a wavering current. As she finished cleaning the table, Kerin stretched out her thin fingers over the sticky cloth and stared at her hands objectively. Her hands looked so old and lifeless. They were the hands of a forty-five-year-old woman, but she was only thirty-five.

There was a time when she had been the attractive one. Not that long ago men would look at her lustfully. Somewhere something had gone horribly wrong. Something had changed for the worse. She no longer felt unique and was letting herself go.

Wrinkles and cellulite were getting the better of her. The wires of most of her bras had already been pulled out because they were pinching her. She had to force herself to shave her legs. Her needs no longer featured on the list of priorities. Her personal desires and lack of self-worth was right at the bottom of the list and there was never any time left in the day to tend to those things.

She slid out of the cubicle, scooped up the bucket and grabbed the mop. She had to get home. Time kept ticking away even when she wasn't looking at her watch. She finished up in the kitchen, and left the restaurant with the waitress apron still firmly tied around her waist. She waved goodbye to the kitchen staff and nodded forcibly at Russel, the shift manager – an emotionless twit who had tried furiously to get into her pants.

The streets were deserted at this hour on a Monday night. Her numb feet were moving fast over the wet tar, occasionally sidestepping puddles and broken glass. She was walking at a steady pace. It always took her twenty minutes to get home. She'd timed herself other nights. The fact that it wasn't raining didn't make it any easier. It was freezing. The ever-present Cape Town wind zipped through the narrow alleys and tugged at her body.

She lit up a cigarette out of habit and only realized that she had been smoking by the time she inhaled the last bit and flicked the butt into the empty street. She had bummed the cigarette from Charl or Simba or one of the others. Staff rotation was such a rampant thing in the restaurant industry that she no longer bothered to remember all the names of the other waiters. They were fired left, right and centre. Such was the nature of the industry.

Kerin felt uncomfortable when she was on her own. She felt stranded and estranged from herself, a one-woman island. Walking down the hollow tubes, sidestepping sleeping vagrants, watching traffic lights change for ghost cars, she wondered if she would ever find a way out of this hell which had become her reality. Life could not be like this for ever. There had to be something more inspiring, more worthy for someone like her. Even the seasons changed. She had been stuck like this for ten years.

She felt as if there was no hope for her; simply surviving already seemed impossible. She felt lonely at least half of the day, and damaged the rest of the time, with a sombre sadness keeping everything together. There was just grief and sorrow present. She could not escape. As much as she wanted to run away, she couldn't. She would never be able to run away. She cried into her pillow most nights, never getting a clear glimpse at the digital clock before she trickled off to nothingness. She had so much love to give, but there was no one willing to listen long enough to hear what she had to say. There was no light and no life. There had been no light for many years.

The door gave way on the fourth shove. She caught it by the handle before it could slam into the wall and wake up the whole floor. She entered, letting out a deep sigh of relief. Another day had come to pass. It was almost 00:00.

The apartment was small, but it was home. The front door opened directly into the living room and an open-plan kitchenette to the back of the room. The doorway on the right led to two bedrooms with a very small bathroom situated between them.

In the living room there were two uncomfortable plastic-leather chairs, an old stained pull-out sleeper couch, square coffee table, side-table and a minute television standing dejected on a stack of telephone directories with an off-cut piece of yellow bed linen cleverly draped over it.

Kerin tripped over a toy which lay near the entrance and, trying to brace herself against the walls, dropped her keys. The clattering of keys echoed through the small apartment. She swore silently. She already felt so clumsy having broken a number of cups at work. The floor manager had roused a spit over the cups, making it very clear that the replacement cost would be deducted from her pay, over and above the normal breakage. Fetching the keys, she wondered what else she would break.

Though the living room felt cold, barren and dark, the small lamp on the side table provided sufficient glow to instil a weak resonance of warmth within the room. Side-stepping an open pencil case and a couple of strategically placed pens and pencils, Kerin made her way through the living room much like a war scout would sneak across a minefield.

In the kitchen, she quickly washed the dishes: cups, glasses, two small pots, plates, cutlery and some plastics. She placed all the items on the drying rack to drip-dry and cleaned off the small counter. She made three ham-and-cheese-sandwiches and packed three lunchboxes for the next day. She put two lunchboxes in a bag with two bananas and yoghurt cups, and placed it on the small refrigerator. She wiped the counter again – almost seeing bits of burgers and chips floating in front of her – and put the dishes away.

The small glass slipped, shattering loudly on the tiled floor. Long slivers of glass scampered into far corners and underneath the old washing machine. A soft groan came from the sleeper couch in the living room, followed by a whisper of a cough. Third time's a charm, she told herself. Was she dropping things because she was just too tired? She had worked so many doubles. Maybe she was slowly burning out.

Kerin didn't waste time on a "woe-is-me" bit. She removed the broom and scoop from behind the fridge and quickly gathered the shards. She quietly moved the washing machine away and with great difficulty cleaned up all the glass beneath it, cutting herself in the process.

Luckily there was just a little nick to the tip of the thumb. She washed the blood off and staunched the bleeding with a paper towel.

"Kerin?" a voice asked from the living room. "That you?"

Kerin lowered herself over Margie's resting figure and pulled the blankets straight.

"It's okay. Go back to sleep."

In a bit of a hurry, she put all the pencils back into the pencil case and moved it out of the way. She also picked up a couple of drawings of trees and animals strewn about the living room, piled them together and slid them into a thin brown satchel along with the pencil case.

"Sorry about that," Margie said. Her voice was so familiar and so warm. "I was still meaning to get around to clearing up the mess. I just couldn't stay up any longer."

Her mother was pointing at the stationary, her curly hair tousled and sticking out in every direction. Her cheeks were red with sleep and her eyes muddy, confused. She was forcing back a yawn with one hand and pushing herself up with the other, ever-ready to do whatever she could wherever she could.

"That's okay," Kerin said softly. "Go back to sleep now. You must be tired."

She forced her mother down with a sturdy hand and adjusted the blankets again. She brushed back her mother's curly hair until she could see the frowns on her forehead. It was so cold in here. The kitchen window couldn't close all the way. The cold seemed to flow effortlessly into the room. Kerin had called the landlord months ago to report the problem, but he was the absentee, unforgiving type and she never paid the rent on time.

She switched off the light and felt her way along the wall to her bedroom, quickly stopping at the other bedroom. She opened the door and looked into the darkness, seeing nothing, everything. There was no open curtain with moonlight streaming into the room, no reassurance of discernment. There was only tranquil warmth that echoed from within, calling out to her through the dark. There was no intelligible way to describe the workings and the yearnings of a mother's heart, its selfless determination to provide, nurture and protect.

She went to her room at around 01:30, removed her work clothes and put on a pair of sweatpants and a light-blue jersey which was two sizes too big for her. There were some cheap furniture about the room, cluttered with papers, unopened envelopes, and perfume.

Kerin sat on the bed with one leg folded back, head tilted sideways. She was ambivalence personified. She was counting seconds again, as if she was waiting for something to happen. They just would not stop ticking away. She was combing her hair slowly, patiently. This moment of self-love was one of the few pleasures she still had left. There was no one else to caress her hair and there was precious little time to sit and enjoy the simple melancholy of the mind. A soft comfortable jazz song was playing in her ears and she was instantly whisked away to a wonderful world. With her eyes shut and the tips of her hair brushing over her back and shoulders, Kerin felt herself dancing with the comb. She felt herself gently, ever-gently, slipping away as she performed for the crowd.

CHAPTER 3

David was drawn from his dreams by a loud sound, his eyes quickly adjusting to the morning glare. He searched the room for movement. He was in a frantic state, confused and out of breath. For a brief moment he was lost between his dream world and the real world, uncertain which was which and when was where.

"Elizabeth?" he called, but there was no reply.

Like so many mornings before, realization hit him hard between the eyes.

He was alone. At the Cullinan. It was 05:00.

The telephone was shrieking. David answered the phone in a gruff voice.

"David, terribly sorry to bother so early," Ray said on the other end. "Can you talk?"

"Mornings, Ray. What's wrong?"

"I went through the paperwork and found some discrepancies. Can you meet today?"

David had a very busy day and had meeting after meeting scheduled. Unfortunately there was no time to listen to Raymond Gallagher faultfinding the reports.

"Not possible. I'm fully booked."

There was a long silence, then` Ray said, "I have some questions that need answering. Shall I contact the board and make a protest?"

David sighed and rubbed the sleep from his eyes. Five o' clock was too early for this type of conversation.

"Brief William about the discrepancies. I'll have Jocelynne cancel my flight and I'll stay another night. If your concerns are serious, I'll tend to the matter tomorrow. That okay?"

"I don't really know why I should speak to William about this."

"He's more than capable to tend to the matter and he's also a member of the board. I'm meeting with him at seven and I'll inform him of your call."

Again there was a terrible silence, so much so that David checked to see that the phone still had reception.

"Ray?"

"Guess that'll have to do."

"Fantastic."

"Sorry if I woke you. I'm sure you understand my concern."

After finishing the call, David sat in bed for a few minutes collecting himself. He took in the silence and fully enjoyed it.

By 06:30 he had finished in the hotel's small gym. In the limited time he had set out for the day, he still managed to do 10 kilometres on the treadmill and 10 kilometres on the cycle. Ten years ago clocking 20 kilometres of cardio in the morning would've been a breeze, but the years were finally taking their toll. At forty-two his body was just not as nimble as it had been at twenty. He was a bit slower and became tired-out a bit sooner than before. The other side of forty presented a whole bunch of surprises, but he had accepted the ageing process gracefully. He was still fit and well-built. He could still fill a room with his presence and he still had many handsome features. Even the light patches of gray hair along the side of his head somehow gave him a stately appearance.

Minutes before seven, William already sat waiting in the restaurant. Painfully punctual as usual. He was busy drinking some awful green concoction.

"Dare I ask what that is?"

William looked up bright-eyed and smiled. "It's a Rooibos and spinach smoothie. Good fuel after a 50 k spinning session."

"*You* did 50 kilometres on a bike this morning? And here you sit smiling about it?" David joined the table. "You have been blessed with a robust backside, my friend. Unfortunately my arse can no longer take the pounding. 10 k is my limit."

"You want some?" William asked, waving the vile-looking smoothie at him.

David grimaced and felt his colour change. "Heavens, no."

He signalled the waiter and ordered a coffee instead.

Over a quick English breakfast, they discussed a number of key business topics and other developments. Most were unimportant issues and were only relevant to the day-to-day running of Harlem Properties. David loved William's professional attitude, his business savvy, and his analytical approach. It reminded him of a younger version of himself.

"Now that we got that out of the way, let's chat about the more pertinent matters."

"Such as?" David asked.

"Asset listings and valuations. Who will be regulating the process?"

"It'll have to be you. I want your eyes on every report and every valuation and every assessment done over the last five years."

"Guess I'll have to cancel my vacation then."

"Sorry about that, but I don't quite trust anyone else. Already had a call from Ray this morning about irregularities he wants explained."

William frowned while spreading a thin layer of jam over his brown toast. "What irregularities?"

"Not sure. Something about the reports. He was ready to call in the board."

"That cheeky bastard."

"Hey, no need for that. He's a good man. Just a bit old, senile. But he's been in this company longer than you. Remember that. Treat him accordingly."

"You're right. Just heard snippets from Wendy about his rumblings and that some of the others weren't too thrilled about the sale either. Nothing serious, mostly questions and petty concerns." William finished the last of his green sludge then leaned forward with his hands clasped. "By the way, who are you selling to? The reports show many agreeable figures and good terms, but no mention of a buyer. You need to disclose this information asap. The board is going nuts."

"Nuts? Everybody stands to make a clean twenty to thirty mill with this sale. What's there to be nuts about?"

"You stand to make a cool 400 mill."

David sat back and gave William a belittling stare. It wasn't in David's nature to use his authority. However, there were times when he didn't tolerate any challenge, especially when it involved his personal remuneration, his love life or his past. The years had taught him to become more and more reclusive.

"420 million," David corrected him. "I could easily hold out for an offer where I get one billion. Do I really need to justify a payout that size?"

"Just hear me out. People get funny when money is involved. You know that. We've had many conversations about this. The decision to sell was solely made by you, the boss. As president you have that authority, but if you'd told me in advance,

I could've worked my magic and had a happy board waiting for you."

"You think I shouldn't sell?"

"It's just very sudden, you know." William looked at the waiter and pointed at the empty coffee cups. "A warning would've been nice. It's the rashness of it that has everybody up in arms. But never mind that now. We are where we are."

After the waiter poured them more coffee, the two men sat in a comfortable silence studying each other.

"The buyer is the Benjamin Property Group in Nigeria. Their expansion to South Africa is a strategic attempt to influence their existing business in Lagos. The Nigerian infrastructure is growing rapidly and adding our portfolio to theirs would really cement their progress. Nigeria needs this move as badly as South Africa needs stronger ties in Africa. It is mutually beneficial. I'm meeting with them in the next couple of days to finalize the deal."

William just sat there poking at a salt shaker, appearing to be disinterested in the specifics of the sale. However, having known his protégé for ten years, David knew William wasn't missing a thing. Every bit of info was sinking in.

"I have to sell. I can't live this life anymore."

"Then so be it. I'm with you on this."

The office was very small, containing only a small desk and a large shelf stacked with files. The smell of cigarettes and ash was overpowering. An air of manly arrogance appeared to seep out of whoever sat in the manager's chair. This could be because a woman had never sat there before.

"What do you want me to say?" he asked. The sarcasm in his voice was hard and heavy.

Kerin masked her annoyance, her anger, her many fears. She just sat there, her mind doing calculations in search of a solution to this new development.

She was the third person to sit in this chair today. While preparing her tables for the day, Sheena and Branwell had been called in, one after the other. Sheena had left the restaurant red-eyed and trembling. Branwell had a deep fury in him, but he was still young enough to conquer that hurt.

What would she do? How was she supposed to react?

Russel stared at her with his droopy over-worked eyes. There was no sincerity present, no real concern. He rested his upper body on his elbows. He was in a confrontational mood – his usual bombastic self – and he was ready for a fight.

"I don't want you to say anything, Russel. I want to know why?"

He scoffed at her. "You know why."

"Do I?"

"Yes you do, cupcake."

She felt like strangling him; squeezing him until there was no more twitching left. It would've been a mercy-killing. Anything this condescending and arrogant would be better off dead.

"Enlighten me," Kerin said.

"Like I said, business is slow. We have to let people go."

"But I've worked here longer than anyone else."

Russel became visibly irate. He slammed his fist down on the table and swore. She always knew he had a short temper, but his current frustration revealed a side of him she had never seen before. This ruthless manager for whom she had worked for years, suddenly looked powerless and tired.

"Damn it, Kerin. You're not the best waitress and you're too old for this work, but I always liked you. You were reliable and consistent and that made my job easier." He finally locked eyes with her. "But you're white. The Labour Department was here last week and they did a Black Economic Empowerment survey. We failed." Russel pulled his hands through his thinning hair. "They went through the whole of Cape Town with a fine comb and checked everybody's BEE ratings. One million coloured and Indian folk will lose jobs before the end of the year, and half a million whites will join them. Sorry." His eyes agreed.

Just like that, Kerin's whole world had stopped spinning. She felt as though all her limbs had been severed and that she was unable to do anything. She couldn't function while facing the wave of emotion within her. She wanted to cry, needed to cry. She was so close to freaking out and collapsing and screaming and laughing. This had to be early signs of hysteria, she thought. This had to be the edge of sanity.

Kerin had no friends. No one to speak to. There were certain concerns she couldn't discuss with her mother and her children. One of the many disadvantages of being a single parent, was the fact that she had no social life. Everything she had wanted and everything she still had planned to do, became unimportant. The To-Do-List she had drawn up after school, had become the Wish List of things to achieve before turning ninety. Survival came first and the joys of life became a distant second.

God alone knew how she had loathed this awful job – the restaurant crowd, the clientele, the management, the entire food industry – but it was work and work was incredibly scarce. She also worked at the club once a week, but that delivered poor income. It couldn't even be classified as an income. How was she going to pay school fees and rental? She still had to call the landlord. She needed money. Money, as was usually the case, was the answer to all her problems.

"I have some money saved up."

"Yes, it's in a provident fund. I've already completed the form. It's there in front of you. You just have to sign at the bottom and the money should be in your account in about three months."

KING OF SORROW | James Fouché

On top of a stack of papers there lay a single form looking at her. Salvation? Or the end of her world?

She had to wait three months for her savings. She could stretch out that amount and add it to her mother's government pension to cope for another two months. It would be a difficult time, but it could be done. The real problem was waiting the three months for her savings. She had very little left in her account and she would only earn another couple hundred after her show tonight, but that was not enough to bring the landlord and the school fees up to date. Where was she going to find another job? And *when* would she find one? She'd been on so many interviews. A single parent with no qualifications and no transport sounded alarm bells to management. She couldn't take another no. But she still checked the classified sections every day. Living on hope.

She signed the form and left. Russel had confirmed that the restaurant would pay out the rest of the month but that would simply not be enough. They worked primarily on tips. The basic was a bare minimum.

Kerin didn't bother saying goodbyes. No one there really liked her anyway. What was the use prolonging the agony?

The walk home was a depressing one. It was eerie how the human mind could turn into the enemy. Kerin was subconsciously condemning herself to a life of misery. There was no fight left in her. She was done. The world was choking her and she couldn't go anywhere to get fresh air.

It was still early when she got home. The kids were in school so Kerin had a bit of time alone with her mother. Margie couldn't say anything to the news. Kerin knew that her mother's view was a simple one: if she could not contribute anything useful to the conversation then there was no use contributing at all. Talking to Margie couldn't remove the morbid feeling in the pit of her stomach. She still wanted to cry. She wanted someone to hold her and tell her that everything would be alright. That was not a selfish thing to ask for. Everyone needed comforting at some point in their lives. She had need of it now. In fact, she had needed it for years.

While Margie rested a bit, Kerin cleaned the house. Luckily there were no carpets in the flat because the vacuum cleaner had broken down two months before. She used the broom to sweep the rooms and she flipped the mattresses and she cleaned the bathroom and she got dressed.

"Where you going?" Margie asked when she saw Kerin grabbing her handbag.

Kerin scanned the flat to see if she was happy with her efforts. Everything seemed clean enough and she had expelled some unwanted energy in the process.

"I'm going to fetch the kids. It's your day off."

She faked a smile, but she couldn't fool her own mother.

"It's still too early."

"I know," she said and slung her bag over her shoulder. "I want to see the principle before school ends."

"What will you do about the school fees and the rent? It was supposed to be paid yesterday."

"I'll get some of the money tonight at the club. I want to see if I can pay half the school fees now and the rest later. That gives me some time to find a job."

"The rent was also due Monday."

"Don't worry about it, Mom," Kerin snapped at her mother. "I'll make a plan."

She turned and headed for the door. Suddenly she stopped in the corridor, her hand clasping the door handle firmly. "How did we get here?" She looked down at her mother, then glanced at the apartment. "Living day to day, struggling to make ends meet? Telling ourselves not to worry when that's all we can do?"

It felt strange to have his feet dangling beneath him, suspended in a wanton manner as if no longer attached to the rest of his body. In an attempt to reassure himself that his feet still belonged to him, Sendiwe wiggled his toes. He should've trimmed his toenails before coming here. They were already turning yellow at the edges. The long nails on the crooked toes had a sickly, ageing appearance that freaked him out.

"How long?" he asked after a long pause.

"I can't say."

Sendiwe shifted slightly and heard the bed creak under his bulk. So many things were going through his mind at one time that his conscience became one giant funnel and nothing was coming through. It was blocked, every thought jamming into the exit and not going anywhere.

"How bad is it now?"

The doctor was a thin man. He looked healthy and well-groomed, a neatly trimmed beard stubble masking his weak jaw line. His eyes were emotionless and kind of funny-looking in that they almost bulged out of their sockets.

For a few seconds the doctor scanned through the file in his hands, just enough to act as though he was looking for something, or as if the file would subliminally supply reassurance to his initial diagnosis.

"It's not looking good, Linden," he said finally.

"Okay, so *guess* how long," Sendiwe demanded while putting his socks and shoes back onto his feet.

Here was the problem with a profession that required years and years of knowledge: at the end of the day they had to resort to conjecture. All those degrees and they were guessing their way through patients. Was it so hard to get a straight and honest answer? Even if they had to admit that they didn't know the answer. These people were becoming worse than politicians. Why the uncertainty, the vague observations, the contradictory views? Why not come right out and say it?

"Three months, give or take."

Sendiwe slipped his left foot into the expensive shoe and stayed like that for a long time. His breath was frozen. Whatever oxygen had still been left in his lungs instantly became a solid block. The sound of his heart thumping echoed in his ears. He was expecting to hear something along the lines of ten years, maybe more. Three months was not a substantial amount of time. Three months roughly amounted to ninety days, which was 2160 hours. Subtract eight hours a day for sleeping and he was left with 1440 hours. That was two months.

He climbed off the bed and put on his jacket, baring an all-knowing smile on his face. How fragile the human body? How weak the human gene? How sad the human condition? The great Linden Sendiwe also had an expiry date and it was closer than he had imagined.

"Three months is such a short time," he said as he folded over the jacket collar. "I must start enjoying it then."

The doctor was still paging through his file. *God help you, my funny-looking friend*, Sendiwe thought. *The answer you are looking for is not written on those pages.*

Before long he was in his limousine again. Upon entering the vehicle he had closed the parting panel between him and the chauffeur. He was in an excessively contemplative mood and he wanted to sit in silence, shut off from everything and everyone. How often did one hear you'd be dead in three months? Not often.

"Now what?" he whispered softly.

He sat looking at the 15-year-old whiskey in the crystal glass, his gold cufflinks, the blank LCD screen in the one corner of his expensive limousine. The luxuries and the lavishness of his life suddenly seemed futile. He had accomplished so much and it would now wither away without merit. From ambition to tragedy in five minutes.

What would it benefit to get a second opinion? He had no doubt that the doctor's diagnosis was right. The decision and the final diagnosis had been approved by a panel of specialists and it had taken them a year to reach their conclusion. The clock was ticking and there was only three months left.

Sendiwe swallowed the last of the whiskey and closed his eyes. He felt the tires rolling on, the vibrations running up and down his spine and through his feet, all the while a terrible sickness sailing through his blood and devouring everything in its path. This sickness was there for the taking. This body would become its very own. Sendiwe, its kingdom. There was ample time; in fact, time was all it had.

The school principal was a pleasantly unpleasant man, terrible at being good and doing well at doing well-to-do. He was painfully verbose, jabbering on incessantly about useless things, like the new facilities, and not allowing Kerin to voice her concerns or to thoroughly explain her unfortunate circumstances. He was resolute about his decisions regarding outstanding school fees and pointed out the obvious fact that if he changed the rule for one parent then very soon he had to change it for all the parents. Mid-conversation he resorted to an elaborate explanation of school policies, upcoming events and the new facilities that had to be introduced to the schooling system before the end of the year. At first he appeared to be genuinely apologetic, but this soon proved to be surface dust on his character which merely shifted this way and that to cover questions about extensions or discounts on school fees.

Kerin perceived him to be a masterful manipulator of emotions and realized that as an unmarried, childless man he had perfected the pity act over his many years of solitude. He frequently illustrated situations with his long smooth fingers while making use of his brows and friendly eyes. He moved his diary from one side of his desk to the other, gently scratched his upper lip with his index finger, played with the pen protruding from his shirt pocket, and occasionally glanced at the blank face of his cell phone as if it was on silent and he was expecting an important call. He shifted in his chair, blissfully unaware of the repetitive squeaks it made. He forced a smile to fake courteousness after saying something that might've been considered to be insulting or rude. Then he mentioned some specific figures when he listed the expenses of the new facilities that had to be operational before the end of the curriculum. He attempted small-talk to counter his true intentions. This back-fired as well. He asked vague questions as conversation warmers and noticeably feigned interest when she replied. And magically withdrew a box of tissues from his drawer when the tears started rolling. This made part of him visibly comfortable, and another part of him uncomfortable. Kerin imagined he disliked women being reduced to a position of weakness, but she also believed that he had been scarred by women and this was probably his only opportunity for revenge on the opposite sex. In an attempt to neutralize the situation he massaged his temples, scratched his forehead, shifted and shifted again while pointing out the municipal troubles he was having with the new toilet facilities which had to be completed by the end of the year, then shifted again. He carefully worded his next approach, covering his tracks to avoid any repercussions. Kerin could see his eyes searching for the right words and she also noticed the thin film of perspiration spreading across his large forehead, when she sobbed loudly into the handful of tissues. He sighed once, twice, shifted uncomfortably and paged through his diary, then correlated his findings with the dates on his large desk pad. He highlighted the complications with the new toilet facilities which had to be in use by the end of the year and explained how an arrangement could be made to avoid further complications. The solution would be to implement a reduced fee structure for the next three months, until Kerin had new employment and until she received the monies from her pension fund. Though this was not ideal for Kerin, the principal presented the option as being the greatest resolution since the end of World War 2. Immediately he fell into his congratulatory mood, making mention of how glad he was to have Megan and Dillon at his school, how brilliant they were and how fantastic the upcoming sports events would be, not to mention the new toilet facilities that had to be operational before the end of the year. The school ended when the bell rang, and as she left the school terrain with her children she couldn't help thinking how marvellous the new toilet facilities would be.

Jocelynne studied David's face as he finished his meeting with Najwa September. She could tell he was exhausted. His jaw muscles tightened occasionally and his eyes were not as bright as usual. Then there was that flash of a grimace when he thought no one was looking; just a quick display of fatigue. He was an enthusiastic man, and people as vibrant as David seemed to defy what everyone perceived to be normal. But he was still flesh and blood, and uniquely flawed, like everyone else. She had adopted this view many years ago when she had met her husband-to-be.

Henk and Jocelynne Venter certainly had a strange relationship. It was that strangeness that gave their life so much balance. She had been raised in a far more liberal household, where everyone said what was on their mind, rather opting for honesty instead of protecting each other's emotions. In both the most trivial personal matter and the most tragic crises, everyone would be considered equal and every voice would be heard. This was not necessarily the best environment for a child, as it was a household without any authoritative father figure. Jocelynne had raised her own children the same way, but Henk was there to enforce equilibrium. He had been raised on a farm and he had worked for the South African Police Services for twenty-five years of his life, so his *modus operandi* as a father was discipline, discipline, and more discipline. They were the perfect opposites. As a result their successes echoed in the lives of their children, all settled and happy and strong in their faith.

Najwa was trying hard not to cry, but Jocelynne knew she wouldn't be able to fight it back. Everyone cried when they received the news. Who wouldn't cry? As far as the economy was concerned, this was a terrible time for South Africa and every household was taking a serious financial knock. When the scale of a family budget suddenly tips to one side, even the strongest person will break, and Jocelynne had to sit there and take notes as the scales were tipped.

Tears streamed down Najwa's young face and her eyes suddenly lit up when the news finally sunk in. She flipped her long hair over her shoulders and wiped the tears away. The fact that she had just been retrenched was unimportant. The fact that she would be jobless was unimportant. The fact that she and her husband had been fighting almost every night because he had also lost his work, was also of no importance anymore. Jocelynne knew that all Najwa's troubles were over.

Because Jocelynne had an intimate knowledge of everyone in the office, the series of exit-interviews being conducted was such an intense emotional ride for her. Looking at Najwa's tender display of happiness, tears instantly welled up in her own eyes. She pushed the waterworks back and made a large tick on her notepad. One more to go.

"Thank you, thank you, thank ..." she whispered and visibly forced herself to stop trembling. "You're a good man, Mr. Harlem. We'll never forget this."

"It's a pleasure, Najwa. Thank you for all the hard work and I wish you and your family all the best."

Najwa stood up and left the office.

David sighed a very slow and peaceful sigh, one that suggested his day was nearing its end. He stretched his neck sideways and rubbed his hands together to relieve the tension in his muscles. When he noticed Jocelynne's eyes on him, he stood up and began to pace around the boardroom.

"Wendy is the last one."

"Good," David said as he overlooked the busy Cape Town streets. "It's been a long day."

She had tended to his diary for the day, while Wendy tended to the other members of the board. There had been meetings with lawyers, the accountants, a brutal recap with William, the insurance brokers, lunch with his financial advisor, and then all the exit-interviews.

David sat down at the table for his last meeting of the day.

"Okay," he said. "Let's do this."

Jocelynne briefly stepped out of the boardroom and returned with Wendy Peterson in her wake. Wendy wore a red button-up shirt and black pants, hair tied back in a ponytail and lips blood red. Her demeanour was professional and she projected an air of confidence.

"Hi Wendy. Keeping head above water?" he asked.

She sat down opposite Jocelynne. "Of course. Business as usual. A bit more pressure, but we can manage."

"It's going to be a busy couple of weeks, but it's almost done. The business will be sold as a running concern. Voetstoots. All contracts of employment will be cancelled or settled. This does not necessarily mean you'll be losing your job. The new management will decide whether to renew contracts. They are satisfied with the structure as it is, but things might change."

"I imagined that would be the course of action. I've already polished my résumé. Seven years at Harlem Properties looks very good on a CV."

David smiled and looked at Jocelynne, "That's Wendy for you. Always prepared."

"That's the way you taught me."

He opened a new bottle of water, his fourth for the day, and took a big mouthful before he lifted a two-page contract, quickly glanced at its addressee and slid it across the table to Wendy.

"Along with the termination of your contract to Harlem Properties, an amount of one million Rands will be paid into your account. Just to say thank you for all the hard work."

Wendy tried to remain composed, but Jocelynne knew that the Peterson household also had need of this little bonus. Though money could not buy happiness, she knew it had the ability to temporarily remove burdens, and Carl and Wendy Peterson had a number of burdens they would remove with the money.

After an emotional exchange Wendy signed the agreement and was on her way. She stopped at the door. "By the way, I've updated William about Mr. Gallagher and the others."

"Is this about the reports?"

"Mr. Gallagher had some concern about the reports, but Mr. Motlante and Mrs. Vermeulen was a little strange today."

"Define strange."

Wendy frowned. "Mr. Motlante was very insistent on sitting in with the lawyers and the insurance brokers. He put up quite a huff and threatened legal action, but William took care of it. I'm sure he'll brief you tomorrow."

"And what's the deal with Josie?"

"Mrs. Vermeulen was visibly irate when I handed her the reports and a copy of the sales agreement. When I asked what was wrong she went ballistic, saying if she's not happy with the figures she'll take the matter further."

David's face showed his surprise.

"Josie Vermeulen? Ballistic? That's uncharacteristic of her."

"I know. Didn't make a big deal about it. Maybe there's something personal going on."

"Well, keep a finger on the pulse and notify William if you hear anything." David was too tired to worry about Damian Motlante or Josie Vermeulen tonight.

"I've got William down for breakfast tomorrow, same time." Jocelynne said.

"You're staying in town a bit longer?" Wendy asked surprised.

"Apparently. Might cancel the Johannesburg trip altogether and send William instead. I'm needed elsewhere to speed this thing along."

"Nigeria?"

"That's correct," Jocelynne answered on David's behalf. "Thanks, Wendy."

When Wendy finally left it was already six o'clock. Jocelynne started flipping off lights and collecting her register, but David remained in his chair.

"One more person to see," he said and took out another contract.

"No, I think that was it. You must go get some sleep for tomorrow. You look a bit poof."

"Have a seat, Jocelynne," he said sternly.

She stopped what she was doing and stared at him. Her stomach was aflutter. Why were there butterflies in her stomach? Had she quietly been expecting this?

He pulled out a chair for her and slid the contract across the table until it was in front of the empty chair.

"And what is this?"

"A little something for you and Henk, to say thank you for all the hard work. You have been my most important asset. After Elizabeth and the boys died ..." He stopped himself short, as if he had said something wrong. "I remember you coming into my office the one time and telling me to snap out of it, to get on with my life." She noticed David's fingers trembling as he spoke. "I was ready to give up on everything that day. I'd condemned myself to a life of misery and solitude. But because of what you said, I decided not to drown myself with pity. You saved me from a dark future, Jocelynne. And this is my thank-you."

She just smiled, flattered and humbled. After an awkward pause, she decided to strike while the iron was hot.

"It's time, David."

A look of utter confusion coated his eyes. "Come again?"

"It's time to dispel solitude from your life as well. I think it's safe to say you can move on now. You don't need to be alone anymore."

David slid his laptop into the carrying bag, saying, "I'm not so sure about that."

"Come now, sweetie. This has gone on long enough, don't you think? I also knew Lizzy and she wouldn't want you to go at it alone. You need to find yourself a partner to make the colder days a bit warmer." She bounced her brow a couple of times and gave him a coy smile. "Know what I mean?"

Absentmindedly Jocelynne took the contract and signed on the bottom line, not realizing that the amount on the contract said five million and not one million. Those were details that she simply didn't care about. It was just money.

"Just think about it, dear. Because if I can't have you, then someone else sure as hell should." She stood up and started turning off the rest of the lights as she strolled out of the boardroom. "You are just too yummy to waste. Now let's get out of here."

How do you steal R350 million without provoking suspicion? To start with: anonymity and plausible deniability. If it couldn't be proved in court, it never happened. Besides the ability to distance oneself from any reproach, deception in general requires a keen sense of knowing what someone wants, then promising it to them in the most irresistible manner. The art of selling an idea is much like selling an audience on a magic trick: pitting their limited data against their power of reasoning, they think things possible which are really impossible. Introducing an abrupt contradiction to theory or popular belief, ensures mass interest.

The property industry was exactly the same. Before a shopping mall can be built, the zoning rights have to be changed to commercial rights. When this is done, the government has to approve the construction based on the blueprints and the impact on the land. Soon investors, builders and retailers come flocking by the hundreds. Lease agreements and letters of intent are signed and money changes hands before the first brick is ordered. On paper, the entire development, millions and millions of Rands in the making, is already a functioning business entity before the first phases of development has begun. This is the nature of the property game. It is near impossible to regulate what was taking place before it actually did, and every action taken consumed a lot of time before being of any relevance to the situation.

Sometimes investing and buying into a possibility, depended on how impossible the possibility was. The government approved it, interest was sparked, interested parties invested money, money laid the foundation, and before long a vision was cast in stone. The crookery of it all would only come to light after the completion of the project. An epic struggle to settle debts and unanticipated losses would occur while a select few would slip into the underbrush of paperwork and assorted legal loopholes with bags of untraceable money. CEO's and Directors would get bonuses that seemed dreamlike to the average individual and no questions would be asked.

Now where did he fit into this picture? He was trying against all odds to plot a cover-up. And what irrefutable evidence would convict him of this terrible crime? In short, his crime was impatience and the evidence lay in the paperwork, a tiny trail of signatures and approvals waiting to be discovered.

Only bribes could accelerate the South African municipal approval process. Many developers and real estate moguls resorted to bribery in order to advance the development of a project. Sometimes information leaked out and became a public spectacle, but when the dust settled it was business as usual. It always came down to one official willing to put his name on the dotted line. Whether it be an approval on a Right of Development, known in the trade as an ROD, or the rezoning of a property. If the price was right, the underpaid government employee on the other side of the desk would be as fallible as any human being with children to feed and debts to pay. Sometimes, though, a bit more persuasion was required.

The Antagonist had kept his eyes on a particular piece of land just outside of Malmesbury, a rapidly expanding town not too far from Cape Town. It was a 200 hectare property, almost 500 acres of vacant and unwanted land. For years he played around with the idea of taking the land while other investors and developers fought over the West Coast region of the Western Cape. He saw potential and he couldn't allow it to pass him by. He wanted the land. There pulsed within him an impure need to obtain it before anyone else could. Only two things stood in his way. Firstly, he didn't have an extra R10 million lying around to buy it. Secondly, the land was zoned as agricultural land and would not be under consideration for commercial development rights within the next two decades.

There was something about this land that made sense to him. The Western Cape was growing fast. Foreign investors had a keen interest in Cape Town and surrounds, with large-scale development extending to the Southern Cape Garden Route area and all along the West Coast which led up towards Namibia. Inland was the next logical hotspot. There was a huge influx of people relocating. Financial institutions were moving head offices from the city centre to Bellville and Durbanville; the CBD was shifting from the Southern to the Northern Suburbs. Soon the government would be forced to issue rezoning rights to instigate growth and development. There was money to be made and he had to get in there first. First in, first out. And if he gained the right type of interest from developers and investors, he could do it quickly.

Getting the money was fairly easy. He coaxed an ambitious young lawyer into aiding him with this part of the deal. He created a dummy company called Elemental 5959 by forging application forms and pushing them through the system. Elemental 5959 Pty Ltd was an offshore business entity with a sizeable portfolio consisting of falsified assets and bogus sureties. All accounts ended in the Cayman Islands, not connected to him. Everything led to a yacht company that didn't exist. Within months, The Antagonist had been able to procure R11 million from various financial institutions within SA. He used the extra R1 million to pay the loan instalments for the first two years so he needed no initial capital outlay to acquire the land. His intention was to get the money to buy the land and to settle the loans as soon as he could flip it again to investors. The lawyer acted as a conveyance attorney who legitimized the sale for the right price – and everyone had a right price. Once the property had been paid for, it was conveyed and registered to Elemental 5959.

Next the property had to be rezoned for commercial use before development could proceed. An ROD had to be secured before retailers would option floor space. The Antagonist had to find someone who could force the rezoning and secure the ROD. It had to be someone with powerful municipal connections, someone ruthless enough to get the paperwork done and not ask questions, someone who would be prepared to do the dirty work without there being any ties to him. The lawyer had suggested he use Roelf Lassen. The man was a common criminal, but he had all the right connections and he wasn't afraid to exploit the system in order to feed his own pocket. Even more encouraging was the fact that Roelf was prepared to wait three months for his ten per cent fee while The Antagonist secured letters of intent and formal lease agreements from retailers.

Tomas Shemingu, a municipal official, went to work early on a warm Tuesday morning. After a lengthy discourse between Good Tomas and Bad Tomas, he stamped and signed a few documents with a heavy heart. He handed the documents to his assistant to process and to submit to the Department of Environmental Affairs. He left the office feeling faint and disappointed with himself. He arrived home before his wife and found a gym tog bag lying on his bed. There were no signs of forced entry, no sign of anything out of the ordinary, just a bag on the bed. When he opened it, he was overcome by joy and gripped with horror at the same time. It was filled to the zipper with R250 000 in cash and on top of the stacks of money was a photo of his wife Belinda dropping their kids off at school earlier that morning.

Tomas spent the next two months distancing himself from the act, finally relocating to Pretoria as an exemplary employee. Six months later Tomas was on his way to Asia, where he took up a managerial position in an up-and-coming gym franchise. If the incident ever surfaced, the property would be half-built and Tomas would be beyond reproach. The project would create more than 1500 jobs when SA's unemployment statistics was at an all-time high. Unions would be eager to aid the fight for the salaried employee and the media would side with the poor souls who stood to lose their jobs if tools were downed to ensue court cases. Calling on past experiences, Tomas Shemingu knew the government would have no option but to allow building to continue. The Antagonist knew this as well.

A study was done to assess the archaeological impacts of the site, identifying risks and checking for burial grounds and graves, and adhering to the National Heritage Resources Act. When the paper work was done, he went to work. He outsourced the drawing of plans and blueprints to an ageing architect, who drew up a colossal three-storied shopping complex with extended parking lots, small hotel and small-scale casino. It was named The Swartland Opus and it was meant to be the crown jewel of his long and thankless career as a retiring architect. The Antagonist paid the man his due and submitted the designs. He contracted a prominent construction company to complete the project.

After this he brought in the letting agencies who, in turn, did what they were paid to do. They beguiled retailers into believing that The Swartland Opus was the surest investment to date. While still recovering from the effects of a tense recession, retail chains were fighting each other to get in on the deal. When one retailer agreed to a five-year lease, it's competitor agreed to commit to a ten-year lease bearing in mind they required confirmation that they would be the only retailer of its kind in the shopping mall. The more retail chains and similar outlets contested for occupancy in The Swartland Opus, the more the ears of investors and developers began to itch. Before long, 70 per cent of The Swartland Opus was let out to a number of key tenants with agreements and binding letters of intent to occupy.

On paper, everything looked too good to be true. He had set the trend before the rest of South Africa. He had created the best investment on paper, and he would sell it for a monstrous amount. Eventually he sold it to Harlem Properties. He was one of the members of the board. He influenced the acquisition on a whim, all the while seeming oblivious to the great deception. Harlem Properties bought the property from Elemental 5959 for a staggering R400 million. Ten per cent went to Roelf Lassen for his part and a portion settled the outstanding loan account. R350 million was transferred from account to account and Elemental 5959 Pty Ltd died somewhere in the process. Tax trails were covered up to avoid any suspicion and soon The Antagonist found himself staring at his laptop screen with a smile on his face. His European bank account reflected that he was earning a handsome interest on his little nest egg. In the glow of his laptop, fighting the greed and contempt stirring inside him, he studied the features of his beautiful girlfriend and her three-year-old daughter. For years his father had told him he would never succeed in life. The Antagonist had proved his father wrong. Or had he? He was unsure how much of what he had done, had been to establish a family.

Then, at the height of his exit strategy, David Harlem returned to Earth as a triumphant king who had overcome his sorrows. After Mrs. Harlem had died in a car crash, David went on a sabbatical and left the company in the hands of William Botes, CEO extraordinaire and Mr. Brown Nose Deluxe. Then, out of the blue, Harlem steps back into his role as President. First course of action: sell Harlem Properties!

The Antagonist only needed a couple more months to conceal the deal. He just had to get the builders building. He had been so close. But Harlem's decision to sell was a major obstacle. In the event of such a large sale The Swartland Opus would form part of the assets and it would be valued by experts. The asset report would very likely flag The Opus for irregularities. The government still had enough time to stop the development and to investigate the ROD. It would be a matter of time before Roelf Lassen was connected to the bribe and then a savage International inquest of Elemental 5959 Pty Ltd would be done. Hence the need for a cover-up.

He had to cover himself as best he could. He already tried convincing rival companies to make elaborate acquisition offers on some of the properties in Harlem's profile, the majestic Swartland

Opus being the jewel of the bunch. Though many showed interest, his efforts had been in vain. His last hope had been Elixir Holdings. Sendiwe made a sizeable offer, but Harlem had rejected it.

Time was limited and he had to do something fast. The only avenue left to him was a rather unpleasant one. If something tragic were to happen to David Harlem, insurance pay-outs would settle outstanding bonds on all properties and, as stipulated in member contracts, all assets would remain frozen for a year. The sale would be delayed and construction of The Opus would be completed. The one person in the business of arranging tragic accidents was also his accomplice. If David Harlem was taken out of the picture, only Roelf Lassen would be aware of his deception. The Antagonist didn't fancy having loose ends, but what was he to do. How does one cover up an accomplice?

The Antagonist now sat in his car, his new bad-guy office. It was already turning dark. The outline of the city skyscrapers obstructed the view of Table Mountain and the faltering light made it difficult to discern the shape of the city. This side of Woodstock was a different place at night and he wanted to get out of there. He stared at the building in dismay. He was dreading this encounter with Roelf. The man exhausted him. It was the blend of stupidity and brutality that concerned him.

CHAPTER 4

She could see his scalp through the patches of hair. Bald men were attractive, but Stanford da Silva was sleazy. He had a terrible paunch, due, in part, to overindulging in his own merchandise. Despite the smiles and the handshakes, the club owner resembled a hyena.

"That's the nature of the beast. You know how it is," Stan was busy saying.

"No I don't understand. This morning I was retrenched from my other job. Now you're telling me the same thing. I'm an unemployed mother. And I'm flat broke."

"That's not my problem, babe. The music wasn't working, had to drop it. You've got a good voice, but who cares, right? I don't." He pointed across the club. "Look there. This was a jazz bar when I bought it. Now you got a bunch of old barflies drooling over tables, throwing up on the dance floor. And that's on a good night. No more live music, okay? No more you!"

"Please, Stan. I need this. Singing is all release I have."

"Sorry, babe, it's over." He stopped what he was doing, looked down at her ass. "Unless you can dance? You know, without the clothes?"

"Please."

Stan turned his back on her, greeting someone in the back with a nod and a wave. She ran down the corridor after him, reaching him as he was going into the men's.

"Please," she pleaded again, putting a hand on his shoulder. "My children."

Stan turned around and slowly looked her up and down. He closed the door to the toilet and stepped right up to her, his nose almost touching hers. His eyes searched for a sign of weakness.

Before she even knew what was happening, his tongue was gliding across her cheek. She felt his chubby hand cupping one of her breasts, then squeezing the nipple so hard that she cringed.

"There is a way a single mother can still make money in this town," he whispered, nibbling her earlobe.

She felt him against her. When she looked down, she saw that the top two buttons of her dress had been unbuttoned and his hand was slithering into the opening, underneath the cup of the bra, groping her breast firmly. She felt her dress being hiked up and another hand moving up her leg, fast and precise, massaging her.

Kerin couldn't believe what was happening. It was as if time had no relevance. While Stan was touching her, Kerin had simply stepped out of her body and considered the financial benefits this could generate for her children.

Tears were streaming down her face. Stan looked at her, stopped his advance. He withdrew his hand and stepped away, pushing the door open, beckoning her to join him in the pale yellow light which hung over the toilet entrance. She could feel his eyes burning holes in her dress, but the fact that his hands were no longer on her, somehow gave her enough confidence to regain control of her faculties. She looked down, slipped the cup of her bra over her breast and pulled the dress straight, not once taking her eyes off a stubbed-out cigarette butt that lay in the corner on the floor. She clenched her legs shut and felt herself shivering. The tear tracks over her cheeks had turned so cold that it felt like dry ice carved into her face.

"I don't have time for this, babe. You want the money or not?" Stan was massaging himself through his jeans.

Kerin couldn't look up, kept staring at the cigarette.

"Go drink it off, you little slut. We'll do this later tonight. Tell Bamboo to get you good and drunk."

The bathroom door slowly closed on Stan and she was left in silence, leaning against the corridor wall. She was still clutching her dress. Nothing about the encounter had left her sexually aroused. Her body had responded to his hands, but she felt filthy and disappointed. Dillon and Megan, the school fees, the rent, Margie's medication, and the fact that there was almost no more food at home kept running through her mind. She was disgusted with herself. But at least this way, she would be doing it privately. No one would know. Margie would never hear of this.

Music started playing as the club doors opened for business. A monotonous thumping, slowly getting louder and louder as it seeped through to her. She snapped back to reality and buttoned up her dress. Hurriedly she made her way back to the bar before Stan came out of the bathroom.

The focal point of the bar area was a large wooden structure with an apt barman behind it, moving from side to side, taking orders. His tools of the trade were an array of coloured bottles containing all types of spirits and liquors. Some pool tables were strategically placed around the open area by the entrance. Beyond the bar area was a very small dance floor with a few tables scattered about. At the back was a small stage – her stage. The piano had already been sold to make way for a new jukebox. Who put a jukebox on a stage?

She checked her reflection in the light of one of the advertising display units and wiped away the mascara lines beneath her eyes with a napkin.

"Kerin!" Bamboo greeted as she hoisted herself onto the barstool. "You good?"

Bamboo was half-Chinese and half-Zambian. He was a total sweetheart, and he didn't belong in a bar serving drinks for crappy tips. He was better than this, but he needed the money to finish his studies.

"Been better," she said.

"Heard Stan cancelled the gig, right."

"Just heard so myself."

She almost couldn't face Bamboo. When she finally looked up at his friendly face, there was an uncomfortable recognition in his eyes that suggested he knew exactly what was going on in her mind.

"What will it be?"

"Whatever is strongest," she said softly and forced a smile.

Kerin felt determined. If she was going to have sex with someone for money, she wanted as little recollection as possible. Better yet, she could write it off as a drunken mistake.

Bamboo looked at her for a very long time. At first he looked a bit disappointed but Kerin perceived a glimmer of sympathy. The mixed emotions and the sensation of his eyes on her, caused her to look down again when Stan returned from the toilet.

"I hear you, sister. I hear," he muttered against the loud music and poured her something terrible.

It hit immediately. Moments later she could feel herself relaxing. Her intentions no longer required justification. Her mind had been made up and she would do what she had to do. She convinced herself that any parent would understand, that this was the only way.

A few times Stan waddled past the bar, studying her features as he went. He was ugly. If only he had been better-looking – no coffee stains, oily hair, beard stubble and greedy eyes. If only he looked normal and had a personality, she wouldn't feel so reluctant to go through with it. The establishment had gone from social jazz club to full-fledged bar full of drunk in no time. Her sanctuary, the one place where she could be herself and shut out the world, was no more. Soon, after Stan had had his way with her, this place would hold no pleasant memory at all.

She had her fourth drink in front of her, something yellow and vile-smelling. She didn't even notice that Bamboo had stepped out from behind the bar. He grabbed her by the arm.

"Time to go, sister," he said. "He's in the back, so you must go now."

He pulled her off the barstool and guided her through the pool area toward the entrance. For nearly two hours she had been sitting at a bar, drowning her inhibitions with hard liquor. She had very little resistance left to fight Bamboo, and simply stumbled along, smiling to herself.

"Get out of here," he hissed at her. "You don't know what you're doing. This man, he does these things to women. You just a thing to him." He gently pushed her toward the door. "Understand? You just a thing, right."

"But I need the money," Kerin whimpered.

"I hear you, sister. We all need it, but you go now and find it somewhere else. Here you'll get hurt. I see it all the time, right. You better than this." He pushed her toward the door again, and said, "Go sleep it off. You thank me later, right."

And just like that she found herself standing outside in the rain. She was twenty minutes away from home. She didn't know what to do. It was an uncomfortable walk in heels and she was not in the mood. She was half-drunk, drenched, broke and jobless. Her make-up was running, dress clinging to her body. Minutes ago she had been ready to prostitute her body out for cash, now she looked the part. The irony of it all was demeaning.

The streets were busy for a Tuesday night. Her feet were moving slowly over the wet tar.

It seemed bizarre that Cape Town was considered to be one of the world's best holiday destinations. Foreigners longed to come to the Cape of Good Hope, to enjoy the beauty and the splendour that was South Africa. She had lived there her whole life and she had never seen it. She loathed this horrible place.

Kerin longed for a cigarette, more than ever before. She hadn't smoked since ... She couldn't even remember when last she'd had a smoke. Thinking about smoking also didn't make the walk any easier. Her feet were cold and numb. Her hair hung in clumps down the side of her face.

Her cheeks were deadened. She couldn't feel the warmth of the tears. The alcohol was messing with her, her head was spinning, stomach contracted and her hands shaking. Kerin thought she was hallucinating. Whatever Bamboo had given her had made her nauseous.

She felt like jumping into the oncoming traffic and ending it. Why carry on with this mess of a life? The only thing worth living for was her children. What would happen to them? She didn't even have a life policy that would pay out in the event of death. There was nothing. They'd be raised by the government and that would be a sad end to it all.

No, she needed money. She needed to survive and pay the bills, to provide food and shelter for her children.

A car pulled to the side of the road in front of her. The red brake lights were bright. She couldn't look directly at them. The passenger window rolled down and a voice called out to her.

She stopped, listened, unsure what to do.

"Hi there!" the man called again. "You working?"

Kerin glanced up and down the street, her mind racing through a list of responses and ideas, thinking the unimaginable, thinking money.

"You paying?" she asked.

The man nodded reluctantly, and unlocked the door by remote.

He had met with the brokers to inform them of the sale and the cessation of relevant policies. No brokerage enjoyed losing business. The cutthroat mentality of financial advisers was common knowledge. They survived on commission alone and competition was fierce. But they had no choice but to relent. At point of sale, the transfer of assets relieved him of insurance obligations.

Then came the lawyers. If his personal legal representative, Carl Jonker, hadn't been present at the meeting, he would've jumped out the window. Those in highly qualified legal positions had a suave way about them, projecting an air of sophistication. They spoke in a manner which reeked of confidence and authority. They were ruthless. At times they appeared sympathetic about the sale, other times they were viscous and blunt about their costs.

Lastly: the staff meetings. Initially he had asked William to do the exit-interviews, but something urged him to do it personally. In some way it felt like giving each employee closure. It turn, it had left him on an emotional high.

Then Jocelynne dropped that bomb. She always unscrewed his cap at the last minute and left him hanging. She had always been a good influence in the office, but why confuse him at the last minute. She had told him not to remain alone.

For a long time he had been aware of his growing sense of loneliness. Maybe it was time to move on, but how? Every woman he met was measured by the memory of Elizabeth, and they always came up short. Moving on was not just moving on. It would never be that simple. There was an ever-present reluctance in him. The only way to break the mould was to force the issue of moving on, just for the sake of moving on. He dreaded that.

He dined at Calibri's Ristorante, one of the most romantic spots around. The food was exquisite. He was seated in an abandoned corner, a table for two. He stared at the empty chair opposite him. The candle flickered on languidly, the shadows looking like two lovers dancing across the walls. The couple at the next table were celebrating their anniversary. Other couples were holding hands across the tables, smiling at each other, eyes glittering like stars.

Dammit, Jocelynne! he thought. *Why did you have to point it out?* David would have spent the night without noticing a thing. He would have carried on with his life, sold the company and spent his days on the farm in George, maybe tried his hand at farming. Now every measure of happiness grated him and every lover's glance annoyed him to his core.

David finished his meal and left the restaurant in a sombre state. Just like that, at the height of his career, his life appeared to be worthless. He took a little side trip, not eager to get back to the hotel. It was not even 20:00 yet, but he was too depressed to sleep. He didn't feel like watching television either. Better to revisit the past.

He drove the car into the shrubs, until it was completely hidden from view and out of the road. He sat there in silence for the longest time. In the distance he saw the lights of Beach Road. With the moon piercing through a break in the clouds, he made out the waves lapping angrily on the beachside.

From his wallet he removed a small photo. Wasn't that where memories were kept? Didn't every family man own a wallet with a little reminder among the cards? Why should a man of stature, a man of accomplishment, be any different? He kept it there like any normal man. When the weight of the world choked him, he took it out and relived the best parts of his life, just to remember once more. He studied the photo and felt himself tearing up. In the picture Peter and Mitchell were playing with Elizabeth, pushing her to the ground, tickling her. David was the photographer, staring at his family and waiting for that picture moment. And then it happened. She turned her head towards him and stared out at him with her deep eyes, elated and smiling. The joy screamed out at him and he preserved it. Now it was all he had left. There was a computer full of wedding photos, birthday pictures and videos, but this tiny picture was the very essence of his joy, and the weight of his sorrow.

He climbed out and stood in the drizzling rain for a few minutes. Looking down he perceived the length of the steep hill. The road had an abrupt curb, with a small section of gravel where the Land Rover now stood in wait. Beyond the section of gravel was a high barrier of shrubs, but beyond that lay instant death: a sharp, yet gradual, twenty-metre drop down the hill.

Even from the top he could discern the tree which signalled the demise of his trusty old Jaguar. At the base of the tree the bark was still scorched black by fire. The drizzle subsided slightly. He ventured halfway down the hill. This was where he had landed that day, where he had woken up. This was how he had survived.

He had finished the grieving process long ago, but memories had an involuntary relationship with grief, a marriage of joy and pain, marred by the inevitable burden of loss.

David gave the damaged tree a quick salute, as one old comrade would greet another, and left. The sound of the car door slamming shut, greeting locking mechanism and shuddering in his grip, was identical to the recoil from a silenced rifle. He closed his eyes, rubbed his face with both hands. Another unpleasant memory he couldn't erase. It wouldn't let him be. Though no longer a reality, it would always be part of him. But he was ready to forget. As before, he vowed never to visit the tree again.

The drive back to the hotel was absolute torture. Once there he remained seated in the car for a while, mesmerized by the swiping wipers and the gentle hum of the car engine. His mind was blank. He had no idea what he would do on a big piece of land in George. Nothing ever happened there. He had enough money to travel the world and live off his investments.

The evening concierge ran up to the driver's side door in his porter uniform, holding out an umbrella. The young man opened the door and looked expectantly at David.

"Sir?" he asked.

David stared at him. "Sorry, I think I'll drive around a bit."

"Of course, sir," the concierge said politely and closed the door.

His mind was all over the place. He wondered what other wealthy bachelors were doing in a city that seemed to vibrate with decadence. Few things came to mind. He imagined he had very little to be mindful of. He had nothing left to lose, just money.

Without thinking it through, David stopped at the first girl he saw. It was a mysterious-looking one. She wore an evening dress, not really the attire he had imagined.

"What the hell are you doing?" he scolded himself as he wound down the window. "You're picking up a hooker, you fool."

As she came into view he asked if she was working. At the mention of money she was in the car, dripping all over the leather upholstery. He studied her, aware that the overwhelming smell of alcohol had followed her into the car. She looked frantic, edgy and drunk. *Great! Loads of prostitutes walking the streets and you had to pick the drunk one.*

"You okay?"

"Yes," she said loudly, as if trying to convince herself. "I know what I'm doing, okay."

"I was talking about the rain. You're soaked." He reached behind the seat, fumbling around in search for something.

"Hey, what you doing?" she asked in a panicked voice, her eyes wide and make-up smudged.

He removed a faded hand towel and gave it to her.

"Oh, your seats. Sorry." She grabbed the towel and began wiping without any aim, dabbing her hair and then the seats.

"I don't care about the seats." He couldn't help smiling at her. "So, how does this work? Do I pay now?"

As the car pulled away from the curb, the girl stopped what she was doing and gaped at him. It was as though she woke up in the car, not sure where she were or what she was doing.

"Listen, I don't know what I'm doing here. I didn't think this through."

That was not the ideal response, even at a time like this. How difficult could it be to coax a prostitute into your car? He just needed someone to talk to, even if he had to pay for it. Now this nonsense.

"Is this a scam?" he asked.

"I must go."

"What?"

"I want to get out. I need out." She frantically pulled at the door handle, but the car was already moving and the locks had clamped down. When she noticed the locked doors, she began slamming her elbow into the door.

"Hey, wait. What the hell are you doing? The door locks automatically. Just relax."

"Don't tell me to relax, okay. I've got kids. I can't do this, I can't!"

David was flabbergasted. He heard that annoying voice in his mind saying, *I told you so*. What on earth was he doing there? Aware that situations could easily spin out of control, he imagined the headlines: PROPERTY MOGUL KIDNAPS HOOKER.

"What just happened?" he asked, pulling to the curb.

"Open the doors!" she screamed, still tugging at the handle. "Open the damn doors!"

"Okay, okay."

Suddenly she stopped. She rummaged through her tiny handbag, ripped out a small red canister, her finger poised over the nozzle. "If you don't let me out right now, I'll Mace you."

David almost burst out laughing. She looked serious enough about drenching him with pepper spray, but the expression on her face was so precious that he memorized it immediately. Her lips were clenched and her eyebrows were scrunched together. Her hair hung in unattractive clumps across her face and shoulders and she was shivering, either from the cold or the excitement. He held up his hands in surrender.

"The doors lock automatically. If I press here..."

He pressed a button and the locks popped up. In a flash the door was opened and she was making her escape. She stopped mid-exit and turned around, rain slanting in.

"I'm not really a prostitute, you know," she said in a defiant tone.

Though it explained her reluctance and her erratic behaviour, it didn't explain why she had climbed into his car. Something was different with this woman. There was something deep, needy and deserving, that couldn't be defined.

"That's okay. I'm not really a client. Just wanted someone to talk to."

Still undecided, one foot on the pavement and one foot in the car, she reasoned with herself, looking for excuses, still clenching the can of teargas.

"I'm drunk. I'm terrible company."

"I think you need a cup of coffee."

She glanced up and down the wet street, then at him again.

"My treat," he said invitingly, maintaining the hands-up pose. "There's an all-night coffee shop up front, a block or two away. I go there when I can't sleep."

"Just talk?"

"Just talk," he confirmed. "Pinky promise."

"R500 an hour?"

"R500 an hour."

The door closed.

"Can I put my hands down?"

"Don't try anything funny or I'll use it."

He drove to the coffee shop with the pepper-spray nozzle still aimed at him. He stopped in the brightly-lit parking lot.

"I'm David, by the way," he held out his hand.

"I'm ... I'm ..."

When he looked at her, he noticed her features had changed. Her face was white and her eyes were glazed over. She put one hand on the dashboard as if that would stop the world from turning.

"Seriously, are you okay?"

"I don't really drink."

And then it happened. She tipped her head forward and threw up all over him. He caught her head before it could bump on the handbrake handle. He held her up until she was finished. Then he felt her go limp in his hands, slowly slipping away. He held her head tenderly, like the day when Elizabeth had a stomach bug. There was life in his hands, the pulse in her neck, her breathing, her warmth.

If he had anyone to point out his mistakes, this would've been a great scenario to recall. But he was on his own, on a rainy Tuesday night in a vacant parking lot, with a passed-out hooker's head resting in his lap. Jocelynne probably didn't have this in mind when she had urged him to move on.

"You do not steal R 350 million without getting your hands a little dirty."

"I don't mind getting my hands dirty, but the insurance ..."

"The insurance is a last attempt to try and mop up this mess."

"You knew the risks ..."

"Quiet," Roelf Lassen said in a calm voice. "Do not speak. For as long as you sit here, do not open your lips again or I'll cut them off."

His voice carried a certain inaudible threat in it, something that seemed to resonate with an underlying violence so fierce that it had no need of being uttered. A man with a voice so subtly demanding was void of emotion. No threat was empty. What was said, was meant. The Antagonist had no desire to test the waters, so he kept quiet.

As if to keep the electricity in the air a bit longer, Roelf elegantly cupped one hand over his mouth and cleared his throat. He leaned back and entwined his fingers over his expanding waistline so that they became inter-locked. Roelf appeared to be the perfect gentleman, but in reality he was a monster – a monster with connections.

"This business we are in normally has need of being conducted with a bit more finesse than the business I'm used to. I was hoping it would remain that way, but things change and we adapt. Those are the risks we take."

The Antagonist was appalled. We, we, we. Roelf used the word as if the two of them had signed a contract, as though they had been working together for years. The Antagonist wondered if the man had any idea how to steal R350 million on his own. Roelf hadn't contributed much to the crime. His role had been to generate legitimate documentation by bribing municipal employees.

That bit of effort came at a steep fee, of course. Ten per cent had seemed fair at the time, but The Antagonist was beginning to reconsider the fee.

Roelf's eyes hardened ever so slightly as he stretched his arms out over the smooth surface of the leather couch.

"My father was a yachtsman his whole life. Don't know if I ever mentioned that. His fingers were like stone, skin as tough as this old leather. He was a sea crab, even walked like one when he was drunk. One thing he always told me, I'll never forget it. He said rope was most important thing on a yacht. It was strong, kept everything in place. But when rope frays at the edges, you have to burn it off to make it hard again, then you have to tape it, or else it breaks integrity of rope. If you don't, rope will keep fraying until there's nothing left. You understand, yes?"

In the opposite chair, his listener sat quietly. The Antagonist nodded slowly, but kept his eyes on Roelf. A rope was such a stupid metaphor.

"Good!" Roelf exclaimed. "I'll help you with this problem. But if it starts to fray, I'll burn everything off and go to work on your family. Understood?"

The Antagonist nodded, clenching his jaws in frustration.

"There will be a fee. We settle on R150 000, yes?"

Again he nodded, grudgingly, quietly fighting to contain his contempt. It was blatant bullying, and thievery. He couldn't just move around small amounts willy-nilly. The last thing he wanted to do was to alert the regulatory bodies.

Roelf dismissed the meeting with a wave of his hand. *Such a bloody diva*, The Antagonist thought. Who waved a hand to conclude a meeting, the Queen of England?

The Antagonist left without a word or a gesture. A storm was brewing within him. He had to get outside and vent. He had to escape. It felt as though a noose was forming around his neck and someone was pulling it tighter and tighter. He had to get away from it, but couldn't. Everything was such a mess, now he had to face the music.

Roelf's two trustworthy bodyguards escorted him out, their lifeless stares and broad shoulders encouraging him to comply.

Once outside, he climbed into the safety of his car. He raced his car as hard as it would allow, the engine flaring up and screaming vehemently. For almost fifteen minutes he kept the pedal all the way to the floor, until the scenery outside the windows changed from high buildings to emptiness. He was well out of the city, far away from the lights. He pulled off the highway and came to a halt on an abandoned road. He turned out the lights and sat in the dark, whimpering softly. Tears were streaming down his face and his body was shaking. Suddenly a deep guttural scream leapt out of his mouth and it kept flowing until there was no air left in his lungs. He punched the steering wheel with all his might. It felt as though he was confronting his dilemma and releasing his pent-up vehemence, a feeling that would pass in time. He kept on assaulting the car, his fury knowing no end. In the frenzy a few drops of blood sprayed over the dashboard from where he had cut his hand the night before.

From afar, the car did not look out of place. It gently rocked from side to side, with the soft *honking* sound of the car horn occasionally audible above the sounds of the night. The rest of the world was oblivious to the fact that something far more menacing was festering in the darkness.

When he finally calmed down, he looked at his reflection in the rear view mirror. With one hand he combed his hair back into place, careful not to get blood in his hair, and forced a smile. He sucked at his teeth, cleaning out an imaginary piece of dinner with his tongue. He collected himself, closed his eyes and sighed.

After what felt like an hour he unlocked the cubbyhole and opened the lid. When the light came on, it reflected off the shiny barrel. He removed the gun from its hiding place. It felt reassuring,

KING OF SORROW | James Fouché

powerful. He slipped the barrel deep into his mouth, until he felt nothing but metal on his tongue, against his teeth, crazy wonderful.

Right now pulling the trigger was the furthest thing from his mind. He just loved the feeling of it in his mouth. It kept him in the present tense. He badly wanted to use the gun, even contemplated using it on himself. He wanted to see the muzzle flare, feel the recoil in his hands. He couldn't explain why. His sickness was growing towards a point of being made manifest. It was terror within the realm of fruition.

CHAPTER 5

She woke up slowly, systematically stepping into her memories and her senses, like a child coming into the world. She blinked her eyes repetitively, then opened and closed her fists a couple of times. Her fingertips felt numb and her neck was sore. Not only was her mouth dry but her tongue felt twice its normal size, swollen.

She was alone in the room. At first she thought it someone's house, but then she noticed the faint beeping of a heart rate monitor beside her, and a drip connected to her arm. Outside the room people were passing by in nurses' uniforms. Then she heard the intercom system calling a Doctor Stevens to reception. Moments later the disasters of the night before seeped through.

The walls were a soft peachy colour. The wooden skirting boards and windowsills had recently been varnished. The bed linen, curtains, chairs – everything had a homely neutrality. She was not sharing the room. There was a bed opposite hers, but it was empty. It was a private hospital, not government, and that meant money.

Kerin forced herself up into a seated position and urgently began scanning the room for her clothes when a tall, handsome young man walked into the room wearing a white gown, a file in his hands.

"Morning, Mrs. Fellows. I'm Doctor Koen," he said in a pleasant tone and gave her a quick smile. "How are we feeling this morning? A bit dry-mouthed?"

"Fine, I guess. Where am I?"

"Medi-Clinic." He stared into her eyes, made some notes. "You look much better."

He picked up her hand to gauge response and gingerly put it at her side. His hands were soft, gentle and warm. He had a caring way about him, but his manner was still swift and methodical.

"Who brought me here?"

Doctor Koen ignored the question. Instead he studied the monitors and the drip, making more annotations to her file. Regular check-up procedure.

"I don't have any money," she blurted out.

"I don't deal with accounts, Mrs. Fellows."

"My name's Kerin."

"Okay, Kerin," he said softly. "I suppose you're curious as to how you ended up here."

"Mildly. I remember throwing up."

The doctor stood at the edge of the bed looking down at her, not even a hint of a smile on his face, an intellectual sarcasm belying his sincerity.

"That's what happens when you drink on an empty stomach. Walking around in the rain, too." He glanced at the file. "Luckily you threw up before passing out."

"Luckily?"

"Yes. Comatose patients are likely to aspirate their vomit. You could choke on your own vomit and you won't even know

85

about it. If it hadn't been for your friend, it could've been much worse."

"That it? I drank too much and threw up. Nothing more?"

"Sorry to disappoint."

"So, just a hangover?"

The doctor, visibly irate, glared at her over his thin-rimmed spectacles, then shifted his eyes back to the clipboard.

"Hangover? Miss, if you didn't get medical care you might've ended up with hypoglycaemia, lactic acidosis, or acute renal failure. Your lack of respect for our efforts affronts me."

Kerin was not amused. She had her own regrets to deal with, but right now she wanted to go home. She wanted her comfort zone back.

"I never asked to be brought here," she snapped. "I just want to get home."

"Home? Alright, let me ask you this, do you have children?"

"Two. Why?"

"How would they feel if someone told them their mommy spent the night in hospital because she drank too much? I imagine Child Services would also like to know."

"You always treat patients like this?"

"Just stating facts."

She instantly became woeful and apologetic. The night before was a blur, but now she was more concerned about her children. There were flashes of Stan's hands on her, a car pulling up next to her, then throwing up. She closed her eyes and sighed.

"I didn't mean to snap." She looked at the man's wedding ring and wondered if he also had children. "This is not me. I'm not a boozer, okay. I just can't remember what happened."

"You don't look like a heavy drinker. Sometimes not knowing is better than knowing."

Kerin said nothing, just stared at the bedding over her legs, contemplating the extent of the damage at home. "Your vitals are fine. A nurse will assist you with the checking-out procedure."

A nurse helped her get dressed. She claimed her belongings from the night before, not even bothering to check the contents of her handbag. What was the point? There was nothing of real value inside. She checked her cell phone: three missed calls from Margie. She made a quick call to her mother at 09:00, using as little airtime as possible. She told her not to worry, that everything was fine and she'd be home soon. The call gave her some relief. She had worked long hours before, but she'd never just stayed away.

At reception Kerin signed out, then went to the accounts department, where she became engrossed in a heated dispute with the admin manager. Her account had been billed to a credit card and settled in full. The payer had requested to remain anonymous, but Kerin put up such a stink and threatened with legal action. Eventually, as required by law, the information of the payer had to be given upon request of the patient.

Then she had her freedom. She stood outside the hospital building, shoes dangling from one hand, purse from the other. For a while she remained there, looking out over the parking lot and the awaiting city, before disembarking on her long trek home. She hadn't made a block on the pavement tar before her feet began aching. She could almost feel the blisters being forced into being. Outside a small cafe she saw a group of waiters preparing their bays for the day. She thought about approaching the manager for work, but she was not presentable enough for an interview. When the smell of freshly brewed coffee hit her she searched her purse for change, only to discover R1000 in notes stuffed into a side pocket. She gasped and smiled, but the rush of elation was short-lived.

She didn't know what to make of the money. All the way home she was mulling it over. She was stumped. Had he paid her for nothing? Or had there been something? She remembered saying R500 an hour. Had something happened while she was unconscious? Had he gotten his two hours' worth without her knowing about it? The thought terrified her. Would she even know if she had been raped? She didn't feel sore. What if he had taken advantage of her, but had been careful about it? If she had indeed been raped she could do nothing about it. *She* had gotten into the car without any persuasion. Whatever transpired after that was better left unthought-of. She had convicted and sentenced herself for bad parenting, possible prostitution, and drunkenness. This was not Kerin Fellows. She had never done this before.

Then another thought: she was not on contraceptive medication. In fact, she hadn't been sexually active in years. What if this stranger had taken advantage of her? What if she was pregnant? By the time a taxi dropped her off at home, she was quietly freaking out.

Margie was waiting for her. Instead of scolding, she greeted Kerin as though nothing had happened. She took Kerin's purse and shoes from her, as the children came in from their room. "Don't worry. I told them you had to work the whole night. They didn't go to school, though."

Kerin almost burst into tears. The sudden relief made her legs wobble. "Sorry about this," she whispered back. "I'm such a shit ..." she began, but Margie cut her short with an embrace.

"Pull it together, deary. Don't let them see you like this. You're their mother."

Dillon blasted around the corner, pushing Megan out of the way. She shared hugs all-round, spent some time with them, then slipped into the bathroom. She locked herself in and drew a bath. As she waited for the tub to fill she sat on the toilet seat. Using her fingers and a loose piece of mirror she inspected herself for signs of penetration. Not knowing was terrible. She had to know.

Kerin had no idea what to look for. Her ex-husband had been rough with her, many times. Their intercourse sessions, though brief, had been the plausible result of consensual rape. She had merely been the mother of his children. She had no self-worth, no urge to stand her ground or to fight back.

She remembered Stan cupping her breasts, and was instantly nauseous. What the hell was wrong with her? Kerin was trying to minimize the blame her guilty conscience was placing on her. But no amount of reasoning would lessen the regret. She had been stupid, childish and naive. She had not considered the repercussions. She could easily have been a victim, formed part of a shocking crime statistic.

After a while she relented and decided that there had been no penetration. Besides, she hadn't had sex in a long time. She would have known if something had happened.

Before climbing into the tub, she examined the piece of paper with the payer's particulars. The credit card used for the hospital payment listed the account holder as a company. On the note was scribbled the name of the company, a postal address and a landline number. Harlem Property Group.

She had to do damage control, had to get her life back on track. It was time to fight again, for her children and for herself. She had to take responsibility for her actions and repay the hospital bill in full. She had to find a new job, soon.

David skipped his gym routine. He was rolling around, staring at the ceiling for prolonged periods, then at the bedside clock, then at the ceiling again.

He was mulling over what had transpired the night before. Never before had he found himself so undecided about a singular experience. He loved it. He loved not being able to explain why things had gone the way it had.

His breakfast with William had been brief. David discussed his trip to Nigeria to meet with the buyers and what would happen in his absence. William prepared for his trip to Johannesburg, taking notes as David gave them.

"Just supervise. Everything is on paper. It's not rocket science. Documenting inventories. Contractual chit-chat. Lawyers are paid to iron out wrinkles. You just nod."

"Are they happy with the terms?"

"They'll get over it when we settle their account." David savoured a short silence. "I am no longer Harlem Properties. It's become an entity on its own. Time to step aside."

David asked the hotel manager to have his car sent to a trusted valet service. Hopefully they would be able to remove the smell of vomit. He had a personal taxi take him to the office, where Jocelynne greeted him with a stack of files for the day.

He gently pushed one boardroom door inward on its hinges, freezing in his tracks when he saw two board members engaged in a tussle near a trophy display case.

Aaron Bala and Damian Motlante were pushing and shoving one another, as one would imagine two kids pawing at each other while shielding their eyes. Damian, having sheer size to his advantage, grabbed Aaron Bala by his collar and pushed him back into the display case. While Bala pouted his lips in defiance, Damian leaned forward threateningly.

"If that's how you wish to resolve the matter, then you're on your own," Damian hissed and gave Bala one last half-hearted shove to enforce his dominance.

As the men glared at each other, it dawned on David that neither had noticed him entering the boardroom. In a gentlemanly manner, and in a subtle play on theatrics, he cleared his throat to get their attention and entered the room without looking at them.

"Gentleman," he greeted, strolling over to the chair at the furthest edge of the table. "I hope this is not business." He put down the files and sat down. "And if it's personal, this is the last place you should be settling disputes."

Both men unclenched their fists and began straightening their suites.

Bala stepped forward in a humbling manner and folded his hands apologetically. Though short in stature, Aaron Bala was an accomplished man with many degrees to his name. He was a millionaire many times over and was even wealthier than David. He had the uncanny ability to feel the way of the economy, to predict dips and rises before they realized. His understanding of the natural flux of business cycles made him a valuable asset to any company. David knew Bala welcomed the news of the sale. He had many other business interests to tend to or future ventures to pursue.

"Apologies, David. This is a personal matter. We shall take it elsewhere." He gave Damian a quick once-over. "Sorry you had to see this."

Damian Motlante, in contrast to Bala, was a big man with a large bald head. He looked like a Rottweiler. He had menacing eyes which had helped to win over many business deals by belittling rivals. He was a bombastic man, but he had one of the smallest shares in the company and he was constantly reminded of this at board meetings. Sendiwe had tried pulling Damian away from David's side with lucrative offers. But who in their right mind would consider playing second-fiddle to Linden Sendiwe and his ever-growing money monster, Elixir Holdings?

As yet Damian hadn't acknowledged David's presence. He kept his eyes stolidly focused on Bala, an unrelenting and unforgiving anger present in his features.

"Yes," he mumbled in a deep voice. "We *will* take this elsewhere."

Damian stormed out of the boardroom, the door swinging shut in his wake.

David and Damian had been involved in many heated discussions about the direction of the company. Damian still thought Harlem should list the company on the Johannesburg Stock Exchange, to make shares available to the public. Some board members shared his view, but David opposed this effort of expansion. He was owner and majority shareholder. He had the final call. By nature, Damian was blunt, rude, and near impossible to work with, but an absolute genius. Genius had place for many flaws. Quickly getting hot under the collar was a minor flaw in the property industry, one easily overlooked.

Bala apologised again and left.

David fell into the paperwork and prepared for his meeting with Ray Gallagher. An empty silence roamed and the hours dripped away like minutes. When he took a break, Jocelynne came in and joined him at the table. She slid a large envelope across the table.

"This came for you a short while ago."

David held up the envelope and given its weight, said, "Great. More paperwork."

Jocelynne wrapped her long nails on the desk, lost in thought.

"Penny for your thoughts?"

"He's here. Early as always." She sighed and leaned on her hand until her cheek forced her left eye shut.

"Good, we can get this over with." David closed his files, methodically stacking them on his left, bottle of water on his right. "No need to punish the punctual by making them wait."

He opened the envelope and flipped through the contents.

"That man is not punctual. He's dangerously infantile." She composed herself and forced a smile.

David had stopped listening to her, his mind suddenly captivated by something far more severe. The contents of the envelope had his attention. He should have been more upset, but he had learned to roll with the punches of the property business.

"Could you track the sender of this envelope with the waybill info?"

"No, it was hand delivered. A guy in a suit. Why?"

"No reason."

She left and returned with Ray in tow. They greeted with a handshake, the first proper greeting in months.

"On time, as always," David said, adding the envelope to his stack of files.

"Bad news?" Ray asked, pointing at the envelope.

"Nothing new under the sun, right?"

Ray smiled and nodded.

"You sounded a bit concerned on the phone. What's wrong?"

"I know you had to change your plans to see me and I appreciate that. We haven't spoken lately, with you travelling across Africa and all that. In fact, we haven't spoken much after the accident."

"Why are we here, Ray?" he asked, making the matter not one of I and me, but one of we and us.

Ray folded and refolded his hands, rubbed his forehead, cleared his throat. "There is this woman ..." he began. "We've been an item for a while. Getting married later this year, to make it official. She has this great kid, Allibeth, sweetest thing I've ever seen. She's turning four soon."

"Four? How old is the mother?"

Ray flashed his eyes at David, a steely look which declared he was prepared to defend himself.

"She's twenty five."

"That's a bit young, Ray. She's younger than your other children."

He began reciting a defence he had rehearsed well in advance. David held up his hand and stopped him mid-way.

"Why do you defend yourself? I don't care about your love-life, Ray."

"But why is age such an issue to everyone. She's very mature and she doesn't mind my age. She's been there for me after Misha died and ..."

"And she's the mother of your child," David said matter-of-factly.

There was a sudden silence. Ray looked down at the table for a long time, contemplating whether to lie.

"Ray? Just me and you here. Is Allibeth your daughter?"

"I hate it when you do that, calling the card before I play it." Ray sat shaking his head for a brief moment. "It happened just before Misha fell ill. She knew about us. We worked through it before the end. It was a difficult time."

The admission of a child born out of wedlock while his wife was on her deathbed, qualified as a sensitive issue. David had learned that the best way to deal with delicate matters was to power through and to get to the end, to accept that no amount of reasoning would undo what had been done. It was either a fact or a memory and nothing could change it.

"Father at sixty-five. Wow, that's something. I think congratulations are in order."

"Doctors said it was a miracle."

David wondered briefly what the opposite of a miracle would be. He imagined the death of Elizabeth and the kids would be just that, the exact opposite of a miracle. It had been doom in all its pain. It was hard to imagine God's hand at play in the woes of life, but the harsh reality was that life was not all joy and butterflies. Life was fragile and tender, and the fullness of grace had to be experienced. Sometimes it only took one accident to flip the switch.

"Yes, God has a funny way. Little surprises when we least expect them."

"I'm not twenty anymore. That child will be the death of me. I can't play with her as a father should. My knees and my elbows keep packing up. I'm just an old man."

Having been away from business for a long time, David had noticed how rapid Ray's age had been flecked open to the world. Droopy eyes, wrinkled skin, puffiness. It reminded him that life never stopped for anyone.

"Well, you made your bed. So how does this tie in with the sale?"

"I was in the process of transferring a portion of my shares to her name, to give her some security."

"Oh, I see." David leaned back in an impartial manner. "I doubt that will be done before the sale, Ray. Besides, it's a move that requires a majority vote."

"I know. Thought we could stall the sale for a while, until I can get buy-in from the other members."

"Paperwork is done. Sale has been concluded. If we stall, we are in breach of contract and the offer is off the table. The media would have a field day with it." David sat forward again. "Have you thought about this, Ray? Your daughter is a minor and there are certain implications. If you wait till after the sale and your marriage is on paper, it makes more sense to leave funds or fixed assets to your *legal* spouse or guardian. Even a trust might be a better option."

He appeared disappointed.

"You wanted to meet with me about your shares? Ray, you stressed how important this was, that there were discrepancies. Meanwhile you were stressing about tax implications?"

"My integrity is all I have left. There might be questions if I change beneficiaries now. I haven't brought the matter to the board yet."

"You should've done that first. The paper trail can kill you. You know that."

"Well, if I knew the sale would be so sudden, I could've proposed it better. You just decided to sell."

"Ray, I'm selling. It's been a long time coming. Make peace with it and let it go. You have to move on with your life and I have to move on with mine."

They sat talking for a while longer, Jocelynne serving coffee and cookies.

"Regarding your dilemma," David said finally, "you have a large share in the company and there's going to be a lot of money when the sale goes through. Your children okay with the new missus?"

"They don't know yet," Ray confessed, a naughty look on his face.

"You naughty bugger. I'll miss you, Ray. You've been an important part of my life."

"I'm going to Australia after this, visiting the kids."

"Then this will be goodbye for now."

They parted ways. David had no idea when he would see Ray again.

William entered moments later, a smirk on his face and his eyes playful.

"Coping?" he asked.

"I'll survive."

"Ray appeared rather docile."

"In a manner of speaking." David walked to the windows and opened one of the side panels. The smell and the sound of the city streamed in, a pleasant cacophony floating on a stench-cloud. "Is your flight to Joburg sorted?"

"It seems the lawyers are coming to Cape Town."

"Is that right?" David asked, tiny hint of sarcasm in his voice.

"As you said, they are smelling money. They wanted deposits and accommodation, but I'll make sure every cent is accounted for."

"Give them their due, William. And get it done."

William put his hands in his pockets and blew out a sigh of relief. He seldom relaxed his rigidity.

"Consider it done, boss."

"Boss? That's a first." David rolled his shoulders to relieve the stress in his neck. "What would I do without you?"

"You'd work yourself to death."

William joined him at the large boardroom windows, his behaviour mimicking David's sullenness. They stood side-by-side, staring out over the mid-day traffic, like two brothers at a funeral.

"I very nearly did. You're a good man, Will."

"No I'm not. I'm as flawed as you, maybe more."

They stood in silence for a long time, then David fetched the envelope. He removed a stack of photos and handed it to William, who paged through them slowly.

"What the hell is this?" he hissed. "Where did you get these?"

William immediately became enraged. In this regard David and William differed tremendously. David had the ability to force calm upon himself, but William had an eagerness to resolve matters, sometimes prematurely.

"Who took these pictures? And when?"

"I don't know. They were hand delivered a while ago."

"Is this blackmail?"

The photo was of two people meeting in a restaurant. Linden Sendiwe, his size and arrogance as evident in photographs as it was in person, was sitting across from the thin figure of Ashraf Parker. Parker was leaning across the table, both hands open, thin fingers orchestrating something.

"Who is being blackmailed?" David asked. "Not you. Me neither."

"You suppose it was meant for Parker?"

"It was addressed to me. Someone wants us to know about Parker's intentions. But who cares about that?"

"At least we know why he didn't pitch for the board meeting."

"Parker flirting with Sendiwe ... What are we gonna do about this?"

David had tried to get rid of Parker many times before but never succeeded. "We do nothing. The sale takes preference. This doesn't change a thing."

"Still, this is not the type of mail you want to get. Maybe we should wait and see what he's up to."

"No. We all know Parker's been getting cosy with the shark. He's been aching for a split and delaying the sale would be like giving a fox a second chance. Besides, he wants a buddy to back him in South America."

William slipped the photos into the envelope. "I never trusted him, David. He is dirty to the bone."

"He's dirty to the soul, and nothing will change him. He'll share in the profit of the sale and that's all. It's the nature of business. Money doesn't ask why or how, it just goes where it's told."

"Come," William said after a while. "Let's grab some lunch downstairs. My treat."

"More of that green slop you drink?"

"You kidding? That's breakfast. This is lunch. By the way, you still going to the farm this weekend."

"Yes, I need to fix the place up or sell it. Still undecided."

"Some serious development happening in and around George. I won't sell if I were you. It's still a good investment."

"Always ahead of the trend. But this investment harbours bad memories."

"It's been a long time, David. Let the memories go."

"Wish I could. I still see her in that house. Still see the kids running through the fields, chasing butterflies. Memories can be a bad return on a good investment."

As they strolled through the office floor, David heard a commotion coming from the reception area.

"You!" someone called out.

When he turned around, he found himself looking at her pointed finger. She flicked her hair over her shoulder and darted at him accusingly.

"You! Where do you get off dumping someone at hospital. What if I'm allergic to something? And I can pay for myself, by the way. I don't need your charity."

Her face was flustered and her eyes were wide with surprise, almost shocked at how her voice echoed. Her nostrils flared slightly and her cheeks hollowed out as she panted. David thought she'd scared herself more than anyone else.

Her eyes scanned the office. Everyone had stopped to stare at her. Her long fingers nervously played with a piece of paper in her hands. Her body heaved rhythmically with what David imagined to be a pent-up rage. He could make out the pulse in her neck, the vein gently pushing against the skin as blood raced through.

Everything in her demeanour appeared instantly frozen when the silence sank in. She appeared to do some calculations before focusing her glare back on him. From experience he knew there were only two ways this confrontation could play off. She could either go on screaming and huffing and he would have to resort to calling security, or she could come to her senses and calm down. David cut his teeth at negotiating long ago. Coaxing the best out of someone only required a small gesture. He had seen something good in her the night before, so he believed the situation could be neutralized.

He folded his hands behind his back and stepped into her territorial bubble, standing beside her in the way a friend might stand shoulder-to-shoulder with another friend. He leaned over until he could smell the shampoo in her hair and the sweetness of her perfume. She smelled soft, confident and pink, not a light pink but a powerful womanly pink.

"Maybe you should've called first," he whispered without looking at her.

"Yea, I didn't think this all the way through," she whispered back, then, "Maybe I should've called."

For no apparent reason he wanted to touch her. He felt that, given the present situation, she had been so removed from her comfort zone that she wouldn't mind if he touched her. His stagnation was personal. He wanted to be in control of himself and rob himself of that personal gratification. He didn't even know the woman. What if she was a convicted criminal?

Involuntarily his hand touched her shoulder and his other hand pointed to the open boardroom at the back of the building.

"We can talk in there."

She lowered her head and marched into the boardroom projecting an air of regret, as if this was a long walk of shame that could've been avoided.

David nodded a few times to get everyone back to work. Jocelynne gave him a thumbs-up and winked. It scared the life out of him.

"Good luck. She looks like a tough cookie," William remarked .

"Tend to business and I'll tend to the tough cookie," David said politely and went to the boardroom. The last thing he saw before closing the doors was William's broad grin.

"Please, have a seat."

Kerin sat down as instructed, her cheeks burning with embarrassment. She looked down at the table, too ashamed to face him. Through the years she had endured her share of uncomfortable situations, but this one would be remembered for years to come. She rummaged through her bag for something, anything worthy of being sought after, trying her utmost to give her arms a false animation.

He sat down opposite her. "How did you find me?"

"I forced them to give me the payer information. They are bound by law to disclose that information, you know."

She zipped her purse shut and looked at him. His eyes were cool, without a hint of concern. She envied his ability to be so neutral.

They sat their staring at each other for a while, no exchange and no real desire to have an exchange. Whatever doubts or fears Kerin might've had prior to marching into the office were almost instantly dispelled when she fell into the depths of his eyes. The worries of this life seemed to crumble without protest.

"I wondered if I'd see you again. It's good you came."

"Good I came?" she hissed. "Listen ..."

"David, my name's David."

"Whoever you are, this is not a social visit."

"Very well," he said and opened his hands invitingly. "So why did you come here?"

"To express my concerns, and to return your money." She began searching through her handbag again. With great effort, she removed her purse. They really needed the money and she'd spent some of it already.

"I don't want the money back."

She stopped and stared at him, half-relieved and half-terrified. Nothing in life was for free. Everything had consequences.

"What do you mean?"

"You can keep the money. To compensate for the inconvenience, and for my stupidity."

She was unsure how to respond. "Come again?"

"How do I say this? I was very confused last night. I was really just looking for someone to talk with."

His demeanour was calculated and reserved, which was dangerously charming. He had a persuasive ease with which he spoke. There was an air of confidence and humility about him. Too most women this was like a natural aphrodisiac, but Kerin was reluctant. She'd fallen for this before.

"Talk? Yea, right."

David smiled, his eyes peering into her, not in a judgmental way. She felt him prying her innermost places.

"I'd never done that before. How else would you ask?"

"Well *I* sure won't know."

There was a brief, leaden silence. She no longer felt uncomfortable alone with this stranger. One thing was certain, she had absolutely no idea what to do next. She had come to say what she had said. Now what?

Then, as she was planning her escape, he asked, "Are you busy later?"

"What?"

"Join me for an early dinner. Six o'clock?"

"Why would I do that?"

David leaned forward and spoke softer. "Do you believe that everything happens for a reason?" She was too confused to respond. "I'd like to know you a bit better."

"Why? I'm not that interesting."

"You don't have to be interesting, you just have to be yourself. Dinner, nothing more."

She was hesitant, afraid that she was considering dinner for all the wrong reasons. What if she ended up drunk again? Would she repeat the night before if there was more money to be made?

Did he want what he couldn't get the night before? Rich men pursued things that were off-limits.

"Dinner, nothing more?" He nodded. "Just talk?"

"Just talk. I promise."

She sighed and closed her eyes, already regretting her answer before she had given it. "Six p.m."

He smiled. "I don't even know your name."

"It's Kerin."

They shook hands. "Pleased to meet you, Kerin."

He gave her his business card and she scribbled down her address: a convenience store's parking area two blocks away from where she lived, just to add distance to familiarity.

As she was walking home, it hit her. She had said yes. Why? She had almost slept with this man for money, now she was doing all forms of stupid over again. He was convincing, but that didn't justify going on a date.

She took a taxi home, paying for the trip with money that wasn't even hers. He *had* told her to keep it, so it was rightfully her money now to do with as she wished. Still, it didn't feel right. She hadn't really worked for it. Or had she? She was massaging her temples and rubbing her eyelids, stressing herself and analysing everything to death.

How would she break the news to Margie? What would her mother think of her? Kerin was expecting various forms of condemnation, reproach and, even worse, disappointment.

"On a date?" Margie asked. "That's great!"

"Not a date, mum."

"Well, what is it then?"

Kerin looked at her mother, a stunned expression on her face. "I don't know what the hell this is. It's just weird. He asked and I said yes. You think I should cancel?"

"Oh no, you don't." Margie pushed her daughter into the bathroom. "Go make yourself nice and pretty for the man. If it's not a date, then it's a free meal. Either way, go enjoy it."

She had been praying for Kerin to find a husband and, more importantly, a good father for the children. Children needed both parents to be present. There were things a father brought to parenting that a mother simply couldn't as a single working parent, no matter how much she loved them. Megan was not really a concern. She had a strong character and ample heart to boot. She did not require excessive disciplining or doting over. Dillon was a different little monster. He was like a little Jack Russell terrier, bouncing this way and that at the slightest excitement. He needed direction and tough love, a strong hand to guide him.

With the children in front of the television and Kerin in the bathroom, Margie lowered her guard for the briefest moment. She almost collapsed on the spot as exhaustion set in. She steadied herself against the wall and took a couple of deep breaths to blow away the dizzy spell. The spells have become more frequent of late.

In the bathroom, she could hear Kerin readying herself. Margie leaned against the door to hear Kerin's voice. She was singing to herself, something she did when in thought, as if it calmed her. Only those closest to her knew of her hidden talent. Margie was quietly relieved that she no longer performed at the club. She disapproved of Kerin singing in a sleazy jazz club where drunken old men ogled her.

Suddenly Margie realized that her age was getting the better of her, not just in spirit but in body. Her joints and muscles felt rusted and weathered, constantly tender to the touch and swollen in the mornings. Her face looked worn. In the greater scheme of things, she had accomplished so little. She always imagined there would more to this life. People accomplished amazing things, made miraculous discoveries and achieved impossible feats while facing terrible odds. She'd done nothing noteworthy with her time. But now that her biological clock was forgetting time or missing a beat now and then, her aspirations were instantly superseded by Kerin's needs.

She went to Kerin's bed and rested her head on the pillow, just for a short while, a quick breather, then she would be one hundred per cent for the kids when Kerin went out. When she closed her eyes the world disappeared at once, like morning fog when the sun breaks through.

Ronnie was the first image she saw when she stepped off the painting of her life. She reached out her arms and embraced her husband. She could feel him in her arms, the arch of his back, the hair on his forearms, his sharp chin gently pressing down on her head. He was alive again. She could see into his eyes, the life inside of him calling out to her. Strange as it was, Margie could almost feel Ronnie's soul coupling with hers, like a spiritual marriage. It was so deep, and intense.

However, this was just a dream. Nothing of it was real. Soon she would rouse from her dreams and she would have to face reality. The sickly self was inescapable. Dreams were exactly that, dreams. They ended abruptly before they even began. More and more there was a desire to remain here with Ronnie, to live the dream in its entirety and to forget the world. She no longer wanted to return. She no longer wanted to leave this dream, but Kerin needed her.

CHAPTER 6

She dreaded the possibility of seeing the Land Rover again. When David arrived in a black Mercedes, she was slightly relieved. The image of the Land Rover parked on the curb, door open, rain slanting in, had been cemented in her memories. She had no interest in being reminded of her recklessness the night before. David opened the car door for her. She wasn't used to that. She took great care lowering herself into the seat, the seams of her dress were a bit worn already. She was wearing her last good evening dress. She hadn't worn it in years, not counting the night in January when she'd worn it to the club. The dress was a short black number, fraying delicately just under the knee and sloping down toward the right. A bit too summery for the Cape Town winter but it was all she had left in her wardrobe. It was a bit tight around the tummy; she could see how her ass had expanded over the years. She remembered being more petite, but pregnancy had left a mark. The dress still made her feel classy, though, and she needed to feel classy tonight.

At the restaurant a portly waiter rushed to meet them. "Mr. Harlem! Good to see you again. It's been a while." He tugged at his green shirt, turned on his heel, menus tucked under his arm, and led the way through the reception area.

She had never been to a five-star restaurant. Not even on her wedding night had she enjoyed such luxury. Charl Fellows, a struggling mechanic, and Kerin Miller, six weeks pregnant, joined hands at the magistrate's office. The reception was a small braai held at their flat, attended by eight people. Her new husband had invited two fellow mechanics who kept hitting on her while he lay passed out in the next room.

The waiter made a sharp turn to the right and they followed, stepping into the life of the eatery. It was a posh establishment, a renowned farm-style restaurant located on a wine estate in the Northern Suburbs of Cape Town. The forty-odd tables, chairs and decorations smelled like money. Even the tablecloths and the waiters' uniforms were rich. She instantly felt completely out of her league. There were two levels, one level two steps higher than the other and separated by a sturdy galvanised metal railing with intricate flower designs. To the left of the building was a section with roof-to-ceiling windows revealing the Durbanville hills in the distance. In the far right corner was a small stage and a piano.

Seeing the stage, her heart skipped a beat. She thought of Stan and the bar where she had braved the microphone once a week to entertain those beyond entertainment. At least that part of her life was over, replaced by uncertainty.

Most of the tables were reserved. Here you booked to eat. It was the type of restaurant where being on the reservation list was already an accomplishment.

Waiters cleared away as they crossed the floor, nodding and smiling at her. Surely no waiter could be friendly just for the sake of being friendly. They made their way up the steps to the elevated section. The table in the far left corner was theirs: decked in red and white, flowers in a vase, candle lit and napkins folded over starter plates. Though a bit more isolated, it was a window seat overlooking a small dam. The dam was encircled by a series of garden lamps which, when viewed from the height of their table, captivated her imagination and briefly sucked her into her own wonderland. It looked like a magical world where fairies lived, the place where children could run around and enjoy themselves to their own heart's content.

David pulled out her chair, waited and eased the chair forward ever so slightly. This gentlemanly behaviour and the sincere preference was intoxicating. She was excited, yet there was a sinking feeling in her stomach, a case of the butterflies and the dread of predilection. For Kerin, wining and dining with the South African elite was like an escalation in the ranks of the social hierarchy.

The special treatment was a bit overwhelming. She had to remind herself that this was just dinner. But how she had missed romance in her life. A woman needed these things, to be treated like a real woman, to be spoiled by a pursuing lover. Her life had been void of all the trivial and wonderful things of love. She had concluded that she would never experience love like that.

They ordered a bottle of wine. When the waiter brought it, David stalled him and poured the wine himself. She traced one fingertip along the base of her wineglass, then turned the stem between thumb and forefinger. She moved utensils this way and that, unfolded and refolded her napkin, all the while her fingers betraying how nervous she was. She felt restless yet confident enough to speak her mind. It was in her nature to be direct. It was unfair to feign happiness when she was harbouring concern. At this stage of her life, she had no time for games. She had to get a job, not a new boyfriend.

"Why did you bring me here?"

"To have dinner with me."

Kerin shook her head. "No, I mean, why me? Why did you bring *me* here?"

"No easy way to answer that, I'm afraid."

"Try me."

"This is going to sound strange." David sipped his wine, editing his response. "I feel we have a lot to offer each other."

"I don't know what you're looking for, but I can't offer you anything substantial." She shifted her fork excitedly, on the verge of succumbing to a fit of nervous giggles.

"I think you can. Let's find out. Tell me about yourself."

"Like what?"

"I don't know. What do you do for a living?"

"That's not a good question."

"Why not?"

"I was a waitress."

"Was?"

Kerin smiled nervously. "Well, Tuesday morning I had two jobs, but Tuesday evening I was an unemployed mother of two. Then I'm mistaken for a drunken prostitute."

Normally a man would signal the waiter for the bill after a reply like that, but David just sat there. His demeanour was neutral, relaxed.

A brief, uncomfortable silence followed. Luckily the tables nearest to them were unoccupied. She gulped down the rest of her wine. It was strange to be out of her comfort zone. She was experiencing things she had no control over. A thunderstorm of emotions were whirling around inside her, beckoning release. She never realized how much she had bottled up. This, the romantic atmosphere and the strangeness of it all, was outage. It was relief, expression and escape.

"Is that what you wanted to know?"

"No," he said calmly. "I don't care about that. I want to know more about you, not your circumstances."

Kerin looked away, forcing back the tears. She didn't know why she was so emotional. She took out tissues from her purse, dabbed at her eyes. "Sorry about this?" she said giggling. "Don't know what the hell is going on with me."

"That's okay."

She closed her eyes, took a deep breath and gathered herself. "What else do you want to know?"

"Tell me about your children. How old are they?"

To her own surprise, she began opening up to this stranger. She told him as much as she could without betraying her reservations. It was intensely therapeutic to sit and talk with someone about the mundane things that made up her boring life. She pictured herself having supper with a psychiatrist. He listened, nodded and asked questions. He was not self-obsessed and seldom spoke about himself. When he did, it was done in a mandatory manner, as if he had grown tired of his life.

The restaurant's choice of music was soft and constant, from big band music to swing to jazz. Without noticing it she was gently swaying her head to the music. They enjoyed crumbed mushroom starters, talking as if they had been friends for years. Kerin ordered a basil pasta dish and David ordered lasagne, surprised that they shared a love for pasta. They ate and drank the hours away. The restaurant became busy and then it died down again. Then there were only a few tables left.

"Heavens, no," she was saying. "Margie wants nothing to do with music. She was a music teacher at a private school. When the school went bankrupt, she was let go. She couldn't get in anywhere after that. I think a piece of her died during that time. She doesn't teach anymore."

"What instruments can you play?"

"I play the piano, and a bit of guitar. You?"

He held up his hands in surrender. "Oh, no, I'm sure I'm useless. Never tried my hand at music. But you love it?"

"I love to sing."

"Really? I'd love to hear you sing."

They looked at each other through the flickering candle, both a little drunk, just enough to enjoy themselves.

"I'm not sure that qualifies as a first date request," Kerin protested playfully.

"Is that what we're doing? Dating?"

She replayed her words carefully. Had she called it a date? She blushed, her mind racing for a quick cover up response. How could she be so blunt? The night was playing off so smoothly that she never even realised her guard coming down.

"No, no," she stuttered. "That's not what I meant. What I meant was ..."

He touched her hand gently, his finger tips just touching her skin. "Hey, relax." He turned his head to the stage. "Would you sing something? They won't mind you using the piano."

"What do you mean?" She looked at the beautiful instrument. "No, I can't do that."

David called the manager with a quick gesture.

"Is anything wrong, sir?"

"No," Kerin whispered shyly. "Everything is great, thanks. Really."

"May the lady play something on the piano?" David asked.

"But of course. I'll turn the microphone on."

"No, hey, wait!" she called as the manager disappeared between the tables. "What the hell are you doing? I can't just start singing!" She was excited, an exhilarated smile on her face.

The microphone squealed to life as the manager stepped into view behind the piano. It was almost eleven o' clock. Many tables were deserted, candles no longer alight, chairs empty.

"Would the lady please come up?" the manager said into the microphone.

"Oh my word," she said and covered her eyes. "I can't believe you just did that."

"Come on, I can see you want to."

"This is going to cost you."

111

"I'm sure it will."

"You have no idea."

She slowly got to her feet and made her way to the piano, all the while thinking, *I can't believe I'm doing this.*

The manager pulled the microphone stand nearer to the piano and adjusted the mouthpiece and cables so that Kerin could sit and sing without having to strain her neck.

She sat down and cleared her throat. The sound echoed through the restaurant. She felt strange on the stage, a cloud of anticipation in the air and her hands suddenly clammy.

She hadn't played the piano in years. She used to sing at the club once a week, but that had been very different. Singing at a sleazy jazz club was just that – singing at a sleazy jazz club. No emotion, no commitment. Musicians changed as often as the other staff. It was a means to an end, food on the table.

Facing the piano, Kerin was shocked to discover that she really wanted to play and sing tonight. She needed this more than anything else. Her hands stretched out over the keys. For a minute she struggled to remember some of her own music. It slowly filtered through.

She looked out over the near empty restaurant. She had the floor, the microphone, the music. And she had no idea where to start. There was just a spiral of notes in front of her, and she couldn't find the beginning.

At first her hands moved clumsily over the keys, but each stroke affirmed her confidence and soon, her surroundings blurred into obscurity and all distractions disappeared. The room became muted. Musician and instrument became one.

Her soul poured into her hands, and with it came the slow seduction of her voice, soft and powerful. Her voice rose and fell, pitching delicately, wrapped in a sadness that almost consumed the mind. A small part of her stood at the edge of a precipice, staring into an abyss. Her sorrow was on display and all that pain was, somehow, lost in the translation.

They sat talking until midnight. They were the last customers to leave.

"I'm leaving for Nigeria tomorrow, a quick business trip," he said as they crossed the parking lot. "But I'm going to George for the weekend. I own an old farm there. I'm trying to figure out what to do with it."

"That sounds like a lot of travelling."

Before opening the door, he stopped, fumbling with the keys, like a child with a secret.

"You and your family can come with, to George. For the weekend."

She stepped back in shock, eyes wide and mouth open. "To George?! You want us to come to George? And then what?"

David was also in awe. He had just invited a virtual stranger to join him for the weekend, but he was so comfortable around her that he couldn't restrain himself. Going to George on his own was not a very appealing notion. Not only could she keep him company, but her presence would take his mind off the sale.

"Then nothing. The house is there. It's standing open. There are rooms for everyone. Food will be taken care of. Wouldn't cost you a thing."

"I don't think that's a good idea."

"Why not?"

"David," she pleaded. "I'm damaged goods. Father died young. Mother worked two jobs. Married a husband who abused me. He left us and died in a rehab somewhere. I'm thirty-five, unemployed, mother of two, and I don't want to upset my life again. Not now, anyway."

"I don't want to upset your life, and I don't want to pressure you. Just think about it. You have my number now."

He dropped her off outside the block of flats where she lived. They said an awkward goodnight. It was casual, no expectations. He drove away and gave the George matter no further thought. Little did he know that Kerin could think about nothing else.

When he reached the hotel, his entire mood changed to a more cautious one. An awkwardness fell over him.

He checked in at the reception desk for messages.

"You have a visitor," said Amid and flicked his eyes toward the lounge area across from the lobby, an uneasiness lingering in the manager's eyes.

He turned slowly, half expecting a man with a gun behind him. Instead he looked at an empty lounge. Then he saw a chair squeezed into a corner behind one door. In the chair was the thin figure of Ashraf Parker, suit and tie at this hour of the evening. There was a thin smile of feigned recognition, that belittling smile of arrogance, a smooth curl of the lip.

Parker put down his cup, offered David a seat.

"For five months I've been told you are travelling abroad," David said matter-of-factly. "Then I find you waiting at my hotel, at this godless time of night." He joined Parker, slipping into the leather chair opposite him.

"I was in Brazil when my office received notice of the sale." Parker always spoke slowly, quietly, engaging the listener with a calm and gentle tone. "Can I get you something to drink? Peach tea with honey, perhaps?" He took a slow sip.

"I'm good, thank you." David raised an eyebrow in mock surprise. "Brazil? So you're operating in South America?"

"My business in Brazil is of no concern to you or the company. I'm doing that in my personal capacity, with other developers." Parker had a way of insulting someone with elegance, but this had no effect on David.

"Developers like Elixir Holdings? Or is that another personal matter?"

For the first time in years, David saw a flash of surprise in Parker's eyes, but he continued calmly.

"Are you spying on me, David? Never thought you had the gall for it."

"Oh, don't get your panties all crooked. I don't care what you do in South America, or what you and Linden Sendiwe are up to. As long as it doesn't involve my company." David stared at Parker, a deep and penetrating stare, one he had perfected over years of confrontations. There was no reaction from Parker. "I will not let you ruin my company's reputation."

"Yet you are willing to destroy it yourself by selling to the Benjamin Property Group?"

"If you had the decency to be present in the board meeting, you would understand."

"I had business to tend to."

"Of course. Yet here you sit."

A waiter removed Parker's empty cup. He declined another tea and settled back into the chair.

"Why are you really here? Why didn't you just stay in Brazil?"

"I want you to stop the sale?"

"Why?"

"The price is not right. Benjamin could pay more."

"It's more than adequate."

"No, it's not. And the Nigerians are not prospects at this point."

"As a minority share holder that's not your call to make."

"I can get other board members to see things in a different light," Parker hissed. "My light."

"It wouldn't delay the sale. I have majority share. I'm of sound mind and the paperwork has been done. It's now up to Benjamin to sign. Harlem Properties is sold as a going concern. What part of that do you not understand?"

"Look, David, we've never seen eye-to-eye on anything. When I joined your little company five years ago, it was a long-term investment."

"In the five years your little investment has nearly doubled."

"And in another five years it would grow exponentially. We can make more money, together. Open shares to the public and the sky is the limit."

"I will not list the company on the stock exchange. You know that."

"I know, but why sell the entire portfolio below market value?"

"In keeping with the nature of the sale, all assets are calculated at twenty percent below market value, to accommodate for anticipatory monetary loss in the transference of assets." David grinned at Parker. "That what you are worried about? Is that why you hopped on a plane and surprised me here? Because you want more money?"

"It's my investment, David. You are stealing food off my table."

"You have enough food on your table to last three lifetimes, Ashraf, and still you want more. The sale is finalized. Nothing you do will stop it."

Parker looked down at his fingers.

"Unless," he said softly. "Unless something were to happen to you. All negotiations would cease immediately if it is within the thirty-day sale period. Insurance payouts might even improve investments."

David didn't enjoy being threatened, particularly not by people from his own company. Few people ever managed to ruffle his feathers, but Parker was something else. He was dangerous, and David had to exercise all possible patience to restrain himself.

"Let me ask you, David, who stands to inherit your shares when you die? Can't be your wife, now can it?" A thin smile spread across Parker's face. "It's my understanding that your shares would revert back to the company and be divvied up among the members of the board. One might say that your demise might resurrect the company."

David hadn't been this angry in a long time. He imagined Parker's face on the other side of a rifle scope and pondered about how good it would feel to pull the trigger. And at the peak of his rage, for no apparent reason, Kerin's face flashed inside his mind. It was the strangest thing. His anger subsided at once. Whatever ill he harboured disappeared.

"I changed it this morning. Anything happens to me and my shares go to the Nigerians."

"On what authority? You can't change beneficiaries without a unanimous vote."

"Then you should've been at the meeting." David stood up, dismissing the conversation as if it had never taken place. "Go back to Brazil, Parker. There's nothing left for you here."

He walked away, took the elevator to his room. It was difficult to be ambivalent about Parker's threats. David was aware that, given enough time, Parker would attempt another dangerous ploy to manipulate or obstruct the sale. But those were concerns for another day. Tonight he had Kerin's voice in his mind.

Curtis expertly flicked his hands over the steering wheel. He had been driving limousines for years. He had perfected the art of guiding his vehicle down narrow streets at a sedate pace without upsetting his passengers. Contrary to popular belief, driving a vehicle that long was unnerving and, at times, costly. Especially when it was your own limousine. Scrapes along the side of the car could cost you a job.

Curtis Mallow offered his clients a high value asset transport service. He was synonymous with protection and transportation for the paranoid VIP, and he was in high demand. His brother and another driver used the two smaller, older limousines for freelance jobs, while he pampered the big fish. It was a steady business and the money was very good. Sendiwe's annual contract alone paid more than he had made in eight years working for the South African Police Service. And now he was his own boss.

His past as a police officer was the key ingredient to securing the Elixir Holdings contract. He was required to wear a firearm at all times, for which he had to obtain a special permit. Besides, he was still a police reservist on standby, so that greased the wheels a bit. Because Sendiwe was a high-profile, high-risk client, the money justified the means. Curtis saw an opportunity in this industry. Sendiwe was just the start to something big.

However, Curtis felt a strange pang in his gut. The Linden Sendiwe he had come to know had undergone several changes over the last couple of weeks. The man was, for lack of a more definitive description, not himself. He studied the reflection in the rear-view mirror, occasionally flicking his eyes down at the road. Sendiwe was slouched over, his elbow resting on the door panel, eyes staring into the night. He appeared lost. And Curtis was sure that he had seen Sendiwe crying in the backseat the day before. It did not bode well for his company. He had a sinking feeling about the relationship between Elixir Holdings and Mallow Transport.

"Have I been good company?" Sendiwe asked out of the blue, snorting.

Curtis purposely considered the question. Few and far between were the times when Sendiwe had treated anyone well. Even his own children and his women. He was without attachments, without decency. He had thrown Curtis with liquor more than once, had used his limousine as a whorehouse to entertain business associates, and he had treated Curtis like a corporate spy. These were all demeaning incidents, but he needed the contract.

"Sure," he said.

Sendiwe hissed loudly and shifted his body sideways. "That is the problem when you surround yourself with liars! You can never expect an honest answer."

Curtis glared at Sendiwe in the mirror. "Alright then. You're a cold, manipulative bastard who looks down at people – but money talks."

"Money?!" he scoffed. "Money tells more lies than people. It doesn't care who wants it, as long as it's wanted. Money will tell you you're special."

Sendiwe loosened the knot of his silk tie and tossed it on the floor, exasperated by the effort. It looked as though he was struggling to breathe.

"I'm a horrible man. I'm a tyrant, and I've never treated you well."

"Well, as long as your cheque clears."

Sendiwe gave him a quick salute to show his appreciation for the man's honesty.

After what seemed like ten minutes, Sendiwe cleared his throat a few times and spat into the handkerchief.

Curtis made another wide arch with the steering wheel and turned into a deserted parking lot. He knew Woodstock well. He could expertly manoeuvre the limousine through the narrow streets if he had to make a quick escape, but there was little cover.

"You sure about this?" he asked hesitantly. "There's no place to hide here."

"Sometimes the best place to hide is in plain sight. Besides, I need to do this one-on-one."

One part of the area was well-lit. He circled a section of handicapped parking bays and guided the car on until it stood nose to nose opposite another car, about twenty metres apart. Without moving around too much, he slipped the Beretta out of his shoulder holster and turned the safety off.

"So you're sure?" he asked again.

"You are here to deliver a service, nothing more. Do this and I'll get you enough business to last a lifetime. I might be a bastard, but I never lie."

Sendiwe struggled to get his bulk out of the car, then walked up to Curtis' open window.

"Be ready. Just in case."

"In case of what?"

"I don't know. I never trusted this person. It's like there's two sides. A good side and a bad side. Someone like that, you never know what they will do." He lingered for a while, then said, "Thank you."

"You told me to come alone, then you don't," he said loudly, glaring at the limousine.

"That's my driver," Sendiwe screamed back. "He can't even kill a rabbit with his tyres. He's useless."

Sendiwe had called the meeting. He didn't like this one bit. He was a bit on edge already. Not really nervous, just on edge, looking down an empty space, not sure what the landing would be like if he jumped. And he wanted to jump. Also, for someone who always liked to be in the know, he did not appreciate being kept in the dark.

It was incredibly cold. The Antagonist had his hands tucked into his jacket pockets, one holding his gun. The weight of the metal in his hand was reassuring. He felt indestructible. He was burning to use it. His index finger was playing with the trigger, sometimes squeezing it a bit to feel the tension.

He had no idea why he brought the weapon. He had no idea what to do with it, or when to do it, but do it he would, should the moment arise. He hadn't really planned on killing Sendiwe. He hadn't really planned on killing anyone, but the concept was becoming more and more agreeable to him. When The Swartland Opus was first etched on paper, he never imagined he would stand opposite the Shark with a gun in his hand. That he had brought his driver along complicated things. He hadn't used a gun before, so he didn't know if he would be able to shoot both men before they could take cover.

They stood opposite each other for a long time before he started the conversation.

"You called me, remember ..." He held up his hands while still nestled inside the pockets.

Sendiwe's eyes flashed down to his hand, the one holding the gun.

"You forced the meet with Harlem. Why?" Sendiwe asked in his heavy voice.

"You could have asked me that on the phone."

"It was a rhetorical question. I already know the answer."

The Antagonist faked a frown and pulled up his shoulders to mock confusion. A subtle panic was brewing in him. Sendiwe couldn't possibly know, and if he did, how much could he know?

Using deliberately slow movements, Sendiwe lit up a cigarette. "Since you called, I asked myself, 'Why is this guy calling *me*? Why should I make an offer to buy properties from Harlem? And why those ten specific properties.' So I snooped around. You tried to sell me your problem. Is that about right?"

The Antagonist felt like ripping out the gun and having a go at them both. Something restrained him. He could see the bullets sinking into Sendiwe's large stomach. He could see the bullets smacking through the glass of the limousine.

"What the hell are you talking about? I saw an opportunity for Elixir and thought ..."

Sendiwe cut him short. "Thought what?! I already have four of Harlem's board members in my pocket, looking for employment after the sale. You are just another vote. I don't need you to think for me."

The Antagonist couldn't respond. His mind was too busy. He ran through the other members of the board, attempting to guess who was in Sendiwe's pocket. He was trying to figure out who he could trust when Roelf Lassen concluded his part of the deal. He was tallying up shares for majority rule, plotting a cover-up.

"I'm just looking for a new boss. That so bad?" The Antagonist said, aching to use the gun, but Sendiwe was blocking the driver. The limousine was a couple metres away. What if he missed? The driver would remember his car, the personalised licence plates. Dammit, why did he get those vanity plates?

Sendiwe offered him a wry smile, sucking back on his cigarette and blowing out the smoke. He finished the cigarette mid-way and stepped on it, as if making a point by stubbing it out under the heel of his shoe.

"New boss? I've gotten myself into trouble many times and I always got myself out of it. I despise blame shifters. If you're ambitious enough you can clean up your own mess."

The wind was blowing full force, adding to his agitation. In the back of the parking lot was a light that flickered. He was indecisive, couldn't think straight. When the light went out, he felt like ripping out the gun, when the light went on, he shrunk back into a shell of contempt.

"I know about The Swartland Opus, the development rights, and Roelf Lassen."

And just like that the house of cards came tumbling down. How could he know? All the connections had been covered up, or lost in a never-ending cycle of paperwork. No one could track it just like that. Unless Roelf thought there was an opportunity in third-party blackmail?

As if Sendiwe was reading his thoughts, he said, "Don't fret yourself. I have ways of finding dirt. You forget who I am."

He wanted to deny it, but couldn't. He lifted his jacket pocket up to where the gun would be level with Sendiwe's chest.

"I wouldn't do that if I was you. Anything happens to me and a letter gets mailed. I plan ahead. You're not the first person to point something at me."

"What do you want?" he hissed through clenched jaws.

"I want you to make it worth my while?"

"What?"

" I want Harlem Properties. I want the whole thing."

"I'll need time."

"Time is one thing I don't have, patience is the other. You see, I have nothing to lose. Keep that in mind."

"What does that mean? You've got everything to lose!"

"If you haven't learned anything in this industry, then learn this: money isn't everything."

The Antagonist lowered his gun.

"I never liked Harlem, but at least I respect him. You are a dog. If you can be a loyal dog, I might have use for you when the dust settles. You have one week before I tell Harlem what's been going on." He pointed a finger at The Antagonist, his menacing eyes narrowing. "Make it worth my while."

"You know, money might not be everything, but it's worth killing for."

"Not if it kills you first. One week."

Sendiwe turned around and walked back to the limousine.

It was so loud in The Antagonist's mind that he almost felt his head splitting open and his eardrums pop like firecrackers. He was trapped by his circumstances and his inability to do anything. He was hyperventilating, feeling the onset of another dizzy spell. As the limousine disappeared, he stammered back to his car and wrestled with the door. His hands were shaking violently, his fingers fumbling with the keys, dropping them, then trying the lock again. His breath was so hot that he couldn't see through the condensation when he exhaled. He got in behind the steering wheel and slammed the door so hard that it echoed through the parking lot. Then a wave of elation came over him: he was catapulted over the precipice, sailing through the clouds of euphoria where sentiment and lunacy merged, exploring the vicissitudes of his individuation, celebrating his becoming, the affirmation of his psychosis.

When he glanced down at his crotch, he noticed the stain spreading out across the front of his pants. He had ejaculated all over himself. He was filled with sadness because he had just purchased the pants, and now he would have to burn it.

CHAPTER 7

David became an orphan when his parents died. He was only five at the time. He slipped into the government system and remained there until he finished school. He was enlisted to join the SA Defence Force for obligatory national service. It was shortly after the Border War and the Army was in a state of flux. His military prowess and acuity caused him to excel up the ranks. As an orphan he had learned to fight for himself, to stand his ground and push back. When others dropped out or gave up, he kept pushing. When there was pain, he shut off. His only flaw: he was a loner. They say no man is an island, but with David no one man is an army. Service was about cohesion, so he had to adjust. David excelled better when he was competing against himself. He preferred alienation. Luckily the army had work for people who performed better on their own.

He progressed to Special Forces, attending a rigorous training at the Oudtshoorn base, where he applied to join the reconnaissance battalion. The *recces*, the golden warriors of warfare. He was withdrawn from combat operations and recruited for stealth missions, replacing team strikes with direct fire force-oriented reconnaissance. Then he was outsourced, ordered to do terrible things. After three jobs the cracks began to show. It was the solo hit in Africa that broke him. After completing the assignment, David locked himself in a room for two days. A week later he dropped out of reconnaissance and within a month left the army altogether. David was good at killing, but he was not a killer.

Then he met Elizabeth, the bridge to his little island. She saved him, brought the sun into his life and then it was over. Elizabeth: here one day, gone the next. And as much as he missed her, it was merely a shadow of the sorrow he kept hidden. The death of his two boys could not be translated to mere words.

The plane shuddered a couple times, then dropped a few feet. David rubbed his eyes. He couldn't sleep. He had dozed off for about ten minutes, but that just reminded him how tired he was. He needed sleep, just to catch up. He had so many things to think about, but whenever he tried to focus he ended up thinking about Kerin. He loathed not being able to control his thoughts Only one other woman had been able to distract him like that, and she was no longer there.

He propped the tiny pillow behind his head, then flattened it again. When he closed his eyes, he saw Kerin's face: soaking wet, make-up running down her cheeks, can of pepper spray clenched in her hand. He pictured her lip curling back, that confused, desperate look in her eyes. Involuntarily, he smiled. Then she was behind the piano, eyes closed. He could still hear her strong voice, picture her long fingers moving over the keys. His smile faded as he recalled her features. There was something intoxicating about her, something he couldn't shake. He found himself inexplicably drawn to her.

When the plane shuddered again, he sighed and pulled his pillow free. What had felt like mere seconds had in fact been four hours of sleep. He felt refreshed. It was about five in the morning and darkness still roamed the skies. Outside the window, between the occasional passing cloud, he saw a dark sheet speckled with the dim lights of fishing trawlers.

The Nigeria flight usually lasted seven hours. He boarded at Cape Town International around 4 a.m. Then he was flying back to Cape Town again that evening, and Friday he was flying to George to spend the weekend on the farm. Monday he had to fly to Johannesburg for meetings. He wanted to get the deal over with. He was a patient man, but his decision to sell had been a rash one, and rash decisions had need of being dealt with rashly.

He briefly thought about the weekend, and whether Kerin would join him. He just wondered. He had switched off his phone during flight, but when they landed he checked his phone with a childish enthusiasm, almost expecting a missed call from her. He wanted her perspective on the land in George. It was so big and empty. Initially he had considered buying a villa in Spain or Italy, but he loved South Africa. George would always be his retirement destination the day Harlem Properties came to an end. And that day had finally arrived. Now he was no longer sure what to do, or where to do it. To someone who ruled empires, the thought of limbo was comforting.

After touchdown he found himself choked by the intense morning heat of Lagos. He stumbled through the rigmarole of Third World airport procedures. He presented his yellow fever certificate and passport at checkpoints, where the contents of his carry-on luggage was scattered across a table and poked at by customs officials. He was looked at suspiciously, studied by the armed guards patrolling the airport. The treatment was standard, but everyone appeared a bit more on edge than normal. David felt instinctively alert. He sensed the strain in the politics, the battle of loyalties and the uncertainty brooding within the people.

In the background, along the walls, large air conditioners were already buzzing, fighting a never-ending battle against the humid tropical climate and the ever-present mosquito. David disliked the extreme humidity. He was wearing expensive chinos and a loose golf shirt, not one with his company's insignia.

Near the entrance stood a short stout man wearing a tight black suit and a black cap. When he saw David approaching, his face lit up. He offered David a wide smile, extending his hand.

"Welcome to Nigeria, Mr. Harlem. I trust your flight was comfortable," he said in a heavy accent.

David gave him a quick once-over and shook his hand.

"What makes you think I'm Harlem?"

"You are the only white man here."

When he looked around, he found it to be as the man had said.

"My name is Chobo. I will be your driver." He scooped up David's bag. "Is this all your luggage?"

"I travel light."

Chobo nodded at two burly men in military uniform. The men lifted their assault rifles and began marching through the airport in an authoritative manner.

"Come," Chobo said as the two men led the way. "We must hurry."

Once outside, the true heat hit him in the gut and he had to take a deep breath to adjust. One could never really prepare for that overwhelming warmth. In front of them, parked at the curb near the entrance, stood two vehicles: a big black SUV with tinted windows and a rugged little off-road Toyota with a modified chassis, large wheels, and a red light unit flashing on the roof. The one armed man had a curt exchange with Chobo, signalled the two of them to get in the SUV, then climbed into the Toyota.

Chobo hurriedly slipped David's bag onto the rear seat. "Please, get in," he said in a friendly, yet pressing tone.

"Why the rush?"

"Don't worry. It's just a precaution."

Chobo and David climbed in and were instantly swept away on the terrifying journey through the everyday Lagos traffic.

Noisy and nerve-wracking, it was loaded with trucks, cars with missing windows and doors, and hordes of motorcycles stacked with two to three passengers, all churned and weaved along the roads in a disorientated mess.

"Is it normal to have military escort?"

"Not really, but the wrong people might know you are coming." Chobo gave David a wry smile. "It is a difficult time now. And you would fetch a good ransom."

David swallowed a mouthful of dried spit.

"Thank you, but I have no intention of being ransomed just yet."

He had kept up with events in Nigeria. The country was facing a critical time. This year alone there had been many politically-motivated bombings and shootings. Rebel forces were trying everything in their power to swing the vote for the next government elections. Adding to the inter-ethnic conflict was the number of violent attacks on local churches, hinting at the possibility of a religious war between Christians and Muslims. David was not a fearful man by nature, but he had served in the Special Forces and knew how quickly a flammable situation could ignite. His visit to Nigeria was not really a high profile visit, but it could raise an eyebrow in the business world. When he began travelling Africa to present a series of development seminars, the members of the board had been less than thrilled. They insisted his insurance be updated, and subtly hinted at the appointment of an acting CEO to tend to matters in his absence. At the time David was still coming to grips with the loss of his family, so he was glad to be relieved of the burden of management.

The Toyota in front of them screeched to a sudden halt mid-traffic. From the SUV, David saw an old green Mercedes blocking the road. The doors of the Toyota instantly flew open and the two armed men snaked out of the vehicle with their weapons aimed at the Mercedes. They were screaming at the driver, who sat with his hands in the air, nonplussed by the fact that they might open fire. As much as the driver was screaming back at the armed men, so the armed men became more vehement in their dialogue.

David slowly unclipped his safety belt, leaned forward and checked for suspicious movement behind the car. Four years in the army had instilled a natural suspicion of coincidence. He still remembered the mantra of the infantryman when under attack: dash, down, crawl, observe, sights, return fire. This had been drilled into every soldier during the first three months of training. David had rehearsed this manoeuvre with such frequency that it became second nature for him to react defensively. He couldn't help it.

One of the armed men turned and gestured for Chobo to carry on driving, screaming and waving his weapon around to stress the urgency. The other man fired a haphazard shot at the ground to let the driver of the Mercedes know that he was not mucking about. People scattered when the sound echoed through the crowd of pedestrians. They ducked into shacks and shops for protection. Screams of alarm followed. Within seconds the Mercedes began sputtering and rolling forward, no longer obstructing the road.

Chobo followed orders and shot through the space, scraping against the Mercs' bumper. He expertly shifted through the gears and sped along a lane which had been cleared after the gunshot had sounded. The Toyota raced by David's window at breakneck pace, lights flashing.

Thirty minutes later Chobo took a sharp right turn and guided the SUV into a dark tunnel, sloping down into a basement parking lot. The two vehicles drove around the underground car park until they reached a shiny elevator door. Outside the door stood two armed guards, clean-shaven and tough-looking. These were not entry-level military men. They were private security, the type that cost a lot of money. Chobo jumped out and jogged around the car to David's door. He opened it with a polite smile and motioned David toward the elevator.

"I take it you will drive me to the airport again tonight?"

"Of course, sir."

"Good."

As he reached the elevator, the doors parted and he stepped into the cubicle with one of the guards. The man had a shaven head, round shoulders and huge hands, one clasping his bag as if it was a tiny purse.

"Hi, I'm David." The man nodded hesitantly. "You guys don't smile much, do you?"

"I'm not paid to smile," he said in a deep voice, then turned around spontaneously and offered David a huge smile, baring the huge gap between his two shiny white front teeth.

David gave an appreciative laugh and the guard reciprocated.

"I needed that after the drive here. People look tense about the election," David said.

"Maybe this time Nigeria will be free again." He glanced at David, as if to search for a threat. "My name is Clifford."

They exited on the fifth floor, walked down a corridor and stopped at the last door. There was an old bronze plaque against the wall but David couldn't make out the engraving. Clifford did a quick survey of the room and handed him the keys.

"You can shower and rest here. Your meeting is at two. Lunch."

There were five other people joining the luncheon. Godfrey Benjamin sat at the head of the table. On the opposite side sat Godfrey's two sons: Ajaka and Chilotam. They looked like younger versions of their father, with subtle differences evident.

Chilotam was the eldest, early thirties with a slight paunch and a heavy gaze, eyes filled with a young wisdom, thick curly hair and a silent humility. Ajaka was the youngest, late twenties, inquisitive eyes.

Lunch was a bountiful endeavour, the mere sight of which made David perspire. He seldom over-indulged on lavish cuisine, but he enjoyed a constant awareness of what he put in, and how much.

This was a feast of astronomical proportions. There were food types he had never eaten before and others he had been introduced to before. There was an okra stew, fried plantains, cassava, garri and fresh pot bread. There was also a delicious Jollof rice dish, heavily spiced with ginger, cumin and nutmeg, and served with tomatoes. David loved the traditional Igbo dish called awaá, which was a type of yam porridge.

"I'm afraid you are right," Chilotam was saying in a reserved tone, his accent sounding more European than African. "The Western Cape shows a lot of promise for future developments. However, a structured growth needs to be implemented in order to sustain those developments with further developments."

"I agree. I slaved along a ten year plan to achieve a feasible mutualism in the property game, particularly in the Cape. But complications are inevitable, unavoidable. I do believe the approach might work better here in Nigeria."

"Nothing works in Nigeria, Mr. Harlem," contributed young Ajaka, but his father reprimanded him.

"Pay no attention to him. That's the pessimism of youth speaking. Still much to learn."

Ajaka withdrew his views with a slight bow of the head.

This was the gist of conversation throughout lunch. David found the engagement taxing. They spoke about investment possibilities, demographics, the diversity of cultures and politics, comparing the aptitudes of the South African and Nigerian governments. This was property banter, a loose conversation conducted in rich-speak. Whether African, American, European or South African, there was a congruent manner among the wealthy and educated the world over.

In many different cultures business was either done over meals or after. One conviction behind this practice was to fill the guest with such gratitude that it would be impossible to deny the beneficial resolution processes of tender contractual pressure points. However, David was not that easily swayed. It took more than a meal to turn his mind on a particular matter. If the purpose of this meeting was to alter the contract, it would be a short meeting. The paperwork had been done. The last thing he wanted was to stall the deal any longer. He wanted his freedom, to start a new life.

After the meal, Godfrey asked David to join him for a coffee, leaving his lead financial advisor and his children behind. This was the actual meeting, the informal wrapping-up of affairs. David preferred to keep things on paper, but Godfrey Benjamin was more inclined to take someone by their word.

The coffees were brought in by a woman wearing a bright green *abaya* wrapper dress, lavishly embroidered with gold patterns. She placed the tray on a table between them and clumsily offloaded the coffees and a sugar bowl.

David loved the aroma of the fresh coffee that lingered in the room. African coffees had such a diverse character, like a complex wine. He loved it.

"I'm told you met with Linden Sendiwe?" Godfrey said suddenly.

David was not surprised. Sendiwe had a famously big mouth and enjoyed rivalling businesses against each other. He had been responsible for many a war of words in the media, resulting in frantic battles between companies, which ultimately lead to Elixir Holdings picking up the scraps for next to nothing.

"Yes. I had no idea what his intentions were until I sat down."

"It's not really my business who you meet with, but when it's him I need to ask questions. Should I be worried?"

"There's no need for concern. Sendiwe proposed that I unbundle a portfolio of select properties, our larger single-tenanted properties in Kwa-Zulu Natal and Gauteng, along with some undeveloped land in the Cape. He made an offer, and I refused. I didn't build up a company just to break it up for small change."

"Ah, but you can make big change if you do it right."

"Money isn't everything."

"How do you know I won't break up your life's work and sell it off? I could sell the entire portfolio to Elixir when I take ownership, and still make a profit."

"That's your prerogative, but I don't think you'll do that. You're a visionary, someone who loves his country and his people. Acquisition is a form of sustainability to you. This is your legacy. Something to leave behind for your sons."

He leaned back and smiled.

"Is that so? You know me that well, do you?"

"Yes," David replied flatly. "You have fingers in the right pies all over Africa. You know exactly how much power you have and what to do with it. And still you spend time in the slums uplifting those who need it. If you were corrupt even a little, you would've gone into politics by now. There's no more lucrative a business than presidency, right?" There was a slight pause and then both men laughed.

"It is as you say," Godfrey admitted. "The politicians have tried to rope me in many times."

"SA needs you as much as you need us. And from a purely professional point of view, it wouldn't make any sense to pawn off the company. We have a near-impossible occupancy rate of 92%, which stayed true throughout the recession. The properties have proven they can provide a constant cash flow in hard times.

Management and maintenance has been outsourced with admirable efficiency. It is a well-oiled machine, and you are getting it at a bargain."

Godfrey rose up. "Let's take a walk."

He led the way to a small boardroom that reeked of teak oil and old leather. It had been furnished with dark wood tables and chairs, with a series of air conditioners hard at work to keep the room cool. Clifford opened the two patio-styled doors. At once the hot afternoon air burst into the room. David followed him along a narrow cemented path and up a series of steps. Standing on the highest step, he found himself looking out over the city of Lagos. It was a magnificent sight. From this height the city was alive and in motion. It looked like a bustling anthill, pulsing, pumping and gyrating.

The entire length of the roof had been turned into a great rectangular outdoor garden. There were rows of trees planted in large terracotta pots. There must have been sixty trees, all of them standing at least two metres tall, forming a dark green wall to either side. These had been placed in three long rows and between the rows were long stretches of grass. Between the pots were other pots with smaller plants, many different flowers and herbs, a mix of scents that seemed strange in a tropical climate like Nigeria.

They walked on the grass, studying some of the trees and talking about a number of things. Three ladies, the gardeners responsible for maintaining the garden, moved about the roof as if it was their home, weeding and watering as they went.

"This is where I pray," Godfrey said as they reached the middle of the garden.

He pulled a leaf from one of the trees and smelled it.

"My advisers still say your company is worth more than the selling price."

David smiled to add a bit of mystery. "Advisers don't do multi-million dollar deals. They are paid to advise."

"That might be, but everything has a fair and decent price. So I ask myself, why the pretence?"

David stopped walking and took a good deal of time to carefully word his response. This was business and he was good at it. It was in his nature to be mindful of what he said and to word it so that he made his point without offending anyone.

"There is no pretence. You need Harlem Properties, I don't. Every board member stands to make a sizeable profit. And, as per the agreement, all legal fees incurred in the acquisition is for your account, and that's no small account. So this will still be business to the end. Fair, decent, and honest."

"Ah, human error. Do you anticipate any of these creeping into the deal?"

Godfrey's eyes peered into his, but this was nothing new to him. Besides, he had nothing to hide. David believed business had to be conducted on the principle of complete transparency. If there were any errors, it would be as much a surprise to him as to Godfrey.

"It shouldn't, but if it does, the price is still fair and decent. I trade by one rule: under-promise and over-deliver. I can take a higher offer and be done with it, but I am here."

Godfrey made a soft grumbling sound and began walking down the path, engaging David in a lengthy conversation about the coming elections. It was evident that this man loved his country. He spoke passionately about the uncertain future and the mutual benefits of expanding to South Africa.

"Ajaka is still young, but he is interested in this type of life."

"You are a fortunate man to have your children follow in your footsteps. This is a rarity among the influential. Normally children scatter what they inherit."

"They are not my children. They belong to God. I provided for them but they are now men in their own right. They chose to follow. Even in their names lies their independence. Ajaka means God is praised, and Chilotam means God remembered me."

Hearing a father speak of his children with pride, touched David deeply. He missed holding his children, smelling their hair and watching them sleep.

"We have our families for such a short time, and then it is over. I'm sure you understand the concept of loss better than most people. Loss is a thief, and it strikes when you least expect it."

David changed the subject. "Ajaka and Chilotam? Is that Igbo dialect?"

"Yes," Godfrey replied, aware that he had made David uncomfortable. "I'm impressed. Not many people would know the difference. The Igbo people were an ethnic group from South-Eastern Nigeria. We embraced Christianity under British colonization. Others didn't."

"How likely is another war in Nigeria?"

"I do not know," he said and folded both hands behind his back. "Hopefully Nigeria will be spared such an inconvenience. I was there during the Biafran War of 1967. It lasted three years. Many died." David noticed an expression of terror creep over Godfrey's usually peaceful face. "My friend, I do not wish to see another war."

At this point David's cell began vibrating. He stared at the display and excused himself. "Forgive me, this is important."

"Of course. I'll be inside."

As Godfrey disappeared down the steps, David took a deep breath and answered.

"Hi, it's Kerin, from the other night. It's me," she said on the other end. Though she was stuttering her way through the greeting, her voice was still so intoxicating that his stomach muscles tightened. He hadn't been this excited in years.

"I'm not sure about this," Kerin complained. "I should be looking for a job."

She was moving about the kitchen, busying herself in an aimless manner.

"Stop it, will you! It's a weekend away. You've submitted your CV to a couple places already. Let it be."

"That doesn't mean I have the job. I need to find work, soon. Have to find another place, another school ..." She was mumbling. "I still need to pay for that school trip. How much was that again?" She pushed her hair back and froze, a frantic expression on her face. "I completely forgot about that. Oh, the money! She can't miss another trip, mom. They'll start talking. I need a job, any job."

"Still your mind, dear." Margie said from the couch. "It's just a weekend. You need this."

Kerin grabbed her cell. "No, can't do it. I have to cancel. I can't go around gallivanting in George. The rent is due and ..."

"And it will still be due when you get back."

Kerin closed her eyes and sighed. "You're not helping. You're actually making it worse."

Margie slammed Dillon's homework down on the couch and jumped up, her curly hair flopping about as she moved.

"Worse! I'm making it worse?! Well, let me get out of your hair then." Margie marched to the door. "Your whole life is flashing by and you're not enjoying one damned minute of it. You've got children, you know. They need experiences, things to remember, like this. Making that call will be the biggest mistake you ever make."

She stormed out the front door and left Kerin flabbergasted, cell in one hand, carrot in the other.

Kerin couldn't remember when last her mother had reacted so passionately. She seldom raised her voice. But the outburst was not entirely without merit. Margie had a point. It was a difficult thing to acknowledge that, after all these years, mother still knew best. She realised that she was being partially selfish in her decision-making. She was trying to control everything, planning the next move. Though her intentions were pure, she was falling short somewhere. She had been so stubbornly focused on her role as provider that she had neglected her role as mother.

With the children visiting friends down the hall, Kerin finished the supper in solitude. Her mind rambled on. She was slicing, mixing, stirring, dishing, clearing, wiping and washing, all the while dreading the weekend away.

Margie and the children returned as the light began fading.

"Didn't mean to scream at you," Margie said after a while.

"It's okay. Guess I had it coming."

And that was the end of it. There was no need to exhaust the situation. They were still hugging when the door flew open. Dillon ran into the room with his arms wide, screaming and making exploding sounds. He was a fighter jet again. This was gentler on the furniture than his bomb tank impression, but far louder.

"Hey, cool your jets, mister," she cautioned. "No bombs in the living room, remember?"

Megan closed the door and gave her mom and Margie each a hug.

"Let's eat."

"What we having?" Dillon demanded, hoisting himself onto one chair.

"Sausage, green beans and carrots."

"URGH!"

Throughout supper, Kerin was fighting an internal battle. Her mind was racing towards a conclusion that made sense. It felt as though she was having a panic attack. Then she looked at her children and the hundreds of thoughts and emotions just stopped. Dillon was playing with the beans and Megan was talking to Margie about something she had seen at school. Their characters depended wholly on what they experienced. They were being moulded into unique individuals and she had the power to staunch that growth or to set their imaginations free.

"Guess what?" she gasped, tears in her eyes. "We are all going on a trip for the weekend."

The children were confused at first, but soon they did what came naturally to children: they embraced the excitement and the suspense of the unfamiliar. They began bombarding her with questions about where and why, and they dined on Margie's inflamed excitement, and they giggled without meaning to, and they ate all their beans.

CHAPTER 8

He arrived back at the Cullinan around 6 am on Friday. He was welcomed back as if he had never left. Home sweet home. He had come to loathe this way of life. Racing here and there, no place to call home. David owned a number of prime residential properties across Gauteng, but they were constantly occupied by tenants. He also owned undeveloped properties in and around the Western Cape, all uninhabitable in their present state.

The only place available to David was the farmhouse in George. But Elizabeth and the boys had called that home. The picnics near the dam, the walks and the many other memories he couldn't shake. His family was still there. Maybe that's why he invited her.

It was now the season of change, time to face the past and to start afresh. During the last couple of weeks, David had arranged with interior decorators and landscapers to make the house liveable before his return. Benny, the caretaker, oversaw everything and kept him updated on the progress. It was time to go home.

He had arranged with Jocelynne to book four extra seats to George, which wasn't too hard to do on short notice.

William sat at the table, health shake in hand, early as always. William was dressed casually; he wore khaki chinos and an expensive blue chequered shirt.

"Another shake?" David said in disgust. "I don't know how you do it."

They had breakfast together and William updated David on the meetings he had chaired the day before. He edited out the legal jargon and gave him a brief summary. Finally all the paperwork had been concluded. Harlem Properties was now in a state of limbo. The entire portfolio was being allocated, verified and transferred to the new owner. Within the next two months every property will form part of the Benjamin Development Group. By the end of the year, David would be free of the contractual responsibilities.

"What do you mean by *off*?"

"I don't know," William said. "Something just feels off, you know? Everybody seems on edge, like they're waiting for something to go wrong. Even Josie Vermeulen was asking questions about the BD Group."

"Don't worry about Josie," David said quickly. "Her husband is one of the best lawyer in South Africa. Asking questions becomes an addiction, especially when your spouse is a lawyer."

"I figured as much myself, but it's not Josie I'm worried about. While you were away, Parker tried rallying the troops in a revolt. He held a private lunch with Annabeth, Damian and Ray. He's fishing for votes."

"Really? What happened?"

"I don't know. Rumours of a vote of incompetence."

"Well that won't help him. I still have majority rule. And hooking Annabeth Girland on a vote will never happen. She knows the business."

"She could get onboard to make a point. Annabeth is more man than you and me put together. Just ask her wife."

"I'm aware of her sexual preferences, but she's still a member, just as Parker is still a member."

"Speaking of Parker, Wendy heard Parker's assistant say he's off to Nigeria to present a vote of incompetence to Benjamin. This was told in confidence, so you didn't hear it from me."

"All that to stall a sale that has already gone through." David shook his head and finished his juice. "One desperate attempt after another to derail it. I don't understand."

"There's more."

"Oh, goody."

"Sendiwe has been hounding me for a meet. Can't imagine why. He's been reaching out to the others as well, like when we bought over the Rightman company. I put the phone down in his ear."

David laughed. "Bet he didn't like that much." Again he shook his head. "Silly business this property industry. Money certainly brings out the worst in people. Remember that, William. Don't let the money bug find you. It never lets go."

William stared at the table as though he was reliving a terrible memory. "How true. Greed is a terrible thing." He sat up after a while and smiled. "Luckily I don't have time to worry about money. I'm training for next year's Cape Argus. I've set up a strict cycling routine and it's killing me. So, when this is over, I'll be taking a little break from business. You should do it with me, man. We could partner up."

"You can't be serious. I'll just slow you down."

"That's alright, I'll do it again next year."

"Has anyone ever told you you're insane."

He flashed a mad grin and hissed, "All the time."

William scratched the tip of his nose with a toothpick, then began picking at his teeth absentmindedly. It was an annoying habit but David didn't mind it. He had become accustomed to William's quirks.

"So when is your flight?" he asked.

"Four-ish."

"I take it you're unavailable this weekend?"

"That's correct. For all intensive purposes, David Harlem is dead to the world this weekend. He doesn't exist."

"Read you loud and clear, boss."

David had planned a gym session after his meeting with William, but he scheduled coffee with an acquaintance instead. The meeting seemed like light pecking and catching up, but David realized, on a subconscious level, that he was systematically saying his goodbyes to fellow property buffs. He was wrapping up his presence in the industry. He was moving on. This was his exit strategy.

After lunch he called Kerin for last-minute arrangements, packed his bag and left. A driver from the office collected Kerin and her family. At the airport David was introduced to Margie. He could feel the tension in Kerin's voice when she introduced him to her children. She kept her arms around both children in a protective manner.

Kerin looked at her bed. She had done a preliminary round of packing, but she had to empty the bed and start all over again. She was not sure what to take and what to leave. She didn't own a lot of clothing, but everything she thought of taking seemed excessive. When she finally began packing, she noticed that her pondering had drawn a crowd of onlookers. Margie and the children stood in the doorway with amused expressions on their faces.

"So are you going to help me pack or just stand there?" she asked.

Megan and Dillon made good time packing Kerin's bags while Margie facilitated the process. It was a joint, exhausting effort. They had just finished packing when a driver fetched them.

This was it. They were going on their first family trip. The gravity of this little revelation did not make the trip any easier. Soon they were all swooped unto a plane and taken to the small town of George.

She couldn't recall when last she had set foot on a plane. She was trying hard not to pass out. At times she had to remind herself to breathe. It was less than a two-hour flight, but it was still a flight. She could hear her heart beating in her ears, her breath grating.

Both children and Margie were fast asleep.

She studied David throughout the flight, glaring at him between panic spells. He sat on a separate seat across the aisle, one row ahead of them. He was tapping away on the small laptop's keyboard, hard at work. She was looking for flaws, motives, and weaknesses. Only a few days ago, she had climbed into his car for the wrong reasons. Just thinking about it made her cheeks warm. But the sad reality was that he had been looking for a prostitute. She could not get that out of her mind. She questioned everything he said or did. Did he see her as an easy target? Wealthy men always want what they can't have. Was she just something he wanted but couldn't have? She didn't want to get hurt again. There was one consoling thought: no other man could ever hurt her more than her ex husband.

On the other hand, she had nothing left to lose. Dillon and Megan were all that remained. She had no money and, having considered prostitution while drunk, she had little dignity left. She had no expectations. She wanted nothing from this man. It was just a weekend away. Their troubles would be waiting when they returned home on Monday. David was not a solution; he was just a plaster for the weekend. She couldn't deny that he was attractive. He had a raw and manly quality about him, yet he appeared kind and gentle. But the most captivating thing about him was the fact that she sensed his pain. As much as opposites attracted, so also kind sought out kind, and pain felt pain.

The plane made a wide arch over the coastline, dipped slightly and touched down minutes later at the small George Airport. They collected their luggage, each child pulling their own bag from the runner and placing it on a trolley. They stepped out of the baggage area and into a small crowd of people. David kept his distance, allowing them the freedom to drink it in as a family, much like a tour guide would tourists in a foreign country.

From the crowd emerged a tall black man. His brown eyes were warm, set in deep sockets and naturally watery. Even though he was a thin man, he had wide, broad shoulders, like that of a boxer.

He shook David's hand. "Welcome back."

"It's that time, Benny."

He introduced Kerin and the family, saying, "This is Benny. He will take care of you this weekend."

He greeted everyone with a handshake, even Dillon.

They were led to the car where baggage was loaded. The small van was a six-seater so they sat comfortably. Fifteen minutes later he drove the van along a dirt road, then turned into a long drive. The decorative stones gnashed under the tires.

Kerin had half expected the house to be a gaudy monstrosity, a symbol of power and accomplishment, a building so unbecoming when compared to the beauty of the surroundings that it would leap out at anyone who dared to look at it. Instead, the house was a modest single storey farm house. Its design was simple, and it seemed so much older that Kerin had a hard time believing David when he explained that the previous owner had built the house in 1995.

"That's when mommy was still married to daddy," Megan said.

Kerin shushed her with a quick glance.

"The stones are new," David said in thought, attempting to change the subject. "It works well."

"Glad you approve. Men from the quarry delivered it a couple days ago," said Benny.

"Money well spent."

"There are still some bushes around the house that needs clearing, but at least you can see the place."

"Sorry about the short notice, Benny. I should've done this a long time ago."

"Have peace, brother. The rooms are clean and there are beds. That's a start."

"Love the house's new colour. Looks like cappuccino froth."

Benny smiled. "Thought you might."

The drive ended in a large loop around a water fountain. It circled past the front door and linked in with the drive on the other side. The water feature was not too dominant, as one might expect it to be. It was a gray fountain with three levels and a spout, which poured over a series of round rocks, pouring water into the lower levels where the pump transported water to the top nozzle. A wide circular bedding of flowers offered an array of colour around the fountain. There were a selection of Marigolds, scented geraniums and common chicory, interspersed with rosemary and trimmed lavender bushes.

"Heavens, look at all these flowers!" Margie said as she climbed out of the van. She stooped down, cupped a hand around one of the marigolds, closed her eyes, and inhaled the familiar smell. "All these colours, in winter. Amazing."

"This is George. Everything grows here, if you give it love," Benny said. "I planted these last month. I couldn't do everything I wanted to do. Spring is around the corner." Benny glanced around the property and sighed. "Lots of gardening to do."

David led them through the house. Benny took the children to the kitchen, while David and Kerin made their way to the right side of the house.

He opened one door and said, "This is your room."

She peered in, hesitantly stepping into what would be her own room for the next two days. She steadied herself against the doorframe and put one hand on a small stand.

"Everything is so clean, so orderly."

"You wouldn't think it, but I haven't been here in over a year."

"Wow," she remarked, swiping a finger over the surface and staring at it in disbelief. "Guess George doesn't have a dust problem then."

"Oh, it does." He slowly brushed past her into the room. "For the last three days a local cleaning agency has been making it liveable. They told me it was one of those mission impossible deals, but ..." He looked at the curtains in an absent-minded manner and continued, "I think they did alright."

Kerin stared around the room. It could have been a luxurious hotel room. There was nothing in the room that had any emotional connection. No photos on the cabinets, no paintings on the wall and no books or magazines anywhere. There were cabinets, a stand and two smaller bedside cabinets, all made with expensive woods. Against one wall was a large King-sized bed with dark wooden posts as high up as her hips. The bedding was a plain striped design, comprising of blue, green and orange. Matching curtains. It looked like the work of an interior decorator.

He pulled back a large wooden door covering the left wall, flicked a locking mechanism in place, and revealed a spacious en suite bathroom. Expensive stone tiles, fancy glimmering faucets,

KING OF SORROW | James Fouché

sensual down lighting, a shower with two heads, a free-standing corner bath, heated towel rails – and this was just the guest room! Kerin forced herself not to be impressed by the material things, but it was difficult when you've never experienced these things and possibly never would.

"There are shampoos and bath salts in all the bathrooms."

"How many bathrooms are there?" she asked.

"Three."

"But the house looks so small."

He followed her into the en suite. Horizontal bars of fading light streamed into the room, angling through the wooden slats of the outside shutters.

"There's a window over here. You can't really see it from the outside when the shutters are closed. Gets a bit dark in winter, so I'll have Benny open them for you."

"No," Kerin said quickly, stepping through the blades of light. "I like it this way. It feels dreamy."

"If you change your mind, just have Benny open them from the outside."

She was at a loss for words. Her senses were overwhelmed by the newness and the wealth. The sheer bliss of it all was surreal. She felt like Alice on the other side of the rabbit hole, strolling through that wonderful dream world. She fought hard to contain herself. All she wanted to do was run to the bed, jump through the air with her arms open and her eyes shut, then delve into the bedding until she disappeared from her life.

There were four bedrooms, three bathrooms, a large kitchen, two living areas and an outside entertainment area with built-in fireplace. Benny stayed in a smaller house beyond the row of trees that lined the drive.

Kerin reunited her family in the living room, everyone stunned to a momentary silence. Margie winked at her and asked what she thought. Kerin couldn't answer. She was too far outside of her comfort zone to care. Whatever her fingers touched, felt so real that she could discern its composition. The powder across the surface of a collection of African clay pots. The smooth surface of a rosewood table. The teak oil on her fingertips. Just for a little while, she indulged her senses.

While Benny brought in the luggage, David showed the rest of the house. The children did an once-over, running from front door to back door, room to room, window to window, toilet to toilet, and back to the front door again. They were well-behaved given their ages. Kerin's mother tagged along in the distance, gasping softly when entering a room. David did a minimalist showing of the house, trying hard not to boast. However, the more he tried to play it down and speed the viewing along, the more they commented on features.

With the guests entertaining themselves and getting to know their own rooms, David and Benny walked around the house. David was still a businessman and this was one of his many investments. Caring for an asset was a given. However, there was something more ingrained than his desire to maintain his financial interests. His time served in the military had instilled a necessary and instinctive caution within him. So, as he frequently moved around, it was in his nature to constantly survey his surroundings in a disciplined manner.

"They painted the shutters?" he asked as they pushed through the shrubs along the side of the house.

"I noticed. I wanted them to paint it white, like before, but something stopped me." Benny closed the shutter doors all the way. "If you look at it like this, you don't see the window at all."

"I see." David frowned. "The slats are flush with the wall."

"You want it white, don't you?"

"I'm not sure."

David parted the doors and closed the horizontal shutters by pulling the metal lever up. When he heard movement inside Kerin's bathroom he instinctively shut the doors and slipped the lock in place mid-way. He stepped back until he stood between the trees.

"If it doesn't grow on me this weekend, we can paint it white. If it grows on me, we patent the design." He stepped into view again, blew out a tiny leaf and wiped at a cobweb clinging to his forearm. "But cut down this tree here. It's blocking the sun." He trailed off, considering the tree for a moment. "And it looks ugly. I want to make the back area accessible for guests."

They spoke briefly about the dam, the sawmill, and some of the other plans David had.

"Food?" he asked after a while.

"Fully-stocked fridge. Meats, milk, bread, eggs. They delivered this morning."

"Gun?"

"In the safe. Cleaned and oiled."

"Phone lines?"

"Too short notice. They'll be here next week. The alarm company wanted to install a radio sensor but I told them to wait until the phone lines were up. Oh, and I got a quote for new fencing along the main road. They can do it before month-end, but it will cost a bit of money."

"Then I'll pay. It needs to be done before I start building." David gave a quick sigh of relief. "What would I do without you, Benny?"

"You would grow old, fast."

"I'm already old."

They made their way back to the house.

"By the way, there's been some outages in the area, so I bought a generator, in case the lights go out this weekend."

"What happened to the old one?"

"That old thing blew when Elizabeth ran it dry."

Both men showed a hint that a nerve had been touched.

"Is it fuelled?"

"Yes, and there is a filled 10 Litre jerry can for back-up."

When they returned, everyone seemed settled and relaxed. Kerin's mother tended to the children while she unpacked. Margie was a natural grandmother, and the kids appeared contented in her care. The children headed for the front yard to study the house from the outside, Margie in tow. While being pulled out the front door, she pointed at a small bag on the table in the foyer.

"Can you give that to Kerin?"

And the door slammed shut.

He expected a blanket of silence to fall over the house, but he still heard their chatter and laughter around the house. It made him feel at ease. David followed the children through the living room windows for a minute or two, smiled and relaxed his shoulders.

He took the bag to Kerin's room. It was already early evening, The curtains were drawn shut and the en suite lights were on. Having been alone for too long he stepped into the room without thinking.

When she gasped loudly, David turned and saw her in the en suite doorway. She was in her underwear, frozen, unsure what to do, hair dangling over one shoulder, eyes wide. They stared at each other, both too scared to move. Seconds felt like minutes.

David hadn't seen a woman so sparsely dressed in a long time. He had no idea what to do. He wanted to look at her, wanted to take in everything all at once. He was fighting the urge to stare at her. His eyes moved over her body, quickly. She was beautiful, every curve, every bit of her. Beauty most certainly lingered in the eyes of the beholder, but to him she was perfection personified. He noticed the scars, what seemed like small cuts and cigarette burns, but they only added to what made her unique. Her lithely shaped body revealed a strong femininity that surprised him. Her natural beauty could not be broken by mere marks or scars.

Slowly, as if discovering her dignity and her shame for the first time, Kerin folded her arms over her chest, covering what her bra failed to cover.

"Oh," David said as he snapped back to reality. He closed his eyes and looked away. "I'm so sorry, so very sorry. Dammit, I didn't know. The door was open. I didn't ..."

He heard Kerin move around. "I tried closing the sliding door but the locking thing is jammed."

David moved closer to the en suite door and freed the clip that locked the door. When he looked down at the sliding door, she was standing in the doorway with a shirt clenched to her body. She looked bewildered but not too much so. She stared deep into his eyes; he felt her studying him, asking questions without voicing them. Something inviting remained in her eyes, something that seemed to say *I like you but I'm not there yet*, something playful but reserved and decent.

He wanted to grab her right there and kiss her, to feel her body against his. With great effort, he diverted his eyes again and held up her bag.

"Your mother said you'd need this."

He rolled the door shut and left the room. He smiled, sighed and smiled again. He felt that burning sensation in his body, starting in his gut and flowing through his limbs. When he looked at his fingers he noticed he was trembling slightly. He shook his hands a few times and went outside.

Suddenly Harlem Properties seemed like a distant memory, and Elizabeth was forming part of a different life. His priorities were changing and what had started out as an infatuation was now growing into something with substance. Kerin was on his mind, only Kerin.

Kerin had been watching Benny and David tend to the fire and the food. They worked well together. Margie and Kerin felt redundant, and a little jealous, to see two men making dinner. They relieved each other at their stations as though they had done this often.

David poured drinks, while Benny lit the fire. There was a large stump that served as a wood chopping block. Benny used a tiny hatchet, the size of a modern throwing axe, to chop the wood into thin strips to start the fire. His hands moved so swiftly and skilfully, like that of a trained hunter. When he had finished, Benny jumped back and flicked his wrist through the air. Margie jumped in surprise as the blade of the little axe ploughed into flesh of the stump. And it remained there for the rest of the night, like Excalibur protruding from the stone.

By the time David came out with the meat, the fire had warmed up the enclosed porch. The two men rotated between the kitchen and the fireplace, one slicing and dicing veggies for a salad, then at the fireplace flipping the meat over the coals, switching places as though they were one person split into two.

Margie and Benny seemed to get along very well. They shared lengthy dialogues, expressing different points of view about all kinds of things. She hadn't seen her mother so at ease in conversation since her father had passed away.

Kerin kept more to herself, reluctant to open up. She concentrated on the children. Occasionally, from a great distance across the fire, she observed their host, looking for flaws and signs of mistrust. When David returned to the kitchen to finish the salad, Benny tended to the grid.

"Something has to be done with it," Benny was saying. "The land is being wasted. Dormant land is foul land."

"Why haven't you done something with it yet? You look capable enough." Margie said.

"You are a kind woman to say that, but it is not my land."

"Personally, I think it's too big."

"It was the right size when David bought it. They were going to turn this part into a big guest house. The rest of the land would be used for farming."

"Farming?" Margie asked. "What would you farm with next to a guest house?"

"Horses. Elizabeth – Mrs. Harlem – always wanted to breed with horses. She loved them."

There was a tense silence. Dillon eventually broke it with his innocence. He laughed loudly at the drawing he had made, said something to Megan and showed it to her.

"Did you know Mrs. Harlem well?" Kerin asked.

"Oh, as well as time allowed." He stared into the coals, no longer looking at the meat. "Elizabeth. And the boys, too. Peter and Mitchell."

"She sounds like a wonderful woman."

Benny smiled, aware of her concern. "How does one measure wonderful?"

"I guess by what others say of you when you're gone."

"She was no different than you, Miss Kerin."

"But you speak of her as if she's still here."

The words had simply slipped out of her mouth before she could stop them. She felt Margie's eyes of judgement on her, but she had to know more.

Benny looked at the backdoor and said, "I can assure you, she is very much gone. Happiness comes and happiness goes." He flipped the grid nonchalantly. "Before long happiness comes again."

"Is there still money in horse farming?" Margie asked suddenly. And so began the lengthy discourse about the future of horse breeding in South Africa.

Kerin finished her wine a short while later. Benny politely offered to refill her glass.

"Don't worry," she said getting up from her chair. "I have to go in anyway"

Inside she stopped near the end of the dark corridor. She could see David in the kitchen. He was slicing celery into thin slices, his hands moving with the grace of a skilled chef. His brow was slightly furrowed, but he appeared to be completely at peace.

She felt as though she was spying on him from the shadows, and she liked it. Something about hiding in the dark, looking at a man so lost in a task, made her giddy. At first she thought it was the wine going to her head, but she'd only had the one glass. And wine did not explain the warm feeling in the pit of her stomach, or the sudden acceleration of her heart rate, or the sound of rushing blood in her ears.

David stopped what he was doing. When he looked up, she stepped from the shadows as if she had just come from outside.

"Is there more wine?" she asked shyly.

"Of course. Let me get that for you."

He pushed the salad bowl aside and took her glass. As he poured, the glass tipped over. It cracked softly and two pieces of glass shot across the marble countertop, followed by a small pool of wine.

Instinctively the waitress inside of Kerin kicked into gear. She grabbed a cloth and began dabbing at the wine, but David reached over and took her hand in his. He had big, warm hands. They were not rough to the touch, but still manly hands. She half expected his hands to have a soft manicured feel, but she had been wrong.

"You don't have to do that."

She just stood there, looking into his eyes, and again time froze.

Dillon ran into the kitchen with his arms raised and his voice deep.

"Spider! Mommy, there's a spider! A big one," he bellowed, latching onto one leg and pulling her toward the back.

"Hey, Dilly. Where's the spidey?" she joked.

"Come see!" he screamed and pulled harder.

"Wait. Mommy's coming."

David smiled, took the cloth from her and threw it over the spilled wine. He scooped the shards up with a paper towel and poured her a new glass.

She mouthed the word *Sorry*, followed her boy to where he had seen the spider, and joined everyone at the fire.

Benny was telling them how he and David had met. He was a masterful storyteller, using engaging words and vivid expressions to convey his emotions. When he spoke, everyone within earshot became part of his audience. He added a sense of drama and adventure to every story, drawing in the children when their interests wandered. At times he amplified the suspense by flipping the meat at a pivotal point in his tale.

He explained how he had been working as a security officer at one of David's properties, and how David had opened up a new world for him. Then he had been caretaker of David's triple-storey mansion in Pretoria for a couple of years. He had bonded so well with their boys that David called him Benny Harlem, no longer a refugee named Bveni Mukarakate.

"Refugee?" Margie said.

"I'm Zimbabwean."

"And what did you do in Zimbabwe?"

Benny's face hardened.

"That is a long story, one I do not like telling."

"Don't mean to be nosy. Just curious."

"My country was falling apart in front of my eyes. I was militia, the opposition. We were fighting Mugabe. It was a short fight. Ai, that man, he ruled in another way. It was fight or run away."

"You didn't *have* to fight. There is no shame in running."

157

"You don't understand, Miss." He poked at the coals as he spoke, the glow reflecting in his wide eyes. "In my culture much lies in a name. My name, it is Bveni. It means guerrilla. I was leader over many. I had to fight. And the fighting was very bad. Then I was leader over not so many. So, I *had* to run. Now I'm South African. No more fighting, no more death."

Margie, nearly the same age as Benny, had grown up in an entirely different world. The trials of Zimbabwe was beyond her grasp. She had little more to say on the matter.

"Benny sounds much better than Bveni. You are not a guerrilla anymore."

"You are too kind."

When the meat was finished, everyone dished for themselves.

For the first time in years, she sat down to eat without a heavy heart. Her face didn't feel tired or tight, her muscles were relaxed and her many woes were temporarily forgotten.

CHAPTER 9

She woke up into a dream world. Her life appeared to be upside down, or downside up. Nothing made sense. The comfy pillows, the lavender smell of the bedding, no police sirens blaring in the distance. The stark contrast between senses and memories played havoc with her emotions.

Kerin wanted to enjoy herself for once. But, as appealing as the thought was, she couldn't. She wanted to remain out of place, to feel as if she didn't belong in this world of luxury and ease. Getting used to something was too easy, but parting with comfort was a far more complicated process. She wanted to be able to give it all up in a second.

It was cold outside, so she put on the only warm jacket she had brought with. She made her bed, methodically tucking in the sheets at the base and taking great care to leave the room as she had found it the day before. This was not her room. This was not her bed. This was not her life.

In the kitchen, still in her pyjamas and the jacket, she prepared a cup of coffee for herself. She struggled to make out the arms on the clock. It was 05:05.

When she stepped outside the back door, an ice blanket wrapped around her body. Though twice as cold in the open morning air, she didn't mind. It was still dark, but the world was getting lighter by the second. Here and there, as her sights adjusted and the sun woke up, she could make out the ridge of the mountains and the outlines of treetops.

The air was fresh. As the sea seemed to be without end, so nature had a way of opening up in front of her eyes. Snippets of the landscape came slowly into view. Before long she was clutching her empty cup and the skies were grey with advancing daylight. When a toilet flushed inside the house, Kerin gave a satisfied sigh, stretched, yawned and rubbed her eyes.

Just then, out of the corner of her eye, something caught her attention. She struggled to find it again, then saw the movement in the distance. As she looked, the object took on the shape of David Harlem. He was jogging along a winding path which ran across the land like a series of separation lines. He wore a light gray shirt, blue shorts and dark running shoes. Even from that distance, she could make out perspiration patches on the shirt. His face seemed completely at peace, as though this was his therapy.

Then her children poured into the cold morning and swarmed around her. She hugged them both, as tightly as she could. She didn't want to let go.

"Mr Benny made breakfast. Come, he's in the kitchen," said Dillon.

Kerin hadn't heard Benny come into the house. The morning silence had blotted out the world.

"Hang on, mister. Did he say we can eat?"

"He said we can eat at seven," said Megan.

"In ten minutes," Dillon hissed angrily, swirled around in irritation and punched the air.

Kerin was shocked that she had been sitting outside for almost two hours. She hadn't even noticed the time flying by.

"What's with you? On weekends you always sleep late. Now you're jumping around."

They stared at him as he began poking at a spider's web spun across one corner of the fireplace.

"Tell him, mom. Since we got here, he's been making more noise than normal."

Kerin jumped and gasped when David stepped into view. He was out of breath, chest heaving and sweat covering his face.

"Mornings. Slept well?"

All three nodded, then looked down shyly, children copying mother. Even Dillon was momentarily subdued.

"Ah, I smell coffee," he said. Then, to the kids, "Let's see if Uncle Benny has finished the food."

At the mention of food, Dillon jumped around again, then shot into the house at lightning speed, leaving the others in his wake.

Breakfast was eggs and sausage, with toast – which Margie didn't eat – baked beans – which Megan didn't eat – and fried onions – which Dillon didn't eat. Kerin had noticed her mother eating less and less with each passing day, as if her stomach was shrinking.

After breakfast, everyone delighted in a refreshing morning shower, except Dillon. If he had his way he would remain filthy for the rest of the year. The family congregated in the living room almost simultaneously and stood around looking at each other, as if they were waiting to go to work or to school. It felt strange not to have an idea what to do. Back home there was always something that had to be done, some rush to contend with. Now the mind was left wanting.

Benny came to their rescue.

"David went to town, but he'll be back soon. Then we can all go to town. In the mean time ..." He trailed off, waved his hands around. "Relax and do as little as possible."

It was rather cold in George and there was snow on the mountains, but the sun was out, so everyone sat outside. Margie and her mom sat in pleasant silence drinking tea while the children went about the business of children, exploring the vastness and doing things that amused their curiosity.

The sounds of nature surrounded them. The gentle repetitive splattering sound of the water fountain, added to the blissful experience. It was heaven and they both felt a little dreamy, taken away by the ease of their surroundings.

"Mom, he saw me in my underwear," Kerin blurted out.

Margie almost choked on her tea, drying her lips with a napkin. "Oh, dear! Was it at least the good underwear? Or was it the white ones with the wires poking out?"

"Does it matter?"

"Well, you wouldn't want him to think about you in that old bra."

Kerin leaned back into her chair and stared at her mother. "Who *are* you? And what have you done with my mom?"

"Oh, come now. You're both warm-blooded creatures, and you're not getting any younger. He's a fine-looking man who thinks the world of you."

"No he doesn't," she said shaking her head wildly, then, "What makes you say that?"

"I've been around. I can see these things when they start. Where there's smoke, there's fire. The kids can see it, too."

They stared at each other, mother and daughter.

"I don't know. It's not a good time now. I guess there's never a good time, is there? I doubt the right moment will ever come along." She sipped at her tea, then added, "You know, we've never spoken like this before, like two friends."

Suddenly a seriousness fell over them both.

"I never wanted to be your friend. I was trying too hard to be your mother." Margie stared into the skies. "When you reach this side of the age-spectrum, things become clearer and, before you know it, everything else becomes unimportant."

Kerin closed here eyes, pushed her shoulders up and stretched out her arms and legs. "Whatever the reason, I like this side of you."

Margie took her daughter's arm and squeezed it gently. "I'm sorry for the way things ended up. I never wanted this for you. You know that, don't you?"

"That's okay, mom. Life has a way of working out as it should. We must just wait for it."

"Don't wait too long, child, or else you'll find yourself looking at a grave with your name on it, and you'll sit and wonder what happened to your life."

They watched the kids running through the fruit trees, exploring the land, their smiling faces tilted back and their screams of joy echoing through all the earth. They were happy.

Megan loved the purple ones the most. They were prettier than the others. She took hold of the stem and plucked it free. Just one; she wasn't greedy. Just one flower was all she needed. She delicately moved one finger over the small purple flower as if she was afraid she might break it. The petals were so fine, frail, unique. She was mesmerized by the life of plants. She could feel something deeper than this world hidden in their beauty. They were so pretty.

Not that pretty meant everything. She knew that pretty could be a bad thing. But in a world where everybody felt so unpretty, she loved to look at pretty things all the time. Out here even the birds were prettier than the city birds. Or, maybe because the buildings here weren't so high up in the sky, she could see them better. Or, maybe because there were less cars, trucks, bikes, and stuff, she could hear them better, too. Their little tweets and twitters carried so far that she thought they were closer than they really were. Sometimes she couldn't even see them at all.

When she exhaled, her breath looked like steam. Dillon did it all the time at home, running around and blowing his steam on everything as if he was steam-marking his territory. Unfortunately he was the same here. Gran always said that some things changed and some things stayed the same, but that Dilly would always be dilly. He was a big baby. Even now, he was standing in one of the sun's rays blowing his breath out to amuse himself, looking at the condensation as if it was his invisible friend and they were having a deep discussion.

It was cold in the shadows, but Megan didn't mind the cold. It was still warmer here than at home. Even if it got colder she would still feel warmer in her mind, because she was far away from home and all that home represented. When she went to the loo, she saw snow on the mountains. That was pretty, too. There had been snow on Table Mountain once, but that was so quick and she couldn't see it with all the rain. Here the sun was shining and the snow was still thick on the peak. It looked like cake frosting, like what they made in Mrs. Adams' Home Economics class, only without the decorative little silver balls that cracked when you bit them.

She put the flower in the side pocket of her sweater, careful not to crush it.

"You like that one?" Margie asked, looking at Megan over the top of her large spectacles.

"It's pretty."

Dillon was running around the fountain with his hands open, like an airplane looking for a landing strip. His cheeks were red and his hair was tousled. When he finally stopped, he collapsed on the ground with his tongue hanging out.

Margie struggled to her feet. Megan felt her grandmother's hand on her shoulder as she balanced herself to yell at Dillon.

"Get up, boy! You'll dirty your clothes and we didn't bring extras."

As if Gran had transferred the caretaking duties to her, Megan marched over to her little brother.

"Come, Dilly," she said tenderly and helped him up. She brushed leaves and dirt from his sweater and pulled his zipper shut, careful not to pull it so tight that it cuts into his neck. "And keep the zip up. It's cold."

Megan worked so gingerly with him, compassionately, protectively, because he was her little brother and he was pretty, too. Even when his nose was running and the green stuff was coming out, he was still a pretty flower. Even when he teased her by putting a dead Christmas beetle on her pillow. Even when he hit her with the remote or pulled his undies over her head. He was pretty. He was beautiful. Taking care of him made her feel warm inside.

Sadly, she was still too young to take care of her mother. There were times she wanted to hold her mother, times when her mother needed someone to hold. It was then Gran told her not to. Gran always said her mommy needed time alone, that it was bad for them to see her like that, that instead of holding mommy she should hold Dilly, and that taking care of him would make it easier for mommy. But then there were nights, when Gran was fast asleep and not there to stop her. Nights where she would wake up and hear mommy doing stuff in the house. Nights where she saw mommy looking over them, lying still as a gecko so she wouldn't know she was awake, until she heard the door close, followed by the soft steps down the hallway, her mommy singing softly to herself. Then her beautiful voice would die down in the dark and the crying would start, soft whimpering sounds, barely audible, but loud enough for her to hear if she put her ear against the door just right. Megan would stand there listening, wanting to hold her mommy, but she would go back and look at Dillon, fast asleep, peaceful, oblivious, free, and pretty. She would just sit there in the silence, looking at the pretty.

Dillon shook himself and looked at her in distaste, his cheeks all puffed up. He pulled his zip down to his chest, an act of defiance.

"It's too tight. I can't move my arms, like so," he mumbled and flung his arms from side to side to make a point. "It's too small."

"Then you must stop growing," Megan said.

"We can get something bigger for him in town," Mr. Harlem said from the front door. His voice was firm but innocent-sounding.

Gran instinctively took up a protective role, putting an arm around Dillon and tugging at his sweater until it looked a bit looser on the shoulders.

"That's okay, we'll manage just fine with what we have."

"It's really ok. I think we all need extra jackets. It's quite cold."

Gran looked at him, almost trying to look through him. Megan had come to realize that Gran's eyes saw stuff that other people couldn't see. She had old-person power vision. Megan had learned early on not to lie to Gran or to hide something from her, because Gran always found out the truth.

Megan saw nothing wrong with Mr. Harlem. He seemed nice. He was good to mom and that was good enough. Since coming to George mom had perked up a lot. She was tense and stressed out at first, but now she seemed happier than before.

Soon everyone was herded into the van and transported to the small town of George. They went to a nursery where they walked through a large herb garden. They had a small lunch. There was a small animal farm with bunnies, chickens, goats and an old donkey called Pit. While Dillon chased the chickens, Megan spent her time with Pit the donkey. She petted it, very gently, like Gran showed her. She had never seen a donkey before, or bunnies for that matter. There were white bunnies with brown spots and brown bunnies with white spots, noses wiggling non-stop and their big feet kicking wildly when she picked them up. They looked petrified. She kept telling them that she wouldn't hurt them, that she just wanted to say hello and touch them for a little bit.

When they returned, the sun was starting its descent. The heat of the day had been enjoyable but it now began to dissipate. Almost immediately, Mr. Benny made his way to the kitchen to prepare supper. Dillon was in hot pursuit, his tiny fingers eager to help. Mr. Benny was happy to make use of Dillon's little fingers. He said that more hands meant better food, so Megan decided to join them. Gran snuck off for a midday nap. Within seconds she was gone, her face puffy and her cheeks red with sleep. Megan knew she was asleep because she had watched Gran doze off many times before. She always slept like a rock. Mom and Mr. Harlem began talking about the house and the land, then went for a walk. Megan wanted to go with but then Dillon also wanted to go with. No, this was better. Gran would be up soon anyway. And she wanted to help with the food. Mr. Benny cut the onions. She didn't like onions. They made her cry and they smelled bad, too. But Mr. Benny was good, and fast, with knives. She watched him through the tears, afraid that he might cut one of his fingers off. At one point he stepped back, pushed her and Dillon away from the counter, and threw the knife into the chopping board so hard that it wobbled from side to side. They clapped hands and Mr. Benny made a little bow, smiling so wide that she could count most of his teeth. She grated a big block of cheese. Dillon collected pizza bases from the freezer and removed them from the packaging. She liked pizza. It felt like weekend food. Some weekends they would eat at mom's work for free, when she was working double, and Megan always ordered pizza. This was different, though. This was a special weekend. She'd remember this weekend for always, and so would Dillon.

David led her through fruit trees and colourful bushes which had been allowed to roam without pruning. Neither bush, nor tree, nor anything growing outside the immediate proximity of the house, had been pruned in a while. She thought the wildness of nature added to the design of the house. Then again, what did she know about gardening or architecture.

He mentioned that he had only been to the farm twice in the last two years, and that he contemplated selling it. He purposely hadn't employed other permanent staff to work the land. He wanted the land to be dormant and wild until he had decided what to do with it. Apparently allowing the land to lie in this way gave it a chance to return to its fruitful self. Benny's function was merely to do some light maintenance and to create the illusion of constant movement.

They turned into a narrow path, the very path she had seen him jogging on that morning. It appeared as though the tall grass and shrubs had been cut back some months ago. The handy work of Benny with a panga.

"Should I be scared of something? You know, animals or insects?"

"There are some snakes."

"Snakes?!"

"Puff adders, but don't worry. Just keep to the path. They come out at night and only attack when threatened."

"That's comforting to know."

After a long walk she noticed light filtering through the growth. It was around four o' clock and the sun would only be up for another two hours or so. The temperatures were already dropping, but the exertion of the walk provided adequate heat. Before long they exited into another pathway which led through grass and around a rise in the land. This morning she had seen David disappear around this part of the path. As they rounded this area, the sun unfolded on her face and blinded her in such a way that her eyes had to adjust to the brightness. She cupped one hand over her eyes and gasped loudly when her vision returned.

Here, beyond the farmhouse and the bushes, the air was unrestrained and full. To breathe one almost had to slice off a chunk of air and eat it. When she finally breathed in, her lungs welcomed the fresh air. She was instantly revitalized by the absence of smog and car fumes or the invisible frequencies that bombarded her in the city. Every unnatural sound was drowned out by the natural.

What she saw appeared to be land without end. She could see no other farms, cars or people. There were a series of flimsy and battered demarcation poles with two lines of rusted barbed wire fixed to them. Other than that, it was just rough country in her sights. It appeared to be bulky, or cumbersomely styled. Kerin only saw freedom.

In the distance, the Outeniqua mountain range encircled the tiny town, like a backbone separating George from Oudtshoorn and surrounds. It's skeletal appearance was because the length of the mountain range was scarred by a series of deep dark ridges and clefts that gave it a haunting and decaying characteristic. In the centre of the range, evidently the focal point from all angles, the highest of the peaks rose up to a crooked point, like a tiny pearl, overlooking the town of George, tiny in the distance. The peak was covered with snow, all the way down to a signal tower where a radio beacon signalled to passing aircraft. The late afternoon bounced off the snow and the white stung Kerin's eyes. The day had been comfortably warm, challenging the fact that the snow had already formed so thickly on the mountains over the last couple of days. David told her George had a moderate temperature and that the snow could cover the mountains today and be gone tomorrow. He warned that tonight would be one of the few colder nights.

To the rear of the land, was a clump of pine trees. Their giant branches and dark green needles stretching skyward. The unmistakeable and intoxicating smell wafted to where they stood, drifting on the gentle mountain wind that pushed back on itself and flitted over the land like a restless falcon. The ageless giants beckoned her to walk amongst them and to listen to the many creaks and rustling sounds within its boundaries.

To the left and the right, the land appeared to be without limit and without use. It was a fruitless grassland from one side to the other; not barren land, but certainly without commercial or charitable function. Throughout the grass was already knee-high and a faded green colour. As she stared at the vastness, that same wind swept over the land, brushing the grass this way and that as it orchestrated an elaborate play just for the two of them, using nature as its puppets and the land as its stage to thrill its audience. She almost applauded and called for an encore.

A short distance from the house, more to the left part of the property, was a large mound, large enough to be a hill, and an abandoned structure that looked like a small house. Here the grass was a deeper green with a more rugged, vibrant appearance. At the foot of the hill some patches of shrubbery and small bushes were visible.

"Why is it so green over there?"

"It's supposed to be a dam, but it's more like a swamp. Some years ago there was a drought in George and the dam ran dry. Now it wells up during winter and dries out in summer." He swept his hand from right to left. "The land slopes down at a slight angle. Perfect to fill a dam. I can rebuild it and open up canals for the water, but that's a costly exercise. Didn't think about that when I bought the land."

"Why buy the land at all?"

David leaned against one of the poles. "We were going to retire here."

"We?"

"Elizabeth and me." He stared into the trees, looking for sanity. "And Mitchell and Peter. Our two boys."

Kerin didn't know what to say so she waited until David broke the silence.

"They died in a car accident about two years ago. It was my first holiday in years. We were going to the beach and ..." He searched for the right words. "It couldn't be avoided."

"What? What couldn't be avoided?"

"A car drifted into our lane. Then we were flying through the air. I wasn't wearing my seatbelt, so on impact I was flung from the car. Everything went black for a second." Tears formed in his eyes, but remained there. The light was quick to reflect the wetness and it brought out the colour of his eyes. "When I came to, I heard Elizabeth screaming. Not like when she screamed because of a spider. This scream cut me to the bone. I pushed through a crowd of onlookers. The car was burning, fiercely. I tried opening the doors but the handles burned into my hands. It wouldn't open, not even when I used my jacket." He opened and closed his hands in remembrance. "I couldn't see the boys in the backseat. There was no movement, just flames. Then she stopped screaming. She just sat there in the flames looking at me." His adam's apple shifted as he swallowed. "I couldn't help her."

"Oh my word," Kerin gasped, covering her mouth in shock. After a while she touched his arm, squeezed it gently, and said, "I am so sorry. I didn't mean to pry."

When he had finished the tears abated almost immediately.

"I didn't know. Must have been hell."

"I understand loss. My parents died when I was young. Then I was in the army. That sort-of prepares you for loss. But nothing can prepare you for the death of a child. After the funeral, my life became a bit disjointed. Life seemed pointless. I spent my whole life accumulating assets. To what end? My estate would be tied up in trusts. I felt like a king without an heir. I always knew what to say and when to say it, as if I had automatic favour. In business, in life, with finances. Things were perfect. And then it was gone. So, I distanced myself from my world, to clear my mind and to disengage." He looked down at his ring finger. "I removed my wedding ring a few months ago. That was all I had left of her. I always thought there was something special about a ring. You know what I mean? Something affirming and binding." An amused smile surfaced. "I've misplaced that ring so many times and she always joked that it was a sign of good luck, that losing your ring was a reminder that it was just an item."

Kerin scoffed. "I wouldn't know. My husband pawned my ring two months after our marriage to buy a motorcycle for one of his get-rich-quick ideas. He never replaced it." She giggled, then composed herself. "Sorry."

"I like that you have a humorous view on things."

"You have to or else you'll go nuts."

"You're right."

"So, wow! No parents, no family and a big business from scratch. I know so little about your life. You have so much to tell."

He smiled and his eyes smiled with him, a patient and reserved smile that rendered the moment immaculate. "Hardly the case. My life is inconsequential. I think I still have so much to learn."

"Geez, you've learned enough." She touched his arm again. "You've endured so much pain and sorrow."

"What can I say? I feel like the king of sorrow.

"If you're the king of sorrow, then I must be the queen of sorrow," she said jokingly. "My life is no fairy tale, either. Guess that makes us human."

He brought his hand up underneath hers and held it there, allowing her to make the choice. Instinctively her fingers pulled his into a firm grip and he closed it with his thumb.

"Come, I want to show you something."

They walked for about half an hour, their light conversation making small change of the time and the distance. At the foot of the high hill she noticed a slight fork in the path. The path to the right led to the white structure. It turned out to be an abandoned house which had been plundered of its roof, window frames and other valuable piping or fittings. Only the skeleton of a lodging remained.

"That was the old servant's quarters," he said before she could ask. "The new quarters where Benny sleeps were built before I bought the land."

"It looks archaic."

"Yes, it's got a certain character. I've been meaning to tear it down, but there are more important things to do."

"Like what?"

"Let me show you."

The path to the left was a bit steeper and disappeared after a while. Here David led the way up the hill. It was a slanted, steep hike, especially for someone who hadn't hiked since childhood. Once atop the hill, the incredible height became evident.

"Whoa! It's higher than I thought."

"It's about 100 metres above ground level, give or take."

Everything within sight, excluding the Outeniqua mountains, appeared to be below them. Between pants she did a 360 degree turn, taking in everything she saw. It was awesome.

At the back of the hill, hidden by its size, was the dam. The upper edge of the dam was a good distance away from the hill. It looked wonderfully flawed. It was filthy, muddy and smelly.

Leaves, pieces of bark and other natural debris littered the surface. It had a decaying quality about it, but not in a gross manner of the word. It seemed natural and the stench of it didn't bother her as she thought it would.

"I need to fix that. It's getting low again."

By etchings and erosion lines in the dam wall, she could tell it was losing water.

"The plan was to dry it out this year and extend it all the way to the tree line. Gonna cost a fortune."

He told her about the plantation of Yellowwood trees beyond the pines, stressing that there was still a large piece of land hidden beyond that.

They worked their way around the top of the hill until the farmhouse came into view again. She pointed toward a large metallic building, the late afternoon sun reflecting off its corrugated roof.

"What's that?"

"The old George sawmill."

"Now that is *really* archaic. How old is it?"

"Not sure. It hasn't functioned as a mill in years." He pointed out a dark patch of earth nearer to the line of trees. "There were more buildings over there, but they were demolished long ago." Leaning closer to her, he trailed his finger across the land to point out another path which led toward the clump of trees. "The loggers felled the trees over there and trucks took the logs back to the mill. There they were scaled, debarked, trimmed and cut into boards. From there they took it to the highway for deliveries." He offered her an awkward smile. "It's much more complicated than I make it sound, of course."

"Of course." She smiled coyly and stared at the building for a while. "Sounds like you did a bit of homework. Ever consider picking up where they left off?"

David shook his head no. "I've been offered a lot of money for those pine trees, but I can't get it over my heart to cut them down. They look so beautiful."

"A developer who doesn't like cutting down trees? Sounds too good to be true."

"Exactly. My wife always thought we should build a guesthouse, with chalets and campsites near the house, and breed with horses on this side. She had this idea of taking guests through the trees on horseback."

She considered the thought. She was no business woman, but the idea made sense. Looking down the hill, she could envision a cluster of cottages, maybe a grid of evenly-spaced camp sites, and the stalls for the horses where the mill now stood.

"That could work. I can almost see it. You'd have to get rid of the mill and build a stable, I guess."

"It's getting late," David said when he looked at his watch. "Wow, it's past five already. Let me show you the mill on our way back. Benny's house is a short distance from there."

"Yes, I'm starving."

The downhill descent went twice as fast but was twice as tricky. Twice she steadied herself by grabbing hold of David's arm when she slipped on the stony path. Soon they were on the path that lead back to the main house.

On the way, they took another quick detour. She didn't mind the side-trip. She found herself scanning the grass for signs of snakes and other creepy crawlies. She'd lost all recollection of time and place. She was simply going with the flow, enjoying herself. For the briefest moment she was the Kerin she had forgotten about.

As they pushed through the long grass, the sawmill slowly came into view. The sun was already gone by the time they had reached the mill. Kerin had to push her sunglasses back over her head to see clearly.

When they stepped into a clearing, she could smell the richness of the earth. It came as a wave of rotting tree bark, saw dust and mould. It had such a pure and natural sense.

"A sawmill in your back yard? Isn't it dangerous?"

"Not really. It's just an empty shell, like the old staff quarters. There's nothing left. The farmer began selling everything off to cover costs, so all the metal and the equipment was taken out and auctioned a long time ago. All that remains are the tattered metal sheeting."

Before long darkness was upon them and David picked up the pace.

Kerin didn't really notice the time. She wondered what the children were doing and she longed to be with them, but she was also trying to take Margie's advice to heart. She wanted to be a mother while she enjoyed herself. She knew Margie would dish up if it gets too late. Her mother kept a stern No Eating After Six rule. She told David that Margie would tend to the kids, so he slacked the pace a bit.

And so they walked, talking and getting to know each other even more. They were comfortable with one another. They spoke openly about private matters, something she never did. As the darkness pressed in on them, they watched the full moon rising up over the Outeniqua mountains like a large glowing cymbal, lighting them from behind and providing a decent light for their feet.

The pain was unbearable. He gripped the railing above his head and grunted in agony, his eyes clenched shut and his body hunched forward. He felt beads of sweat popping up across his forehead. All the muscles in his body contracted furiously. Each terrible spasm only yielded a drop or two. He couldn't take it anymore. His body felt as if it was on fire and there was nothing to quench it. He held his breath and pushed again. *Out, damn you! Get out of my body!*

Nothing.

He groaned loudly as another pulse of anguish rippled through his body. He had been standing there for almost thirty minutes. *This is absolute madness.*

"You okay, boss?" a concerned voice called from beyond the door.

"Do I sound okay?" Sendiwe shouted back, out of breath and trembling. "Stay outside and mind your own business!"

He looked down at the urinal and his shriveled manhood balanced between thumb and forefinger. He was shaking so badly that he couldn't even hold his own pecker steady. Another drop of urine slowly crept through his urinary tract and fell into the ceramic bowl. That little drop felt like a brick being forced through a straw.

He gave a sigh of relief and decided to wait a couple of hours before attempting another visit to the urinal. Maybe he should drink less fluids. But life without alcohol was a bleak thought, even if life only meant a number of months.

When he had spoken to his doctor about this new development, he was told that it was a urinary tract infection which was common in patients suffering from multiple sclerosis. He also said the problem would become more severe in time. Sendiwe couldn't imagine anything more severe. He suspected he would soon be looking forward to the sweet release of death. Another three months of this seemed unbearable, even to him.

He was trying to understand his condition but what good would it do educate himself on the mysteries of physics and biology. Knowing everything would not benefit him in the least. Besides, not even the doctors knew why or how. They had nothing concrete on paper and they only ventured speculative theories. They simply gave him blank faces, empty stares, which he resented, followed by apologetic gestures, which had no merit. He hated not knowing.

They had diagnosed him with a rare form of multiple sclerosis. In his life rare usually meant special, or very expensive and sought-after, like a rare wine. In this instance, it meant unimaginable pain and accelerated death.

As he understood it, multiple sclerosis was an inflammatory disease which affected the ability of nerve cells in the brain and spinal cord to communicate with each other effectively. The man mentioned something about an interruption in electrical signals and his body's own immune system attacking the fluid around the spine and his brain. *What does that mean?!*

Last week, the fears had been possible disability at age sixty, but when the tests came back on Tuesday, things abruptly went from bad to worse in a matter of seconds. His tests had indicated a steady neurologic decline indicative of a progressive relapsing subtype of multiple sclerosis. *What the hell does that mean?!*

"It means it's moving faster than normal MS. Because you've had no superimposed or symptomatic attacks before, we've been unable to diagnose the disease sooner. I still don't understand why it hasn't revealed itself sooner. I'm afraid it's progressed so far that there's nothing we can do to decelerate the decline," the doctor had said.

"Like I said, what the hell does that mean?!" Sendiwe had demanded.

"It means that you are staring fatality in the face. It means that you will not win this fight. This particular form of MS is not just rare, but it's moving so fast. So very, very fast..."

And then, three months was such a short time left to live.

He stared at his face in the mirror. He had lost weight, rapidly; almost twelve kilograms over the last two weeks. His eyes were set in empty, hollow sockets and his cheeks were no longer puffy. All that in just two weeks! Many times he had tried a diet for a couple of weeks, but it never worked. He always ended up gaining weight instead of losing it. Now his body was wasting away in front of his own eyes, minute by minute, day by day, month by month by final month, into the casket and into the afterlife.

He had been thinking a lot about the possibilities of a spiritual realm beyond the physical. He envisioned dreamlike specters floating around a magical landscape, but figured he would never get to see it. Sendiwe didn't doubt that his destiny had been cast downward by his earthly conduct. His sudden musings about Heaven and Hell was nothing shy of an attempt to justify his wrongs.

Washing his hands no longer felt like an obligatory task after a quick restroom stop. It felt like a religious experience, the water flowing over his fingers in slow motion, removing all the dirt and then trickling away into a gaping abyss. Redemption seemed like an impossible feat to him. The great Sendiwe had so many skeletons in the closet and so many wrongs to right that three months was hardly enough time to attain true redemption. It would probably take three months just to write everything down. What would that accomplish?

Harlem was on his mind a lot. He had wanted Harlem Properties with every part of his being. He had longed to acquire it, to gulp it down and savor the taste of accomplishment. He loved the smell of victory. He had lived for the kill. What he couldn't kill, he kept pursuing until he sensed defeat. Harlem had been that little irritating itch that no amount of scratching or ointment could remove. Then Harlem decides to sell. Now there were only three months left to rule his kingdom. How futile? All that fighting, for what?

Sendiwe pondered about his meeting in the Woodstock parking lot. He had come away from the meet with The Antagonist feeling even dirtier than before. In his colorful life, Sendiwe had encountered all manners of men. There had been those who cowered behind the limitations set by governments and different industries. Those who could destroy you when you looked at them wrong. Those who would keep fighting and never let go, no matter how hard you hit them or how difficult you made it for them. Then there were those who were immaculately protected by darkness. They moved among the shadows of the world and conducted many different evils with the greatest of ease, sometimes without them ever being aware of their obscure power. They remained hidden, so that they could never be found when they were being hunted. These were dangerous men, and dangerous men influenced the murderous men.

It was when his old acquaintance, Roelf Lassen, sat opposite him that alarm bells began ringing. He knew all the murderous and barbarous monsters in South Africa. Lassen was as murderous and criminal as a crook could possibly get in this godless country. Soon after Sendiwe became aware of Harlem's intentions, he went fishing for information or any dirt he could use, as he always did, as a shark would prowl the waters when it smelled blood. Soon enough his bait reeled in a surprise response from the sleazy crime world. Sendiwe fought hard to hide his astonishment when he walked into his office one morning, only to discover Lassen sitting in the waiting room with a sly smile on his face.

Naturally Lassen didn't disclose anything of worth. However, the fact that Lassen was there in person, responding to his queries about the Harlem sale, was proof enough that something foul brewing. Lassen had been unaccommodating, avoiding all his pursuits to pry open his involvement with Harlem Properties.

Rousting a murderous man eventually draws out the true culprit, and, lo and behold, then the shadows suddenly gave way. Sendiwe, spurred on by his own arrogance and insolence, had braved the depths of corruption and had peered into the darkness. It was then that the light was cast down upon the dangerous man in his midst, revealing the true identity of an antagonist in hiding. Now, knowing who was pulling the strings, Sendiwe was simply biding his time – a luxury he didn't have.

In the distance shone a light, small underneath the moon. Kerin squinted to adjust her eyes. She made out a structure. When there was so much overgrowth to contend with, distant lights were misleading. It could be that of a stationary car or the huge spotlights of a nuclear plant and it would emit the same glow.

"What's that?" she asked.

"The light? That's Benny's house."

"Wow." She sighed and sniffed.

"What?"

"Nothing. We're almost at the house. Back to reality, back to life."

She did not want to leave this place. She felt free and at peace here. Going back to the city was a terrible thought to digest. Megan and Dillon loved it here. Even Margie loved it here. *She* loved it here.

"And that's a bad thing?" he asked.

She remained silent, absentmindedly kicking at what looked like a small rock. It clattered along and came to rest in a patch of shrubs as if it was meant to lie there.

"That bad, huh?"

"It's so magical here. I can't stomach the thought of the city."

David stared at the ground. "You're welcome to visit when city life gets too much. You and your children."

Kerin was torn up by the invitation. In that moment, he seemed so sincere, and he had endured a lot. She was drawn to him on every level. He was wealthy. This could lead to a lifetime of provision for her children. Deep down, she still felt obliged to remind herself that men were manipulative. She had been burned before, badly. She could handle another roll of the dice on her own, but not with her kids. If something went wrong this time, it would affect the children negatively and she would never forgive herself for doing that to them.

"Where do you see this going? Me and you?"

David didn't answer. He kept his eyes focused on Benny's house. She had seen that contemplative look before. He appeared to be considering her question carefully. "I can't imagine an answer that would make sense."

"That bad, hunh?" she imitated his earlier reply.

"No, that good. You have no idea how good it feels not to know where this is going. It's new for me. I just know I like you, more than I ever thought I could."

She glared at him in the glow of the moon and felt all her defences give in. She couldn't explain it. At one point there was a brick wall between them and then it was gone. There was no wrecking ball, pieces of cement or debris. That instinctive defensive mechanism just stopped functioning, as if he had pressed a button that deactivated it.

His face was placid and confident. She wanted to touch it. She wanted to feel his skin, his lips, and look deep into his eyes and lean into him.

"I like you, too," she said shyly, hair covering her eyes. "But I think we should get back to the city and see how things go. I don't want to rush. What do you think?"

"I agree."

And that was the extent of the matter. They were two grownups, each carrying their own emotional baggage. They were attracted to one another, but they were reluctant.

The stony ground turned into grassy patches as they neared Benny's small house. The smell of lavender crept into her nostrils. She sneezed and smiled at him.

"Bless you."

They rounded a section of the house that served as a small kitchen. The windows were open and the lights on, revealing cupboards and a small microwave. The back door was open and the light guided them along a short cemented walkway.

"I feel like putting up a chair, making a cup of coffee and sitting outside until I can't feel my legs anymore," she whispered.

"Read you loud and clear. Hey, Benny! Can we order some coffee?"

Kerin playfully punched him on the shoulder and they giggled like two children.

"On the other hand, we should probably get home. I'm just worried about the kids."

David nodded and entered the kitchen ahead of her. He stopped dead in his tracks, so sudden that she bumped into him. A remarkable rigidity fell over him. She sensed his muscles tightening, saw his back arch into her.

"Benny?!"

Kerin tried to look over David's broad shoulders but struggled to see what he was seeing. When he fell to his knees and crawled across the kitchen floor, Kerin gasped as blood filled her sights. She was instantly consumed by dread. She couldn't move. Her legs and her arms were frozen stiff. She was arrested by the metallic smell of death. She was consumed by so many terrible thoughts, and nothing made sense. She was instantly sick to her stomach, so much so that she felt her intestines spasm involuntarily. She fought back the urge to throw up as her stomach began to lurch. This was a dream. No, it was a nightmare. It had to be.

183

The Antagonist felt uncomfortable. He disliked not being in control. The two men in the front were personal bodyguards, not his. They were both armed, below average intelligence and emotionless. The one was steering the big BMW, the other fumbled with his hands in a distracted, impatient manner.

Roelf Lassen sat to his right, filling the back seat with his bulk. Roelf was staring out the window, humming some horrible repetitive tune. It gave him the creeps. As the car bumped along, the extra layer under Roelf's chin trembled, sending tiny ripples across the excess skin and down his thick neck.

"We're almost there," Roelf said in a gruff voice.

"Where?"

"There."

Roelf's phone rang and he answered it in German. It was a brief conversation. He ended the call and sighed. "It is done."

"What's done?"

"Harlem, you fool. Harlem is done."

"Dead?"

"It is happening as we speak."

The Antagonist leaned back into his seat, experiencing a disturbing blend of shock and joy. He had no idea how to react to the news, in part because he feared Roelf's unpredictability.

So Harlem was out of the picture. He never wanted matters to get this complicated but it couldn't be helped. There was no way to keep the money, stall the sale or sneak away with the loot, without something terrible happening to David Harlem. Now he was gone.

Roelf took in a mouthful of smoke. He blew it out slowly, spiralling downwards so that it hung in the car. He did this purposely, so that the pinnacle of annoyance could find purchase with the one being annoyed. "You have created big problem," he said, puffing on the cigarette.

The Antagonist coughed loudly and felt his eyes tear up. He hated cigarettes and despised smokers because it reminded him of something terrible: his father.

Smoke was synonymous with the smell of a wet towel, the warm sting where the towel would strike, and the taste of blood in his mouth. He thought about his father's drunken eyes bearing down at him, judgement lingering in them, tied to a chair, beaten with a wet towel. "It should've been you," his father would say. "Not your ma. It should've been you."

His mother had died at birth and he was to blame. It had been the two of them, alone in that house. When his father suffered a stroke, he became a question mark, an empty vessel sitting by the window of a care facility, glaring at the world through cloudy eyes, mumbling to himself. Some days The Antagonist would stand in the doorway of the lounge, staring at the thing in the chair, not sure what to think.

"It should've been you," Roelf said in a menacing voice.

The Antagonist, caught between past and present, gasped. His eyes were wide, heart racing. "What?" he began in a trembling voice. "What was that?"

"It should've been you. You should have cleaned up your own mess."

"Don't you mean *our* mess."

"Quiet!" Roelf screamed. "Shut your lips when I speak."

He couldn't help thinking about the times he had been allowed to speak freely in Roelf's company. When he had offered Roelf 10% of R350 million, the German had been willing to chat about the most mundane things. Now he was prepared to exercise his power and belittle his partner in crime just for the sake of fluffing his own feathers.

"There was no problem before you. Now I have many problem." Roelf blew a mouthful of smoke into his face and smiled. "Now I'm stuck with you."

The Antagonist opened the window to let fresh air in, sucking frantically at the opening. Seconds later he heard a faint metallic sound coming from the front. He stared intently at the front passenger side window. When the big car drove past a streetlight, the last source of light before the road changed from tar to gravel, there was a quick unmistakeable reflection in the window. Fight or flight.

In a flash, The Antagonist reached into his underpants and pulled out the gun he had hidden there. He flicked the safety off and lifted it up. The man in the front seat flipped around, gasping softly when he saw the barrel pointing at him. He froze in his seat, half-turned and uncomfortable. They stared at each other. Roelf also sat there, cigarette burning into his fingers, wet lips shining in the dark, agape with surprise, not sure what to do next.

"What's wrong?" the driver asked when nothing happened, interrupting the stale mate.

Then the man's hint of panic disappeared and anger flooded into his cold eyes.

"*Schwein!*" he screamed and lifted his weapon.

The Antagonist didn't hesitate. His gun echoed in the confines of the car and the slug tore through the headrest of the front seat. The man in the front seat rocked forward and slammed into the dashboard. The windscreen turned into a web of cracks, followed by a messy spray of blood.

The recoil of the weapon was not as bad as The Antagonist had expected. His ears were ringing, but he was still fully aware of what was happening. He was in control.

The driver tugged at the wheel, which sent the car reeling over the wet gravel. He fought to gain control of the car while trying to push the dead body off the gear lever, but couldn't.

Roelf flung himself at The Antagonist, smothering him with his bulk, one big hand gripping him around the throat, the other trying to wrestle the gun from him. When The Antagonist began to see tiny stars drifting into view, he took aim with his foot and launched a potent kick at the driver's head. Just missing the headrest, he struck the man harshly at the nape of his neck with the heel of his shoe. The driver dropped his hands from the steering wheel and fell forward onto the car horn.

Immediately the car veered off the dirt road and the wheels responded to a rougher terrain, bumping and rattling as it sped onward. And so the car went blaringly into the dark night, missing trees as it crept deeper and deeper into the Tokai forest, where the insects crept around in the undergrowth.

Roelf relented the grip around his throat and stared out the bloodied windscreen. He said something in German which didn't sound very optimistic. In anticipation, The Antagonist pulled his seatbelt down and held on tightly, awaiting the inevitable impact. Roelf turned his body this way and that, looking for something.

The car slammed into a small tree at an angle that caused the back of the car to bounce up and pull across to the right. Both front airbags shot out and inflated. Roelf, strong as he was, had somehow managed to steady himself between the back seat and the front seat. However, when he turned his attention back, the look of derision on his face confirmed that he should not have distanced himself from The Antagonist.

He kicked Roelf back into the rear-side window and raised his weapon. He fired twice. The bullets drilled into Roelf's chest and flung him back into the passenger door. Roelf took three quick breaths, as if he was choking on something.

For a long time The Antagonist sat looking at the body, the way in which the blood streamed from the gunshot wounds, making slight sucking sounds beneath his thick jacket. There was nothing about it that seemed fake or dreamlike. Everything had a very real and very disappointing quality about it. The Antagonist had expected the blood to look like tomato sauce, but it looked like normal blood. He had expected the bodies to burst into pieces and to gush blood in every direction, but it didn't. The body just lay there, slowly accumulating a puddle of blood on the leather of the back seat. It looked like road-kill.

The Antagonist sat up and gathered himself. His body was burning with adrenaline. His arm burned where the safety belt had tightened around the bicep and the forearm, but luckily there was no blood.

He studied the driver for signs of life, but the manner in which he slouched over the deflated airbag and the fact that his eyes were focused intently on the speedometer indicated that he was not concerned about the speed anymore. The large piece of plastic protruding from his neck served as confirmation.

The Antagonist struggled out of the car, coughing repetitively. On impact, the seatbelt had forced all the air out of his lungs. He rested on his haunches, took a few deep breaths. He put the gun in his jacket pocket and surveyed his surroundings. It was unlikely that anyone had heard the crash, or the gunshots for that matter. This section of the Tokai forest was deserted at night, and it was too cold to be strolling through the woods. But there was no point in taking chances. He had to be quick about his escape.

He hurriedly began wiping away his fingerprints with a handkerchief. He understood the importance of covering his own tracks. After a lengthy search he recovered all three shell casings. With extreme caution he searched Roelf's body until he found the cigarette lighter in his corduroy jacket. He went through the driver's pockets, careful not to leave clues or to get blood on his clothes. He found a cheap plastic lighter and began to giggle with delight. Initially he had planned to push material into the fuel tank filling line and light it but there was a small sieve preventing entry. The lighter was a blessing in disguise.

The Antagonist removed Roelf's jacket, scanning the night for movement every few seconds. Ironically enough, the thick jacket had the least amount of blood on it. He bundled it up and placed it on the floor of the backseat. He put the lighter over the jacket and smashed it with a large stone. Before the lighter fluid could evaporate, he lit Roelf's lighter and threw it into the vehicle. The dark corduroy lit up at once, flames snapping wildly at the air in search of more things to consume. Thick smoke and the smell of burning blood poured out of the window. The Antagonist waited for the fire to take then threw in a towel he had found in the boot. Before long the fire began gnawing at the back seat and the leather chair. As he watched, the fire enslaved the car, increasing in intensity. It had taken only fifteen minutes to execute. The seats were burning and with it, any evidence of him having been there. No one had seen him getting into the car and no one had seen him climbing out.

Satisfied, The Antagonist set off into the woods. He removed his shoes at the car and ran along the gravel where no footprints could be seen behind him. When he reached the gate, he put his shoes back on and left the road. Within minutes he was a good distance away from the crash. Looking back at the abandoned car, he became aroused by the scene. One headlight shone forlornly into the depths of the forest. The long fingers of fire flowed out of the open rear window and into the dark night. He felt himself becoming more and more aroused by it. He was burning and he was so turned on that he struggled to contain himself. He kept on giggling. The giggle became a grating laugh, a menacing cackle that bounced off the trees and echoed through the forest.

He expected the car to explode but he never heard the bang. It was a bit of a letdown, an anti-climax of sorts, but it made no difference. He had left nothing incriminating at the scene, nothing that would tie him to the crime. Whether the car eventually exploded or not was rather inconsequential. The deed had been done and no one would ever know.

He headed down a hill and made it to the highway a while later. He marched on, diving into the bushes whenever cars came by. Within less than an hour's walk he was back in the city. As it was still early enough, he signalled a passing taxi to take him to the deserted parking lot where he had left his car.

The Antagonist drove home as always, obeying the speed limit, using his indicator when turning. When he arrived home, he put all his clothes and shoes in a bag and threw it in the trash. He had a relaxing shower, switched on the T.V. and fed the dog. He prepared a microwave lasagne for supper. His girlfriend had purchased a variety of freezer meals the day before she had left. To go with the meal, he poured himself a full glass of wine. It was a fruity merlot. He had been saving it for a special occasion.

And that was murder. That was how it was done. He didn't see what the huff was about. Killing someone was easy, and invigorating. He found himself thinking about Linden Sendiwe in an entirely different way. Sendiwe was the only other person who knew about the Swartland Opus. With Lassen, Harlem and Sendiwe out of the way, there was no link to him. He wouldn't hesitate again.

The wine was good, but it was not complex enough. No wine would be complex enough ever again.

CHAPTER 10

This was a nightmare. It had to be. David realised that his breathing was relaxed. He felt as though he was on the treadmill at gym, looking out over a parking lot, shutting off from the world around him. He was zoning, instinctively preparing to demand impossible things from his body. He imagined himself looking through the scope of his rifle, undisturbed by the world, bracing for impact.

He looked up at Kerin, who stood frozen in the doorway. Her eyes were glazed over, absent, hands covering her mouth as if she was holding back a scream.

"Stay there," he said softly.

He was on his knees, looking down at Benny. There was a pool of blood around the body. Benny lay without grace, one arm trapped under him. David saw numerous deep cuts to the body, and a long panga next to Benny's head.

He looked up at Kerin. "Farm attack," he whispered.

There hadn't been farm attacks in the Garden Route. Just petty crime and vandalism. Nothing as savage as this. This wasn't even a farm, and he hadn't been there for years. The house had been standing open. Why would they attack now? Had they been watching him? Had Benny made enemies in the local townships? All valid questions, but they did not merit an answer, not now. He shuffled forward on his knees to inspect Benny's body, to search for a pulse or evidence. Then Kerin screamed at him from the doorway, "My kids! My kids! Shit, where are my kids?!"

She flipped around and disappeared into the night.

"Kerin!"

He scrambled to his feet in haste, but slipped in the blood. He crashed into one of the cupboards, blocking the blow with his elbow. He pulled himself to his feet and ran after Kerin.

She had an indescribable haste in her. So much so, that David had difficulty closing the gap between them. He caught up with her just shy of the point where the house came into view. He grabbed hold of her arm and pulled her back behind an elevated section near the trees. At first she resisted, but when she saw his lips shushing her she came to a halt.

He crouched behind the cover of the trees and she followed suit. Her eyes were wide with panic and she was shaking all over.

"My kids," she hissed at him.

He shushed her again and slowly crept nearer to the edge of the mound. He motioned her to follow him.

"The children are still inside the house," he whispered and leaned close to her so that he could align her line of sight with his pointing finger, as a hunter lining up his prey with a rifle. "Look, to the front of the house, where the drive splits."

Coming from Benny's house, he had noticed the movement around the main house. He had seen them as though they had been walking around with spotlights over their heads. His eyes had been trained for this. Even after all these years, his eyes were still sharp, still able to discern. He saw them, hiding in the bushes. He instantly knew they were preparing to take the house.

Ten metres clear of the fountain and the garage, there was another quick movement. For a brief moment the bushes moved. Looking hard enough, allowing the shadows to fall away, the leaves and the branches formed lines and betrayed bulges.

David saw Kerin strain her eyes, then she gasped softly.

"There are two of them, one behind the other," he said.

She nodded frantically. "Yes, I see them."

He redirected her gaze to the other side of the house, beyond the garage doors, the furthermost section of the house.

"There are two more. In the bushes near the van."

He kept his finger steady until she could make out their shapes. Only when one of the men broke cover to give hand signals to the others, she began to nod again.

Four men. As far as he could see, there were no more than that. They were awkwardly placed around the front of the square-shaped house. Two men covering the front, other two men covering the kitchen door on the far side. The windows on that side of the house looked directly into the living room, the kitchen and his bedroom near the back door. From the front they could only see into the living room, maybe into the children's bedroom. Kerin's room was nearest to the trees where they were hiding. There was no one covering the section along the trees.

They were planning a surprise attack, not concerned with the back door. David clenched his jaws and balled his fists.

"They're wearing masks and camouflage," Kerin said. "I don't understand. Why are they wearing masks?"

"Because it's not a farm attack."

"What do you mean?"

"It's a full-frontal attack, like a raid. Farm attacks are without tact. Hate crimes. These are trained men performing a hit."

"A hit? What the hell does that mean?"

"I don't know."

He looked around, moved back a couple of paces, gave the house another once-over and came back. There was very little he could do. He considered different attempts to prevent the attack, but every option seemed futile. The best alternative was to initiate *and* control the attack as best as possible. To take charge of the battle, so to speak. Definitely the best option had he been alone, but he wasn't. If only he could face them alone, he could try to evade them or lead them away from the house. But they were cut off from the house and the children. He had to get into the house. That was the only way to take hold of the situation.

When he turned to Kerin, she was searching her jacket pockets.

"What you doing?"

"Dammit! I left my cell phone in my room."

"We're thirty minutes away from the nearest police station. Calling them is not a priority. If these guys are professional, the cell phone signals are probably scrambled."

"That doesn't make any sense. Why scramble the signal?"

As they sat looking at the house, Dillon's unmistakeable loud laughter drifted to them. David flicked his head up and studied the masked men for movement. They stared at the house in anticipation, poised for something and not sure what. It felt as though he was looking at them through the scope. When Dillon laughed again, the two men covering the front raised their silenced weapons in response. The leader on the other side of the house, motioned them to lower their weapons. This gesture of restraint gave David instant relief.

"Why are they not moving?"

"Because they are waiting."

"What for?"

"Me."

He moved back out of sight and scrambled towards the trees, Kerin hot in his tracks. They moved down the side of the mound, stopping short of the slope leading into the trees. David didn't want to lose sight of them just yet. If they slipped into the trees, the density of the leaves would shield them, and he would have no idea what they were doing.

Kerin grabbed his jacket and pulled him back. Her face was close to his, eyes filled with panic.

"Who are you, really? You a drug dealer or something? Tell me now."

He put his hand on her clenched fist. "You *know* who I am."

There were tears in her eyes. Her desperation was so endearing, but he could offer her no reassurance. He didn't know what to tell her. He simply couldn't remove her pain or dispel her fears. He could do nothing.

"My kids," she whispered, tears now streaming down her cheeks. "My kids?"

He took her face in his hands. "Kerin, listen to me. Listen. It's going to be okay. I will not let them hurt the kids. I'll die before I let them hurt the kids." Without realizing what he was doing, David leaned in and kissed her forehead. "But I need you to be here, right now. I need you to focus. I need *you*. Okay?"

She gathered herself, closed her eyes, took a deep breath and wiped the tears away. She couldn't stop shivering.

"Okay," she gave a long, steady sigh. "What must I do?"

"I have to get into the house. I think the back door is open. I'll have to sneak around the braai area and circle the pathway. But when I break the tree line I'll be exposed for a long time. I don't like that."

"What about my room? The bathroom?"

"If I break the shutters open it'll make a lot of noise."

"Benny opened the shutters for me this morning. I left it open for fresh air."

His face lit up. "You're a genius."

He began down the slope but stopped when he felt Kerin behind him.

"No, no. You stay here." He gently pushed her back to make his point.

"Don't begin that shit with me. Where you go, I go. My kids, remember."

He didn't even try again. She was resolute.

They snuck down the slope and made their way through the trees at a sedate pace, constantly searching for signs of movement. They followed a cleared section through the trees to avoid rustling leaves or crunching branches. Absolute stealth was their only hope of remaining unnoticed; remaining unnoticed was their only hope of getting everyone out of the house alive.

When they reached the edge of the trees, each picked a broad tree trunk and hid behind it as though they were bark. They were out of breath, more from exhilaration than exertion.

From their position, he could not see the front of the house, nor any masked men. He felt confident that they hadn't been noticed. He made a gesture with his hands, urging Kerin to wait. He slipped out from behind the trees and crept up to the house. The shutters were closed, but, as Kerin had said, they hadn't been locked. When he pulled one of the doors back, it made a soft creaking sound. He cringed and Kerin disappeared behind the tree.

He slid the window all the way back in its track, emitting another unwanted sound. He gave Kerin a quick nod. She broke cover and made her way across the side of the house toward the open window. She would be first to enter the house.

He hoisted her through the opening, then froze when he heard the sound of a Velcro strap being loosened, followed by footsteps.

Kerin shielded with her hands but it didn't stop the fall. She greeted the bathroom tiles with a muted *thud*. A shiver of pain shot through her body and her one arm went numb for a couple of seconds.

She was still rolling out of the way when David jumped up and pulled his body through the opening in one swift move. He shot into the room, pouncing on the tiles, grunting as he knocked into the opposite wall. Without a moment's hesitation he leapt to his feet, pulled the shutter doors shut as quietly as possible and crouched down. He closed the slats by slowly flicking the metal lever up.

Scarcely did the door slip into place when she heard the scrunch of leaves outside the open window. David leaned back and seemingly disappeared into the dark shadows. He became one with the wall.

Kerin felt obliged to hide, but opted to remain stationary instead, sprawled out across the bathroom floor, tiny bars of moonlight cast down over her body, holding her arm and her breath, listening to the approaching sound outside.

The sound of slow, determined footfalls approached the window. Aware of her countless limitations, Kerin was convinced she could hear the man's heavy breathing. It was accompanied by a soft metallic rattling sound, almost in sync with the sound of his boots. The man passed the shutters, stopped short of the trees for a terrible moment, his breathing strained in the cold air, then turned back and passed the window again. She heard the laboured whispering over distance.

"I don't see him," said one.

"We can't wait any longer."

Instantly she began to panic again.

The man continued onward. After a while the footsteps died away and filled the bathroom. They sat staring at each other in the dark, anxious but reluctant to move in fear of making noise and drawing attention. Her stomach muscles were tight, her mind racing like crazy. The suspense of the situation was enough to last her five lifetimes.

David waited another minute before sliding the window shut. He led the way through Kerin's room and into the dark corridor. He stopped short of entering the glow of the down lights. They remained out of sight. The living room was to their right. She could hear the children convincing Margie to play another round of pick-up-sticks.

He rested his head against the wall and sighed. He gave Kerin a long stare, as if he was working out a plan, while wondering how to tell her what he was planning.

"There will be shooting tonight. They will try their best to kill."

"Shit," she said softly and closed her eyes. The words were scarcely more than a sigh, said more in acceptance than in alarm. David had given her worst fears voice. She had hoped to avoid this reality; after finding Benny's body, seeing all that blood, she had been telling herself that all will be fine. That nothing bad will happen, that no harm will come to her children. But she had to step over the threshold and accept the inevitable. She had wanted David to come up with a solution, to fix the situation. All Kerin kept thinking was that they should not have been there, on a farm in the middle of nowhere, surrounded by gunmen. They should have been at home, the city she had come to loathe.

She looked at David and nodded.

"We need to be ready for them. They'll hit the front of the house."

"Yes?"

"You and the kids have to go out the back door. I will draw them in."

"How will you do that?"

"I'll go another way. Obviously they are here for me." He peered into the room. "If they want me, they'll have to come get me."

He stooped low and sneaked another look around the corner. She watched him wait for the perfect moment, then he made the hissing sound of a snake, followed by a shushing sound. He did the come-hither with his index finger and seconds later Megan lurched into the corridor with a huge smile on her face.

They pulled her into the shadows before she could say anything. Kerin couldn't restrain herself. She pulled Megan close, kissed her on the cheek and held her so tight that the child had to gasp for air.

"Mom? You're crushing me..."

David, still crouched low, took Megan by the hand.

"Hey, sweetie. Everything's okay," he whispered.

"Then why are you whispering?"

"We are hiding from someone."

"Who?"

"The bad people outside."

Kerin gaped at David. She began shaking her head in disagreement.

Megan looked from David to her mother, who stopped shaking her head and forced a smile.

"What bad people?"

"Megs, we need to get grandma and Dilly out the house quickly and quietly. You understand?"

She frowned, shifting her eyes from Kerin to David, not sure what to do.

David looked at Kerin again, briefly. His eyes were different, more calculating. "Go in with her. Relay the urgency. Get ready. Wait for my signal," he said.

"Won't they attack when they see me?"

"I don't think so."

199

He got to his feet and walked down the corridor, remaining in the shadows.

"What signal?"

He stopped and turned, a shadow himself. She vaguely made out the whites of his eyes. It gave her quick chill.

"When the lights go out, run."

Then he disappeared.

Kerin got up, looked down at Megan, suddenly lost. She tried to compose herself.

"You going to help me?" Megan nodded reluctantly. "Okay, let's do this."

Kerin sat down opposite Margie, and squeezed her mother's hand mid-sentence. Margie knew that squeeze all too well. She stopped what she was saying.

"What's wrong?"

"I can't explain, but there are people attacking the farm," she said faking a smile. "They are outside, waiting."

"I don't understand."

"Stay calm, they can see us."

"Who can see us?"

"Not sure. We saw them outside. They killed Bennie."

Margie's cheeks instantly went white.

"Mom? You okay?"

Margie kept her head down, eyes staring blankly at the coffee table, her breathing laboured. "A farm attack," she whispered.

"Mom?"

"What are we supposed to do? Sit here and wait?"

Kerin let go her mother's hand. "We wait until the lights go out and then we run."

"I can't run around like that, sweetie. With the gout and the stiffness, I won't make it across the back porch. I can't even get off the couch without help."

"What do you mean?"

Margie was rubbing at one knee, the knee she had been complaining about since winter began.

"I can't run around like that, child. I'm too old. Maybe I can hide."

"Don't say that!"

A sullen compliance fell over Margie's features. She nodded reluctantly. Her reservations appeared to have been forced aside for the sake of her daughter.

"Yes, dear, it will be okay," she repeated, gingerly brushing Dillon's hair back.

Kerin told Dillon they were playing a game with the men outside, that when the lights went out they had to run into the field and hide from them until uncle David came to get them. It was the only way to get his buy-in. He was rather subdued by the excitement, carrying on as normal. Megan was a rock. She had a potent personality, a strong character. She tied Dillon's shoelaces, zipped up his jacket, preparing him for the run that would follow. When it seemed that Dillon could jump up or do something silly, as young boys tended to do, she pulled him close and whispered something to him to keep him excited and ready. "We gonna hide real good. Your shoes tight enough? They will never find us," she said.

Kerin had no idea when her daughter had become so mature. She couldn't recall teaching her daughter anything of the sort. She was hot, then cold, then shivering, then numb. She thought about Margie and how difficult this must be for her, then the safety of her children leaked into her concerns, and then she wondered what David was doing, if he was still inside the house, what if he had already snuck out the back door, leaving them there to die, or what if she died and the children was left without anything.

Then she saw movement out of the corner of her eye. It was David, entering the kitchen, gun in one hand, his big body crouched low. He had mentioned being in the military, but she never imagined it would look so convincing in actuality, so smooth. His movements seemed rehearsed.

Suddenly, as she watched him move around the kitchen, in the middle of a potentially volatile farm attack, she wished she had kissed him earlier. It was a totally random thought, serving no real purpose other than to remind her that she was still a flesh-and-blood woman and that she had indeed longed to kiss him, to feel his lips or his closeness.

She shook her head, looked at her children. The thought of David perished instantly and she was back to waiting for David to tell her what to do.

"Get ready!" he called.

She pulled the children together, and waited.

He had seen two men along one side of the house. They could easily see into his bedroom, so he kept the lights off, crawling towards the closet. He opened it and went to the small electric safe hidden behind shoe boxes. He pinned in the passkey (Elizabeth's birthday) and removed a Beretta 9mm from inside.

He hadn't felt a gun in his hands in a long time. It was cold and heavy. He checked the weapon, pushed the magazine in all the way, pulled back the slide to chamber a round, and pushed the safety off.

He remained in the dark closet for a while, his eyes closed and his breathing alarmingly steady. He thought about his scouting missions in the army, the fighting in the bush, the evasive manoeuvres they had been trained to remember at times like these. Then that memory popped up. The rifle sight, the shot. His one and only assassination by rifle. It didn't get more personal than that. It was about timing the shot perfectly, becoming one with the person on the other side of the glass, then pulling the trigger. Taking a life for the sake of settling foreign political disputes, finishing the contract, completing the job. He had resigned the next day, and he had vowed never to kill again. But someone had to die tonight, and he was prepared to fight.

He kept his eyes closed. "Please God, give me power, direction. Guide my hands, my feet. Let no harm come to Kerin and the kids."

Crouching low, shuffling slowly forward, David made his way to the bedside drawer. He was surprised to see that his cell phone still had reception. He called the police and reported what had happened, giving as much detail as possible.

He went back to the corridor and snuck into the kitchen. Soon they would see him. If only he raised his head a bit, his position would be known to the men outside. He grabbed the van's keys which lay on the counter and moved toward the side entrance to the kitchen. It was already locked from inside. He positioned himself next to the fridge.

From there he could see Margie, Kerin, and the kids. Dillon had no idea what was going on. Even Megan was putting up a wonderful performance. Margie, on the other hand, was ashen, eyes shaky with fear, as if she had been dreading this moment all her life. Kerin, head bowed, seemed to be doing a difficult mathematic calculation, weighing up all possible solutions to the problem.

For the first time since the accident, he had been truly happy. Now this. He had endangered this woman and her family because he had taken them away from their normal life and thrust them into his world. He was responsible for everything.

David hooked a finger around the kitchen towel and jerked it free. He counted the seconds, heard his breathing grating in his ears.

"Get ready!" he said, loud enough to make sure only Kerin heard him.

He stood up slowly, stared out the windows until he made out one of the masked men. Their eyes met and everything seemed to freeze for a few seconds. Then the look of surprise disappeared from the masked man's eyes, replaced by steel, a cold and angry steel.

As the man lifted his handgun and took aim, David flipped the trip switch on the switchboard panel. A sudden darkness fell over the house and an immediate silence came with it. From outside David heard a solitary gunshot, tearing the silence in two, followed by a crack of glass. As before, with the clapping sound came that haunting image through the rifle's sight. He almost felt the tremor of the recoil travelling up his firing arm.

"Run!" he shouted, then pulled the refrigerator away from the wall.

He tipped the heavy unit over and pushed it back towards the kitchen door. It connected with the door so hard that some of the glass panes cracked. This would serve as a momentary confusion. "Get to the hill and stay there until you hear the sirens."

Kerin didn't hesitate. She grabbed everyone and ran down the corridor toward the back door.

David moved into the living room, brushing past them as he went. He leaned against the section of wall between the front door and the living room windows. He ventured a quick peek through the sheer curtains, knowing that the full moon was working in his favour. With the house lights down and the bright moon up, he could see out but they could not see in.

Just then a number of the small kitchen windows cracked loudly and a brief cloud of bullets whirred through the room, slapping into the walls, paintings and new cupboards. The gunfire sounded like handguns, no rifles.

While two of the men were attacking the kitchen, David took up a secure position overlooking the drive and the van. The glow of the moon aided him in locating the two masked gunmen near the van. They were following the assault with the others, preparing to launch themselves across the drive. He had a few seconds of surprise left, only seconds. He took aim, not knowing whether he still had the accuracy. It always took a few shots to get an eye in, but when the eye was in, everything would become a target. He trusted he still had it.

David took a deep breath, his heart beating in his chest, steady, controlled and constant. He focused his eyes down the side of his arm, over the back of his hand, down the barrel of the gun, across the clearing, until his sights fell on one masked man.

He pressed the button on the van's remote alarm to create the decoy. When the van's indicators flashed brightly, both gunmen whipped their heads around and began shooting at the van.

In response, David squeezed the trigger, firing off four rounds in quick succession, the loud reports ringing out again and again throughout the farmhouse. The first and second bullets went astray, smacking into trees or shrubs. The third caught one gunman in the shoulder and knocked him off his feet. His last shot struck centre mass, punching into the second gunman's chest so solidly that it flung him sideways and dropped him down in front of the garage doors, decorative stones scattering into every direction as he slid across the drive.

He watched Kerin and her family opening the back door. They had to move faster. They had to get to safety as soon as possible.

The other two gunmen doubled back and joined their fallen comrades. Seconds later a storm of bullets was unleashed. David dived to the ground amid a shower of broken glass, using the couch as a shield. The white sheer curtain flapped in the dark as the bullets tore it apart. Every now and then he heard the loud boom of a shotgun, followed by a puff of cement chips or a spray of wood splinters. When he looked up again he saw a gaping hole in the front door where the buckshot had punched a hole.

David stared longingly at the door near the far corner of the living room, the one which led to the garage. He had to get in there. Every garage contained a number of unsuspecting household products that could be used to assemble small explosives or decoys. Reaching the garage was his only hope of distracting the gunmen while Kerin and her family made a getaway.

Then, still in thought, he heard Kerin and the kids scream loudly. The screams were cut down by a fresh burst of gunfire that echoed down the corridor. His heart skipped a beat and his chest tightened in suspense.

The lights went out and they were instructed to get to the hill and to haul ass in doing so. Then the gunshots began, terrifyingly loud and bone chilling in essence. Dillon, perhaps only a young child in mind and body, realized that he had been swindled, that something more sinister was afoot, because he stopped dead in his tracks, mesmerised by the loud blasts.

"Guns," he screamed. "Mommy, guns."

Margie picked up the boy mid-sentence and followed Kerin unto the back porch. Reaching the fireplace, Kerin spotted a masked man off to the left of the house, hiding in a raised bed of aloes and other ficus plants. The man, involved in the action along the side of the house, was so caught unawares by their presence that he spun around in the bedding. He struggled to find footing, slipping on the rocks and stumbling into the aloes, pricking himself numerous times on the sharp thorns.

Amidst a barrage of swear words, the man leapt out of the bedding like a ninja on the attack. He soared through the air and landed uncomfortably on the paving, just shy of the porch steps, his murderous eyes flashing up at them.

Megan and Dillon screamed in unison, the sound of horror in stereo.

"Inside!" Kerin shouted at the top of her voice.

Bullets sank into the walls and the doors around them as they ran back down the corridor. The bullets whirred over her head, like huge cockroaches buzzing past her ears.

David was still in a hunched position behind the couch when he heard the screams and the gunfire. He crawled through the glass and debris until he could see down the corridor.

"Kerin!"

He made out their shapes coming down the dark corridor, all four of them, Kerin and the kids in front, Margie bringing up the rear.

He hadn't seen the man guarding the back door. He wondered briefly how he had missed him. However, when engaged in battle, there was no time for deliberation. Bottom line: there was a fifth shooter and he had to adapt. He had to rethink his plan to raid the garage. First priority was to protect Kerin, eliminate the threats.

As Kerin came into view, he saw the vague outline of another gunman standing in the doorway behind them. He heard a gun barking loudly, the muzzle flash betraying his location. Bullets zipped down the corridor.

Instinctively he flipped his weapon into position and screamed, "Get down!"

Kerin awkwardly spilled into the living room. She collapsed to the ground, pulling the children down with her.

There was another burst of gunfire, then Margie fell down involuntarily, her face a grim picture of agony as she toppled forward.

Dave was quick to follow when his sight was clear. He fired off two shots. Even in the faint glow of the moon, he saw the man's head rock backward and then the figure in the doorframe keeled over dead.

He signalled Kerin to remain on the ground. The children were crying and whimpering, scared and confused. His weapon focused on the back door, he kneeled over Margie. There was nothing he could do.

Margie was still warm to the touch, but the moon shining into the living room revealed her still eyes staring up at the ceiling. Upon closer inspection he noticed that the back of her head was a mess of mangled flesh and shattered bone.

He took Kerin by the hand. "Come, quick."

"Is she ..." she started but couldn't finish.

"Yes."

A series of fears and concerns bombarded her at once, attempting to push her into a state of stagnation. But she was stronger than that. As hard as it was for her to see her mother on the floor, Kerin did what she had been doing all her life as an independent woman: she kicked into survival mode. She had to be strong for her children, they needed her now more than ever. She took the kids by their hands and followed David.

He led them down the corridor for a second time. At the back door, his eyes fell over the dead gunman. Gray balaclava, gray trench coat. He dropped to his haunches. Working quickly, he reached for his weapon. He looked at Kerin, her eyes wild, breathing tense. When he touched her shoulder, he felt her shivering wildly. He leaned close to her ear.

"Don't deal with it now," he whispered. He flicked his eyes to the children. She nodded bravely.

The Beretta felt twice as heavy when he held it out to Kerin. He didn't know if she would take it but they had no choice.

"Point. Shoot. It is a gentle gun. Smooth, no force needed."

Their eyes met once again.

"Go!" he said. "Go now!"

Kerin – gun awkwardly in hand – led her children away. They moved quickly and quietly into the night. As soon as they made it to the series of paths which ran through the fields, they disappeared. The darkness seemed to wrap around them, swallowing them whole.

David realised that he was holding his breath. He exhaled softly, then backed into the living room once more. Slowly, he removed the magazine from the gun he had taken off the dead gunman. It was another 9mm. Nine shots left. Enough for what he had planned.

A sharp whistle sounded outside. Then grunts. David slipped back into the kitchen and looked out the window. Outside one man wearing a gray mask screamed something in Xhosa, pointing towards the back of the house.

"No," David whispered to himself. "No, no, no."

He leaned over the zinc until he could see the other men. Near the front of the house, rounding the corner of the garage, he saw two men. One had a limp shoulder, blood shimmering in the moonlight, and the other, a smaller man who moved with a lot of authority and confidence, was pushing the injured man on.

"No survivors!" the man screamed.

Suddenly panic set in. They would not let her go. They would kill everyone. Benny and Margie were already dead. They had no intention of leaving the farm without doing what they came to do. The nightmare had only just begun and the fight was far from over.

Everything was happening so fast. She was running back into the house, Margie pushing Dillon into her hands, falling to the ground, David shooting down the corridor, then Margie was gone. She only saw part of her mother's one arm protruding from the corridor, a ripple of blood spreading over the wooden floorboards.

David said that the hilltop was still the best option. She trusted his judgment.

They ran down the steps toward the path David had run along that morning. The path was sandy with patches of trampled grass, which was good because it hushed their footfalls. The fresh smell of fynbos on either side of the path tickled her nostrils. She led the children away from the house at a steady pace, holding Dillon in her arms at first, then letting him run free. Surprisingly enough he kept up with Megan well enough, only once stopping to ask, "Where's Gran?" Kerin ignored the question, as did Megan.

They continued running for a long time before Dillon began screaming for his Gran. Kerin took a quick break, their second stop since leaving the house, explaining that Gran was right behind them, lying to her own son.

They were a short distance from the hill. Behind them, they were already looking down at the farm house and the land. Where they had once been able to see the tiny lights of gunfire around the house, the night now seemed as dead as ever, but then, when all seemed calmest, peaceful and safe, there was a loud explosion, and bright fire filled her eyes. As the sky over the house lit up she noticed a man in the field, about half a kilometre behind them. At first she thought it was David, and was briefly overcome by relief, but when she made out the gray mask and the weapon, her whole body began to tremble. A charge of electricity shot through her spine. She felt like shooting at him, but why bother? Not only would she betray the fact that she had a gun, but she would waste whatever ammunition there was. If killing had to be done, it had to be done at close range, face to face. If that was the only way to make doubly sure that bullet met gray mask, then she had to find a way of distancing herself from the kids. Drawing the villain to her was the only way.

Then she spotted David running from the house, about a kilometre away. He wouldn't be able to close the gap in time.

With newfound conviction, she hoisted Dillon into the air and ran along the path. They carried on until they reached the part where the earth shot up into a steep slope, forming the side of the hill. She pulled them behind a patch of wildly grown bushes and pointed up the hill.

"Get to the top," she said, more to Megan than to Dillon.

"No," Megan began, but Kerin wasn't having any of it.

"Shush. You listen, Megs. Get to the top and hide. Now! You hear me?"

Megan was shaking her head, teary-eyed, cheeks white as snow and her nose pink from the cold. Dillon stood flabbergasted by his sister's sudden concern, mumbling to himself, "Where's Gran? Mommy, where's Gran?"

"Megs?! Do you understand?"

She nodded, but held on to her mother's hands, not wanting to let go.

"Take care of your brother."

Another nod.

She hugged them, as tight as she could. "I love you both so much. Go now, quickly."

She watched them scamper up the side of the steep hill, then began searching for the gray mask behind them. When the children were well out of sight, she broke away from the cover of the bushes. Almost immediately she saw the gunman racing through a difficult dip in the path, the same dip she had endured a few minutes ago. He was not far behind, making good time.

In as clumsy a way as possible, she scrambled along the side of the hill, grunting loudly and kicking rocks this way and that to draw the man's attention. Not only did she alert the man, but he seemed to accelerate when he spotted her figure moving cumbersomely along, like a cheetah sensing the kill.

She ran to the dilapidated structure at break-neck pace, legs pumping wildly, driven by the thought that her children were no longer there. Every metre she pulled the man away from her children was a metre of certainty that their lives were no longer in danger.

Her pursuer was gaining ground, closing the gap so fast that she almost screamed with delight when she rounded a slight bend and came upon what was left of the old servant's quarters.

He observed the three men from the kitchen window. One took off after Kerin and the kids. She had a good lead on the man, but the kids would slow her down. Luckily he had shown her some of the pathways.

He had to do something, had to buy some time. Remaining in the house until the police showed up was not the best resolve. He had to get into the bush, take cover, distract, survive.

David placed a shot ahead of the running man to slow his pursuit. Dirt shot up a few metres ahead of him. He stopped and jumped sideways into the shrubs, out of sight.

Eight rounds left.

In reply a sudden onslaught of bullets riddled the kitchen, the rat-tat-tat outside followed by a clanging here and thumping there on the inside. Slugs whirred past his head so near he could trace their path across the room. Whether divine intervention or not, none of the bullets had gotten hold of him. Again the loud call of a shotgun rang out and the resulting pellets blew open the refrigerator door, spraying milk, condiments and meats across the tiled surface.

In one swift motion, he rolled off the counter and scrambled towards the garage door. Once there he tucked the gun into his pants at the small of his back and went inside. Near the door he found the metal jerry can of gasoline where Benny had left it. He opened the latch, forced the kitchen towel into the wide mouth of the container, wet it thoroughly with petrol and searched the drawers of the workbench for a lighter. Once armed with a strange type of Molotov cocktail, he went back to the kitchen and squeezed off another round at the man hiding in the shrubs. Whether he was still there or not didn't really matter. The sputter of gunfire aimed at the kitchen window renewed, however the entire party outside was becoming an increasing threat. While shooting at the kitchen, one man moved to the rear of the house, the other towards the garage. This made it difficult.

While the noise and attention was focused on kitchen, David made his move. He rushed to the front door, went onto the little porch and lit the cloth protruding from the jerry can. He gave the flame a few seconds to take, then tossed the metallic container in the direction of the van. It landed just shy of the van's sliding doors with an astonishingly loud thud and skidded under the mid-section of the vehicle, leaving a trail of fire in its wake.

He shot at the van, just one round to pierce the petrol tank. The slug punched a gaping hole clean through the back of the van and downward through the tank, a thin stream of petrol quick to escape.

The assault on the kitchen ceased at the sound of his gunfire. David, his sniper's eye now as effective as it could be, aimed at the can. When the first gunman appeared around the corner of the garage, David pulled the trigger.

It was the second bullet that pierced the tough metal exterior of the jerry can.

There was a loud whooping sound indicative of flash fire, then an instantaneous orange-yellow ball of flame crawled out from under the vehicle and enveloped the entire van. Tongues of fire shot out at the two approaching gunmen. They ducked down in fear of being overcome by the heat or the secondary explosion that would follow.

David was quick to make good on the distraction. He raced down the corridor and shot out the back at full pace, unfazed by the possibility that there could be someone hiding in the dark. He didn't care. He had to protect Kerin and the kids. Besides, a moving target was the most difficult target to shoot.

He ran as fast as his feet could carry him. In the distance ahead of him he made out movement. Running as wildly as he did, his eyes struggled to discern the source of motion.

He had barely left the confines of the house, when a loud explosion rocked the land. He felt the tremble under his feet, followed by a faint puff of air on his back. When he turned around he saw a fireball climb into the dark night. He hadn't expected the van to cause such a large explosion, but he didn't mind it at all. In a manner of speaking it had sounded the alarm. No doubt the other farmers and residents along the main road, not to mention the air traffic controllers at the George airport, would have heard the explosion, seen the pillar of fire crawl skyward. The police were already on their way, now they had a signal which pinpointed the location of the attack.

Taking advantage of the sudden light, he looked to where he had last seen movement. It was Kerin's bright blue pants, disappearing and reappearing among the shrubbery and the wild plant life. They were nearing the bottom of the hill, a good distance between them and their pursuer. David saw him, too. Gray mask, green jacket, moving up and down along the path ahead of him, racing after Kerin. With a heavy heart David realized the man was too far ahead. Catching up with him was impossible. And he couldn't take the shot from where he was. No handgun bullet could execute that shot.

He continued running for a couple of minutes, pushing himself to his limits. Then he heard gunfire. At first he thought it was Kerin's pursuer opening fire, but there was a number of puffs on the ground behind him which convinced him otherwise. He turned and saw the two other gunmen in hot pursuit, no longer wearing masks. They had darted away from the car explosion, rounding the rear of the house, chasing after him. The shorter of the two men, ran as though there was a swarm of bees after him, racing along the path at a scary pace. The man with the shotgun limped along, clutching his shoulder and grimacing with every other step.

David began running with renewed vigour, fresh urgency in his gait. There was no possibility of out-running them. They were making good ground, better than he was making. His only objective was to reach Kerin's pursuer and to delay him, but that would not happen. There was nothing he could do. Local authorities have been alerted, the explosion expressing the urgency, but they were in the bush now. Here it was survival of the fittest, or the smartest. It was now a race against time and stamina.

The man with the gray mask disappeared in a dip along the path. Kerin was already at the bottom of the hill behind the kids, but she was not following them to the top. She seemed to hasten them on, urging them to get to the top as fast as possible. Kerin separating from the kids was a clever move because her attacker had lost sight of her when he went into the dip. David gave a quick sigh of relief when he saw the children scamper up the hill, the two small figures fading into the muted texture of the growth. Then, much to his disdain, and even more to his relief, she took off to the right of the hill, running fast, heading toward the dilapidated structure he had shown her earlier. While the children made their way to safety, Kerin's bright blue pants led her attacker away from them. When the gray mask came into view again, he was following Kerin. She had bought her children valuable time.

David had narrowed the distance between him and Kerin, but so had the two men behind him. He was outmatched and not fit enough to compete with their pace. He abandoned his pursuit of the gray-masked man and drifted off to the right of the path, slipping into the tall grass, leading them away from the hill and away from Kerin.

He was beginning to tire rapidly. His breathing was hoarse and his chest was paining with the strenuous exercise. Sweat was pouring down his brows. He had been running at full pace for a long time, yet the short man behind him had closed the distance to a small gap, just a couple hundred metres of rugged terrain to cover. Even if he ducked down now, he still wouldn't be able to surprise them in a way that would catch them off guard. They were too close. The grass was almost chest height here but that was not enough to provide full cover at close range. He had to find obstacles, hindrances to confuse the enemy with.

His only way to get the upper hand was to make it to the old sawmill building, which lay to the right of the land. He could already see the broken zinc roof of the sawmill rising in front of him, the moon reflecting off the shiny metal surface as though it was a sign from above.

CHAPTER 11

His eyelids resisted. He pushed harder until they succumbed, parting slowly. When he opened his eyes, his world was pain. His eyelids closed again involuntarily, as if someone else was pulling the strings and he was simply obeying. But whoever or whatever had control of his body, did not know him. He was a monster in his own right. No force on this earth could hold him down when forces from above wanted him to rise up to defy the norm. It was not yet his time.

Benny forced his eyelids open a few more times until he had full control over them. The blurriness subsided slowly, until he could see properly. He surveyed what he saw, fighting hard to eliminate emotion from the equation as a tinge of horror set in.

He was lying in a pool of blood, one arm outstretched, bloodied fingers curled into a fist, other arm trapped under his chest, half-numb. The house appeared to be deserted; he heard no sounds, no footsteps, no talking. Silence roamed so utterly that not even a cricket could be heard.

With immense difficulty he rolled over, propped himself unto one elbow, looked down at his body and saw many deep cuts across his chest and legs. These were *panga* cuts. Serious injuries. His life as a soldier had taught him the difference between fatal serious and false serious. What the mind imagined to be serious was not always the real deal, but this time he was in bad shape.

He tried to swallow but his mouth was so dry that he couldn't. He tasted blood on his tongue, over his teeth. Instinctively he opened his mouth and pulled his lips wide apart, as a horse would when adjusting to a snaffle bit. Using the tip of his tongue he cleaned the blood off his teeth and spat sideways, then cleared his throat.

In an attempt to take stock, he gave himself an once-over, slowly moving his arms and legs, then probing each wound to see the severity of the blow. He had a bullet wound in his left shoulder. It was a big hole, meaning a big calibre weapon.

He was trying to replay everything, to work it out, but his memory was not forthcoming. It came in little bursts. He remembered closing the fridge, hearing something at the door. When he turned, he saw a man in the doorway, wearing a black balaclava. He remembered being kicked in the face, like one of those karate movie kicks, followed by a bright white flash. He fell but jumped to his feet again, disoriented but ready to fight. Then there was the muted *tjoop* of silenced gunfire. He was flung sideways by the blow, collapsing on the floor amid breaking cups and kitchen utensils. He felt the stings all over his body, sharp pangs shooting through his body as the *panga* struck flesh. Immediately he distanced himself from the pain, cutting off, going to another place in his mind where the physical had no power. The last thing he remembered, before his world went black, was the loud clang of something dropping near his head.

Recalling the clanging sound, he turned and stared at the *panga* lying on the ground. It was a rusty, homemade weapon not unlike a machete. It had a broad arched blade the length of a man's forearm, fitted with a cheap wooden handle. Having worked in the sugarcane fields in Kwa-Zulu Natal, Bennie was a master with the *panga*. He knew it well, understood the rhythm with which to use it effectively. The *panga* could sever someone's head as easily as it could a sugarcane at the hard base of the reed. Whoever had used it on him, had been inexperienced with it, or else he would have been dead.

Balancing himself on the counter, he slowly bent down and picked up the weapon. He marvelled at the sight of his own blood dripping from the blade, a fresh surge of adrenaline pumping through his body. He growled and pushed himself away from the counter. They did not know him. They, whoever *they* were, had no idea who Bveni was or what he was capable of. They would soon find out. He stammered into the cold, dark night. Time was of the essence.

The house was not far away. Given the extent of his injuries, Bennie had no idea if he could make it. He had surprised himself before, but this time even he had his doubts. He was dying, yet he knew David would be next, and that stirred something in him, like a brotherly concern.

But there was more to it. Bennie's motivation was more poignant than coming to David's aid. There were people in that house who did not belong there, who did not deserve to die this way. The old woman and the children were at risk. They did not deserve to go this way – not if he had any say in the matter. He thought of the two children and felt his heart welling up. His feet were leading the way. He had no control. He found himself praying as he placed one foot in front of the other. Every step was a small prayer of gratitude, a cry for power to finish the task at hand. There was that silent whisper echoing in the back of his mind, "Protect them. Please protect them."

Mid-stride he stumbled over a rock and fell to his knees. Pain shot through his body and crawled up his spine into his skull.

He almost threw up then, but knew that it would consume time and drain strength. He forced it back.

His body was going into shock from the effort and the rapid blood loss. He felt anxious and restless, sweating profusely. His heartbeat was abnormally fast and he was so thirsty that he swallowed a mouthful of blood just to taste liquid over his gullet. He was breathing so quickly that the sight of his own breath pumping from his mouth looked like the puff of a steam train. His hands shook wildly. He felt like giving up but couldn't. He simply couldn't. There was still ample adrenaline reserves available to him, but his body was broken and weak. He had to endure until he could endure no more. He had to fight until he could fight no more. He had nothing left to lose. His fate had been sealed. This was his final act.

Slowly Benny rose up again, grunting loudly. He steadied himself with the *panga* until his world stopped spinning, then carried on. When he crossed over the border of trees, he stopped and stared up at the house. The lights were out. He saw no movement and heard no sound, just an empty house lit by the dim glow of the full moon. The house had been vacant for months, but tonight the sight of the deserted house was far more ominous than before. Bennie noticed the broken windows and the smouldering wreckage in front of the garage, he knew they had already been there.

Upon closer inspection, he saw that the van had been blown to bits, pieces of metal scattered about the front of the house and glass splinters shimmering in the moonlight, a lonely flame flickering here and there. The water fountain had been blasted sideways and water was shooting out of the ground where the hose had been ripped from the pump. The front of the house had been blackened by the explosion. While the garage doors were unscathed, a section of the wooden balustrade was alight, crackling softly as the fire ate away at the surface.

Benny raised his *panga* and went to the open front door. He stumbled into the dark, empty house. The smell of fighting and death hung in the air like a cloud of smoke. It was still fresh. Bullet holes marked the walls, glass all over the floors, furniture shoved aside or overturned. The living room and the kitchen both looked wrecked by gunfire. Carrots and tomatoes lay near the front door and an entire front wheel with flattened tyre lay wantonly on the one couch, having been blown through the front window when the van had exploded. What was left of the sheer curtains flapped eerily in the light breeze.

Sorrow gripped hold of him when he saw the bodies in the corridor. The shape was unmistakable. The old woman was dead. He went to her body, looked down at her lifeless eyes. He had liked her. She had been of the old type of people, those who said what they thought, who loved life.

Further down the corridor, sprawled out across the doorway, was a masked man. In vain he began searching for a weapon. He pulled at the man's expensive camouflaged clothing. These were military men. It was a sham, an attack with a purpose, staged to look like a farm attack.

Benny's confusion was interrupted by the loud bark of shotgun fire in the distance.

He went to the back porch, waited for more sounds to show him the way. The night was silent for but a moment before a number of gunshots sounded, coming from the old sawmill.

He went to the wood chopping stump, where the handle of his trusty little axe protruded into the night, beckoning him. He took the axe from the wood, deceptively light in his hand. He took a deep breath and began down the path, *panga* in one hand, throwing axe in the other. He drew upon all the strength his body could muster up. Once more, into the fight, mumbling to himself as he went.

When she looked back, Dillon was gone. He had fallen behind. She went down a bit and found him sitting behind a bush, gasping.

"Faster, Dilly," she whispered. "Faster."

Her little brother was so out of breath, he couldn't form a reply. He just huffed and wheezed, his tired eyes glaring up at her in disagreement.

"No," he hissed, then mumbled something about Gran again, but Megan shushed him.

She came down to him, took his hand, and helped him up the hill. The terrain was a bit harder on the slope. She felt the ground crunch under her shoes. Near the top, roots of one of the bushes pulled free and she slipped. The weight of her brother pulled her back and they tumbled down the hill. She grabbed at rocks and shrubs in search of leverage, scratching open her arms in the process.

Finally she got hold of a sturdy branch, halting her descent. In the struggle one nail had torn into the flesh beneath the nail, so deep that she had to bite her lip. It didn't hurt that bad at first, until she saw it, then it burned fiercely, like biting into a raw onion, which she would never do again. She felt like crying, even tried to make that moaning sound before the tears come, but it came out like a hiccup, and then she began to panic. She tried to cough but the wind had been knocked out of her. She couldn't move, couldn't get up and couldn't breathe. The harder she tried to breathe, the more difficult it was to get fresh air in. Then, all at once, her lungs opened up and a gush of air sailed through her airways, her alarm subsiding for a brief moment. She sat there for a while, gathering herself, until her breathing was back to normal. She struggled to her feet and looked for Dillon. Off to the side, she noticed his body in the bushes. He just lay there. Still. He was never still, only when he was sleeping, and even then his face twitched the whole time.

"Dilly?" she called softly, whimpering, reluctant to make too much noise. Her mother had warned her to be quiet, but Dilly was not moving.

She crawled to where he lay and kneeled next to him, tears drowning her vision. She wiped at her eyes and stared at him. He lay still, both legs spread out and his arms folded close to his chest. His blonde hair was covered with blood and his eyes were shut. Dillon was her responsibility. She couldn't allow something bad to happen to him. He had to be alright.

"Dilly, get up, silly." She poked him a couple times, but got no reaction. "Get up."

The moon provided enough light for her to take a closer look at his head. There was a cut across the back of his head, not too deep but bleeding a lot. Rolling down the hill, Dillon had slammed his head against a protruding rock, rendering him unconscious.

She studied his chest like the nurse had taught them at school. She noticed he was still breathing but his body felt cold where he pressed against her knees.

"Dilly," she whispered into his ear.

To her utter relief, she heard Dillon groan softly.

There she was, scratched and bruised, halfway up the hill, her brother out cold. She was on her own. She tried to look to the bottom of the hill, hoping to see her mother. But a strong burst of wind rushed up the hill and hit Megan in the face, cutting across her cheeks and almost stealing her breath away. Her eyes began to water. She blinked a couple of times and went back to Dillon.

Mom had said Gran was right behind them, but Megan knew Gran wasn't coming. She had seen Gran in the house. She had watched the pretty fade away in front of her, saw it in Gran's eyes, no life in them, just death, so unpretty in the darkness when the soul was gone.

223

Now she was in the dark herself. It was much darker here than in the city. The flat was cheap, but it was home, and the sound of the city was always there, a constant droning. Here it was a deathly silence and a deep darkness. At least she could see the stars better, and they were pretty. She sat and waited, the darkness closing in around her, the stars getting smaller and smaller every time she looked up at them.

David's lungs burned. When the sawmill came into sight he was a bit relieved, and surprised that he had made it here so quickly. He was still in one piece, but when the height of the grass dropped to knee-height, it was as if he could feel the bull's-eye on his back once again.

He ran past a series of wooden tar poles protruding from the ground. A protective wire fence had once been strung to demarcate the sawmill from the farm. Some poles were skewed, some broken off close to the earth, with coils of partially rusted barbed wire glinting in the moonlight. The rest of the terrain around the sawmill building was completely open, except for the odd abandoned logs scattered about. Underfoot the harshness of sand and shrubs changed to old bark, coarse wood shavings and sawdust. The earthy smell of mould and rotten wood was like Heaven to him.

He rushed across the clearing into the building, exhausted and a bit dizzy. The air was cold, and his body ablaze with adrenalin. The contrast was taxing on his body. He rested on his elbows for a few seconds, catching his breath, then surveyed his surroundings, taking stock and making plans, picking out objects, vantage points, imagining what would happen next and how. He had to be quick about it, only had about two minutes left, not enough time to set traps. But every second helped.

The building was rectangular in shape, the length of it facing the way David had come. A front entrance, the smaller of two entrances, was centred between a series of large jagged squares, which served as crude windows. The second entrance was off to the left, at the back of the oblong building, large enough to accommodate logging trucks. It was a deep dark hole which seemed to drop into the dark of night, like a pit leading to certain death.

There was a flimsy wooden staircase leading to an elevated section above the dedicated loading zone of the second entrance. The level floor hanging over the pit was either where management oversaw loading and production, or a convenient storage area. It would now serve as a position from which to orchestrate an attack, having height advantage and the cover of darkness. He only had four bullets left, not enough to make a stand.

Again he searched the building for anything useful. He had little to work with. There were two small enclosures on either side, made with wooden beams, presumably to hold off-cuts or wooden blocks. Then there was another structure along the front of the building. It appeared to be an incomplete runner for large beams. There were two rails, five metres apart, leading up at an inclined angle. The incomplete appearance was because the metal and machinery which had made it an immaculate refining tool in the logger's arsenal, had been removed and auctioned off years ago.

The other side of the building was just an open space, with dark spots which evidenced that a number of large and expensive equipment had once been there. No other place to hide. No other objects to shape into weapons. Nothing.

The moonlight fell through the rutted window openings and cascaded into the building at a warped angle, creating a collection of elongated shadows across the two small enclosures, wooden staircase and incomplete railing system.

225

David removed his jacket, flung it over a broken beam of one enclosure, and adjusted it to catch a bit of moonlight. At a glance it could be mistaken for a man hiding in the shadows. Satisfied that it would serve as a momentary distraction, he made his way to the staircase. He picked up a large piece of wood and waited. Almost immediately he heard the two men crunch through the shrubs and long grass, entering the clearing very cautiously.

He raced up the staircase as fast, and as quietly, as possible, keeping close to the wall, blending into the shadows. He silenced his rasp breathing, calmed his heart. The roof's broken, rusted metal sheeting creaked softly above his head. Becoming one with his surroundings, David almost heard the multitude of insects moving around the building, like a symphony of creeping and crawling. If tension had a sound, this would be it. He felt the terror, the segue to the madness.

David threw the wood into the darkness, near the spot where he had displayed the jacket. It *clanged* loudly against the metal housing, sounding like a muffled gunshot. He took aim at the smaller entrance, waiting for them to enter his sights, but they remained outside. He willed them to step into the light, so that he might remove their light. He prayed that it would be this easy. A simple aim and shoot and goodbye. He was waiting for them, patiently waiting for them to come for him. For nearly five minutes he kept his stance, primed, ready, finger crooked around the trigger. When everything is poised and tightly wound, five minutes felt like a decade of waiting, and every second like an interrogation. In anticipation of the showdown, sweat was streaming down his forehead and across his forearms. Since removing his jacket, the cold night air clung to his long sleeves like bacteria. It felt as though he was frozen in his pose, rigid, cold, icy air inhibiting his mobility, yet he was perspiring like crazy. The suspense was killing him, slowly.

He waited another two minutes before moving. He abandoned his hopes of a quick shoot-out and adapted accordingly.

His calves were cramping up because of all the running. He moved slowly over the decaying wood, flicking his eyes down at the floor to avoid stepping on rotten patches or broken boards. He remained careful not to reveal his position or to lose his footing, keeping near the wall, in the shadows, like a personified whisper. Not once did he emit a sound the human ear could discern.

After a gruelling few steps he found himself in the corner overlooking the entrance to the loading area, as well as the staircase.

There was no sign of the two gunmen, no sounds.

He was preparing himself for a long wait when he noticed movement below him, directly beneath the elevated section. Within the impenetrable darkness of the loading area there lurked something. He could hear it, a faint crunch of rubber over old wet bark. He could sense it, but couldn't see it. And if he couldn't see it, he couldn't shoot it.

All around the dilapidated structure lay old bricks, broken ladders, buckets, and other building rubble. Kerin stumbled over the obstacles, until she reached the white building, entering through what would have been the front door of the house.

It felt strange standing inside a house without windows or a roof. She felt exposed. She wanted darkness, safety. Moonlight fell on everything, providing little cover. There were many places to hide, but they were all temporary, and dependent on the approach of the attacker. She could hide behind walls, but if he walked around the building her position would be a plain sight.

The old servant's lodgings had two small bedrooms and a larger room with a broken down fireplace. She saw no room where a toilet might have been, assuming that there had to have been an outside toilet. She contemplated finding the toilet and hiding there, but she hadn't seen another building.

Each room was filled with bricks, bits of plaster and wood. In an enclosed section of the large room, which looked like an old kitchen, there stood an abandoned wheelbarrow missing a wheel, filled with dirt and weeds. Tall grass flowed out of every crack in the plaster, sprouting through missing bricks, as though nature was devouring the manmade structure, consuming it whole, sucking it into the earth.

She knew her time was up when she heard footfalls in the distance, followed by heavy breathing. Kerin cowered down on all fours and forced herself into the old fireplace, the only hiding place with some substance and depth, the only part not missing bricks or riddled with holes. From there she looked out over the room, unable to see what was happening in the two bedrooms. She also couldn't see beyond the extended section of wall covering the kitchen.

Only then, finding partial comfort in her choice of cover, did she remember the gun in her hands. It felt hard and heavy in her small hands. She didn't want to use it. She hadn't fired a gun in all her life and she hadn't planned on ever using one, until today. Now she faced a daunting reality: the weapon had to be seen as an object of self-defence. They had killed Margie without hesitation. This man with the mask was a cold-blooded murderer. She had to convince herself that he would kill her, and then the children. This was survival. Him or her.

She stared at the gun, half expecting it to come alive. It was a cumbersome object, not at all friendly to the feminine hand. She slipped a finger around the loop of the trigger and tried to aim it at the open doorway. She couldn't keep it steady at that angle. It was just too heavy, and she was trembling so badly that the muzzle moved from wall to wall.

One big toe was throbbing where she had kicked a brick. It was quite possibly broken, but a broken toe was the least of her worries. There was a masked man in the dark, a murderer, a monster. She would kill him, point the gun at him, pull the trigger, and kill him.

At the height of stimulus something crawled across her hand, something big, heavy, hairy. She waved her hand, smacking at the shadows, numbed by the eeriness of it all. Her fear of insects and rodents became a distant second concern when the masked man slowly filtered into view, like a shadow stretching across the tar on a hot day.

He stopped short of the house, out of sight, reluctant to enter. She could see him through the gaping windowless holes. He had big juicy lips, and he wore that awful gray mask as though it was grafted to his face. She couldn't see his eyes, just dark, empty sockets. The moonlight revealed his large weapon, an assault rifle. She wanted to shoot him through the holes, but couldn't steady the weapon.

There was more movement outside. She edged closer to the edge of the fireplace, taking extra precaution to remain in the shadows. From the front of the house there came a bump, followed by the unmistakable sound of something being kicked, then rolling away and slamming into a wall. She estimated he had tripped over a brick, the very one she had tripped over.

"Dammit," the man hissed.

She tracked his movements around the back of the fireplace, keeping as quiet as she could. She listened intently for footsteps, for any indication of his whereabouts. Then, as though he sensed her ears reaching into the night, the masked man became incredibly quiet, no discernable sounds available to her. She composed herself, calmed her breathing, and strained her neck to listen outside.

Nothing.

The last sound she had been able to follow was a rustling sound behind the fireplace, then nothing. He was gone. There was a brief moment of elation, then she realized he was waiting for her to make a move. He didn't look like the type to give up.

Something else entered her mind, something she couldn't stop. She should have stopped the thought at its birth, but it was raw maternal instincts kicking in. She thought of her children, alone on the hill. What if he had abandoned his search for her? What if he was going for the children first? Kerin knew she had to concentrate on staying where she was. She forced herself not to run out of the house to her children. As the seconds ticked by she became more on edge, waiting for any sign that the man was still stalking her, anything that would put her fears to rest. A long time passed before she heard gunfire in the distance, coming from the sawmill.

David searched the dark for signs of his foes. His fingers were tingly with the anticipation of finding a target in the dark. They had circled the front of the building, entering through the loading bay entrance. He didn't expect that. This was the darkest section of the building, confined and constricted by the elevated floor, providing perfect cover.

David spun around, his eyes searching the broken sections in the wooden deck, eager to find movement. Nothing. He anticipated their approach, weapon ready, senses tuned for accuracy. With only four bullets he couldn't afford to shoot in the dark. Wasting bullets at this juncture would betray his position and tip the advantage. That would be the end to it all.

But everything changed when he heard the faint sound of bark cracking under pressure, at the precise spot he had been aiming. Everything inside of him felt certain about the shot. There was a man there. It would be worth the bullet if it found flesh. But he never got to fire his weapon.

From the front entrance he heard an echoing shotgun blast, saw a flare of fire. The enclosure opposite the entrance burst into splinters and his hiking jacket was torn to shreds, white puffs of goose down floating in the glare. Involuntarily he shifted his aim from the impenetrable dark to a sure target. He took aim at the figure holding the shotgun, fired. The slug punched through the corrugated zinc panels beside the man's head, another beam of moonlight piercing the darkness.

The man leapt into the building, disappearing among the shadows. David tried to follow the figure, but movement at the bottom of the staircase distracted him. It was the second man. He had been ambushed. His breath caught in his throat.

Before he could take aim at the man racing up the staircase, there was a number of flashes, loud gunshots. Bullets whirred passed him. This was it. He could do nothing else, so he simply fell forward.

He crashed into a rotten section of the deck, the wooden floor boards instantly giving way under his weight, just as the shorter man exited the top of the staircase, flash after flash lighting up his angry face.

David burst through the deck, dropping into the never-ending abyss of darkness. He succumbed to the fall, embracing the weightlessness, aware that it would come to an abrupt end. It felt as though he was in flight, suspended and void of a single concern, for but a second. He was trying to fall as cleverly as possible, but there was no real style to falling or landing, especially when the ground was invisible. It was a matter for the laws of gravity. Being such, he was brought down roughly, a graceless collapse. He was able to hang onto his weapon successfully throughout the fall, clasping it around the butt and the hammer for a firmer grip.

What he had done wrong, was to shift his weight to his left shoulder. A loud snap sounded as he touched ground. The humerus bone cracked. A wave of pain shot through his body. His stomach muscles tightened and his legs pulled up to his chest. He screamed in agony, instinctively dropping the gun and grabbing his left forearm to restrict movement. Using all manner of restrained, his scream died down to a whimper, then turned into a guttural growl of anger.

There was a haphazard shot from the deck above, then nothing. David fought hard not to make a sound. He was gnashing his teeth together in an attempt to control the agony, but it wasn't easy. Almost immediately a tingly feeling crawled across his skin. The accelerated pace of his heart indicated that he was going into light shock.

He reached to where he had left the gun, searched the ground with a trembling hand. He found it without much difficulty, pushed himself into a seated position. He kept as quiet as possible, careful not to draw attention, teeth grinding the pain away. He rested the gun on his lap and slowly, and as quietly as possible, pushed himself toward the wall, deeper into the darkness.

He leaned against the cold metal sheeting, gathering himself, fighting to remain conscious. He closed his eyes; not necessarily the best option, but the only option available at the time. He distanced himself from the hurt, cutting it out of his mind, thinking about things that would burn out the pain. And then he saw her face. Kerin filled his mind, all at once, like a whooping whirlwind, drowning out his senses, the feeling in his arm subdued to a constant numbed throb.

He unbuttoned the button nearest to his navel and carefully guided his left hand into the opening. He allowed it to rest freely there, hoping it would restrict movement and support the broken bone. He didn't know the extent of the break, but every time his arm moved, a shiver of pain was quick to follow. Though quite severe, the pain was more of a nuisance than anything else. Kerin was still in danger. He had to get up. He had to get outside.

The entire sawmill had fallen into an abrupt silence. David kept his focus on the deck, occasionally flicking his eyes down in search of the second gunman. It was as dark on the deck as beneath it. In contrast, the mid section of the building was a mess of obscure shadows and beams of light. Every shadow seemed suspect. As hard as he tried he couldn't make out a thing. He took comfort in the thought that his assailants were experiencing the same thing.

David began shivering. He could feel the gun rattling in his tense grip. He held it in front of his face, followed the barrel as he tried to penetrate the dark. Nothing.

The only thing he could do was to slip out of the sawmill loading bay and into the grass. From there he could make it to the hill to help Kerin. But getting out of the building without being detected was virtually impossible.

Then there was a loud thud followed by a scurrying sound ahead of him. He wanted to shoot but it would betray his cover. Replaying the sound, David imagined the shorter man had just disembarked the wooden deck. He had to be a couple of metres away from him, still he couldn't see a thing.

He placed the gun in his lap, quietly searched the ground with his good hand, and picked up something hard. *Timing*, he instructed himself. *Timing and precision.* One man at a time, one bullet per man. Only one good hand.

He took a deep breath, calmed his nerves, constantly pushing away the pain. This was it. Make or break.

He threw the object into the dark, grabbed the gun and took aim as it ricochet off the rails of the runners. Loud shotgun fire came from beyond the deck enclosure. Dave returned fire and heard a groan of agony.

The man stumbled into a beam of light, revealing himself, one arm hanging limply at his side, the other wielding the shotgun. Before David could fire again, he saw the man's eyes freeze in absolute horror. His body stiffened and his stomach bulged forward. He made a bone-chilling gargling sound, and slowly turned around in the glaring moonlight, as a drunkard would when searching for something, clumsily shuffling his feet.

David wanted to shoot again but he was transfixed by what he saw.

Protruding from the masked man's back was the hilt of a homemade *panga*. On the other side of him was the tall, dark shape of Bveni. There was a look in Benny's eyes, something David had never seen, and something he would never see again.

The man made a coughing sound, lifted his shotgun in a manner befitting a little child, moving in slow-motion mode. Benny arched his body back and flicked his wrist, like a spin bowler aiming for a wicket. His little throwing axe whipped through the air and struck the man mid-sternum, ploughing through the breastbone and into his chest cavity with such force that the axe head completely disappeared. But the shotgun blared once more, as though in response to a final muscle spasm. Benny was flung back, a spray of buckshot ripping through his body and riddling the metal sheeting with tiny spots of moonlight. The man who had shot him was also pushed back into the dark by the recoil, both instantly deceased.

At this point David heard a slight grating sound directly behind him. He pushed himself down, lying flat on his back and took aim over his head. There, in the dark, he saw the outline of the short man, faintly visible in the large opening, and contrasted by the tall grass behind him. From an upside-down angle David opened fire, relieved to see the short gunman fall to his knees, then slowly topple over in a heap.

Megan was trying her best to pull Dillon out of the shrubs. He was just too heavy. And she was too tired. She was numb and sweaty all over. The cold night air had turned the patches of perspiration under her arms into ice packs. Worst of all, her old blue jacket was torn under the armpits. It was her favourite jacket.

Moving at mere centimetres with every attempt, she managed to pull Dillon halfway unto a clear patch across the slope of the hill.

She lay there panting, half of her brother's chest across her legs. She brushed his bloodied hair back. "Everything will be okay," she whispered. The bleeding had stopped a while back. That was a relief. She was too scared it might start bleeding again, so she didn't touch the back of his head at all. As she propped herself up into a seated position, Dillon's head lolled to one side. In the moonlight, he looked as though he was sleeping, dreaming about something wonderful. He was so pretty, and peaceful. She wanted to make it all right, but what more could she do. At least they were safe there.

Then she heard the gunshot coming from the bottom of the hill, loud and booming. Even Dillon rolled to his side and moaned irritably. Megan pulled her legs free, struggled to the top of the hill. Without drawing attention to herself she leaned over the edge, staring down at where the sound had come from.

She vaguely made out the white structure below. The building had no roof so she could see movement inside. She was sure she saw her mother's wavy hair, but even that was warped by the shadows. Megan wanted to run down and help her mother. Grandma had told her not to worry about mommy, to worry only about Dillon and herself for now. Then again, Grandma was dead.

Megan turned back, forcing herself not to watch what was happening inside the broken down house. She kept her eyes shut, tried hard not to cry, but the tears formed anyway. The harder she tried, the harder the tears flowed. She didn't want to lose her mother as well. She asked God to take care of her mother, to stop what was happening. "Please don't take my mommy. Please don't take my mommy," she whispered, crying, lost in the nightmare.

When she heard Dillon calling out her name, a renewed sense of usefulness and purpose jolted her into action. She jumped to her feet and ran down the hill to where she had left him. What she found, was not what she had expected to find at all. Who could have predicted that things could take such a horrible turn for the worse.

He lay there for a couple of seconds, taking everything in. He shook his head in disbelief, not comprehending what had just happened. He threw the gun away, pushed himself up with one hand. With a struggle, he made it to his feet, fighting to keep his balance. He was dizzy with pain. He shook his head to regain some focus. Because of the impenetrable darkness, no step he took felt like a sure step.

He went to where Benny lay. His caretaker, his friend: bloodied, broken, chest blown apart by the shotgun blast. David was confused by a sudden rush of emotions. He simply didn't know what to make of Benny's death at that point in time, or Margie's death for that matter. They were only supposed to come for the weekend, to enjoy themselves. A couple of hours ago Benny had still made a fire for them. Now it was a mess.

He heard gunfire echo across the land, and snapped back to the present.

Kerin!

He left the sawmill, running back the way he had come, back to the path. In his rush he neglected to search for a loaded weapon. He just ran, inhibited because of his broken arm, but motivated by the fact that Kerin was in trouble.

David was unaware of the poetic manner in which present was reliving past, the merging similitude. So many old memories had stirred inside him. He noticed tiny resemblances. Even the slant of the hill reminded him of the slope down which the Jaguar had crashed.

She couldn't wait anymore. She had to get out of that creepy house.

Kerin was about to get up from the fire place when she heard something, a scrunching sound, much closer than any other sound she had heard. He was inside the house. He was close, too, in the kitchen, and she couldn't see that section. Kerin froze, her fingers clutching onto the edges of the fireplace started to ache. She was crouched in a half-sitting, half-standing position, not sure what to do. She could probably make it to the doorway if she ran quickly. But if he came around the corner, there would be no escaping him. She would be trapped.

She sank back into the darkness and struggled to get a grip on the gun. She lifted the weapon with both hands, aimed it at the wall jutting out from the left. Her heart was beating loudly, adrenalin pumping through her veins like poison. She trembled fiercely, mouth dry, legs cramping, waiting.

Still contemplating a dash across the room, as she stared at the edge of the wall, right in front of her eyes, she saw the gray mask taking shape, slowly forming out of nothing. The entire mask came into view, snaking around the small wall, two vacant eye sockets concentrated in the darkness, the faint light casting the shadow of his head on the opposite wall.

"I find you," he whispered menacingly, unaware that she too had a gun.

Kerin pulled the trigger and the weapon responded, echoing so loudly in the confines of the fireplace that all sound became instantly muted. She was forced back by the recoil, slamming into the inside wall of the fireplace with such force that it drained all the air out of her body.

The slug bore into the wall a centimetre clear of the masked head, blowing out pieces of brick and plaster across the room. On impact a sharp piece of plaster splintered off, shot past the gunman with such velocity that it cut through the gray mask and sliced open his cheek. He reeled backward, stumbling over the broken wheelbarrow. He tried to regain balance, but succumbed to the rule of gravity and fell across the kitchen floor, losing his gun in the process.

Her eyes had been clasped shut since the gun went off. When she opened her eyes she saw the masked man's weapon sliding across the floor. Ears ringing, coughing, she tried to hear what was going on. All was silent. For a brief moment she hoped the gunman had gone, but it was not true.

For what seemed like an eternity, Kerin sat listening for sounds. Her ears were still ringing from the gun blast and her back pained fiercely. She kept the gun focused at the wall with renewed spirit, still shaking from the initial shock of having actually used it.

She heard a series of coughs from beyond the wall, and soft groaning sounds.

"Bitch," the man said in a gruff voice. "You pay for that."

Kerin heard him struggle to his feet.

What to do next? Her cover was not safe at all. She had to buy more time, get out of the house, distance herself from her attacker. If she wanted to make a run for it, it would be now or never. She mustered up all her willpower and leapt out from the fireplace enclosure.

As she rose up, she saw him. He was shaking his head, heaving loudly, as if choking on something. The mask was torn apart across the left side of his face, blood pouring from the cut. She froze in her tracks, lifted the gun over the wall and took aim, but he was on her in a flash. It happened incredibly fast. She could not react in time.

He tackled her across the chest, agonizingly hard. They flew backward. Because he was much taller than she, his shoulder-width nearly twice her size, she was able to straighten her arms and slip out of his grip mid-flight. In doing so, she pushed herself away.

The man slid into a pile of rubble near the centre of the room. Kerin tumbled to one corner, knocking into the wall. The gun skidded across the floor. She had lost her grip, and for a moment, in shock and in the darkness, she could not see anything. She groped about her, but only grabbed hands of cold rubble. She would not be able to find it in time – she could hear the masked man struggling to his feet. Kerin stopped groping and pushed herself up. She could feel her back harden against the wall, as she tried to bore backwards, but she was trapped.

He got to his feet, his arms waving about as he tried to regain his balance. He bellowed something senseless at her, his eyes wide and excited. It was the look of a woman-beater, she had seen it many times before. But this time she was ready for it. Kerin parted her legs slightly to get a solid stance. She shifted her arms as though she knew karate, and screamed, "Come on!"

Instead of attempting another tackle, he approached her with a bit more caution.

It was all an act, but it must've been a convincing one. She noticed a hint of surprise, a slight hesitation, and that was all she needed. She charged at the man with her fists balled, forearms vertically across her chest, screaming at the top of her lungs. The man instinctively raised his arms to shield himself, which was exactly what she wanted him to do.

When close enough, she stopped dead and kicked the man with all her might. She had placed her kick strategically, striking his crotch area with full force. He caught her foot with one hand, pushed her back with the other, hard enough to knock her off her feet. She fell back into the corner, her head banging into the wall.

Momentarily crippled, the man dropped to his knees, gasping for air, both hands clutching limply at his manhood. He was in excruciating pain, but fuelled by anger.

Again she looked for the weapon, but couldn't find it. Instead she tried to make good on the advantage by creating distance between the attacker and herself. She scampered toward the bedrooms, but the man had a long reach. His hand caught hold of her pants, pulled at it so hard that she could see her panties' waistband. She kicked wildly at his hand, falling backward with the effort. Again she slid across the floor.

He was on his feet again, still holding his crotch. He jumped toward the entrance, expertly scooping up his weapon. As he took aim, she ran to the bedrooms. A series of tiny explosions sounded. She heard and felt the bullets smacking into the wall behind her as she ran.

She slipped into one room, a wandering bullet flying into the area behind her, smacking into the wall opposite her. She hugged the wall tightly, exasperated, terrified, and disappointed by her efforts. She almost burst into tears.

To add insult to injury, the gunman fired another round into the room.

"Stupid bitch," he moaned. "I get you through window."

He limped out of the house. She was an easy target, no place to hide.

Megan had difficulty taking in what she saw.

Dillon sat up straight, looking at a patch of grass in front of him.

Her eyes picked up movement in the grass, followed by a soft rustling sound, and then the puff adder slithered into view. She gasped and felt her stomach tighten. Though she was glad to see Dillon awake, she almost wished he hadn't woken up at that moment. "Dilly, don't move," she said firmly.

Dillon stared at the approaching snake, his eyes wide and filled with alarm. His face was white.

The snake rolled completely out of the bushes, slithering towards her brother at a sedate pace. She didn't know snakes, but she didn't like this one. It seemed grumpy. It displayed a reluctant inquisitiveness, as though confused by Dillon's presence. But it also had a defensive manner, inspecting everything with a tilted head.

Megan didn't know what to do. She was frozen with terror. It was the strangest sensation to be so enslaved by fear. She knew she had to something, but she couldn't move. It felt as though an invisible hand had closed around her chest, squeezing her body, simultaneously keeping her hands and feet shackled. She willed herself to make a sound, to distract the snake in some way. She could see herself jumping up and down, screaming, but she was not. She stood motionless, mouth agape, fists clenched. She was terribly scared, and didn't dare move.

The snake pulled back into a taut "S" shape, and remained that way for a few seconds, taunting Dillon. Not satisfied that Dillon didn't pose a threat, the snake formed a slow loop, folding back on itself, then pulled itself forward again, edging closer to where Dillon sat stupefied. It made a terrible hissing sound, a sound that chilled the nerves. Strange as it might seem, that sound kicked Megan into gear.

A fresh dose of adrenalin hit her bloodstream like a shot of ice water. She snapped out of her trance, looked anything that could be used as a weapon.

"Don't move," she whispered again, taking a few steps back.

She reached down slowly and picked up a big rock, as big as she could hold above her head. She hoisted it above her head with all her might.

The snake coiled again, moving closer to Dillon, emitting another sinister hiss.

Megan began stomping one foot on the ground, luring the snake away from her brother, while balancing the rock on her head.

"Away. Shoo."

She kept making noise, until the snake tilted his head sideways, shifting his gaze to her. Those lifeless eyes seemed to glint in the light of the moon, burning with a supernatural evil. She almost dropped the rock when it hissed at her.

The snake rolled its body into the shrubs, again winding into an "S" shape, then shot forward, gunning at her shoes. The snake sailed forward, shifting across tiny stones and grass patches. Megan thought it would move faster. The puff adder seemed to enjoy the slow approach, goading her, snapping hostilely at the bigger stones, hissing and puffing as he charged.

When the snake was close to her, she noticed its slow approach was pure deception. The snake suddenly picked up momentum, sailing across the terrain as though it was skipping across the Atlantic with turbo jets, preparing for the strike, mapping its prey. The snake stopped in front of her, pulled back into its striking pose, wound its thick body so tight that it looked like a ram's horn.

Mid-attack, seconds before the snake could launch at her, a handful of tiny stones scattered across the surface of the ground, knocking into the snake from behind. Its flat head flicked around as though jolted by electricity. The snake glared at Dillon, hissed, vehemently.

"Hey," Dillon called, and that was ample.

The moment's hesitation was all Megan needed. She capitalized on the moment, lunged the rock forward and downward, as hard as she could. There was a dull crunch as the snake's head disappeared under the rock, hissing no more. As the rock rolled down the hill, the moonlight revealed a mess of snake flesh. It was writhing, caught in the throes of death, and no longer a threat to either of them.

But they were far from safe.

From the sawmill he could see the blue lights racing up the drive, encircling the farmhouse. He almost ran to meet the police, but decided against it. He went to the hill instead. Kerin needed him.

He was running as fast as he could, which wasn't very fast. When he left the sawmill, the intensity of the cold night really struck him. His arm was swollen and half of his body was numb, but that made the pain worse. The adrenalin was only enough to keep him going at a steady jog. He had no weapon, either. He only hoped that Kerin was still alive. He couldn't give up on her.

When he wiped sweat from his brow, he noticed his hand was covered with blood. He inspected his head as he ran. There was a deep cut across the scalp. He could not remember receiving it. Yet, there it was, as deep as pain and leaking life.

He broke away from the path, forcing a shortcut through the shrubs. He put his hand out to cover his face, crashed through a barrier of myrtle bushes, and stumbled into the clearing around the broken-down structure, bumping his arm in the process. The pain instantly died away when he saw the gunman a couple metres ahead of him, screaming at shadows, waving his gun at the open windows.

David, running at full pace now, stooped low and picked up a broken brick among the rubble. He rose his arm high, as though attempting a tennis serve.

When the man heard him, it was too late. He turned around just as David brought the brick down on him. It smashed into his face, crunching through skeleton and nose, driven into his skull. A random shot rang out as his muscles tightened, smacking into the ground beside him. The man gargled, became lifeless, then toppled over.

David dropped to his knees, next to the man's body, spent and broken, exhaustion finally getting the better of him.

"Kerin!" he called, out of breath. "It's me."

She reluctantly crawled from her shelter behind one wall, searched the terrain with wild curious eyes. "David?"

"Hey," he said, smiling wanly. "You're okay now." And then, succumbing to his body's demands, he passed out and fell forward.

Her relief had been short-lived. Seconds ago she had been looking at the dying snake with a sense of accomplishment. Now she was looking at Dillon, who lay on the ground clasping his right ankle, screaming hysterically.

She had looked up just in time to see another puff adder retreat into the shadows. As before, she was shocked into silence. It took her a while to comprehend that there had been two snakes.

Megan knew snakes were dangerous and after tonight, she would hold unto that fear for the rest of her life.

"It bit me! It bit me!" he screamed.

Again Dillon's manic screams gradually coaxed her back to reality. She shook her head, then ran to him. She pulled her brother away from the shadows, to a rocky section where the shrubbery were not as dense.

Dillon was going ballistic, rolling around, hitting his right leg with clenched fists. The more she tried to calm him, the more he screamed; the more he screamed, the more she panicked. As she watched he became more and more sluggish in movement. His screaming turned into a spine-tingling moan. Soon he just lay there.

"Dilly, you're making it worse," she said, then she did what any other child would do. "Mom! Mom!"

She was calling her mother. Only Mom could help. She kept calling until her voice was hoarse. Then, rounding the corner below, she saw her mother rising beyond the shrubs. Megan jumped up and ran to meet her. She broke down and began crying when she felt her mother's arms wrap around her.

"Snake," she said. "It was a big, ugly snake."

"What snake? What happened?" Kerin asked in alarm.

"Dilly was bit, mommy. By a snake."

Her mother went to Dillon while Megan recounted what had happened. She began inspecting his swollen leg. She hadn't dealt with snakebites before, but she could tell there was need for concern.

David felt a degree shy of comatose. His muscles burned. His body was exhausted. He was hot and cold all at once, his mind not sure how to feel.

"Wake up, dammit!"

It was the second slap that reached into his dreams and sucked him back to reality. He sat up straight so violently that he head-butted Kerin in his confusion. His breathing was hard, frantic. His eyes were wide, scanning his surroundings. He was in a poor state.

"Elizabeth?" he whispered, but she was nowhere to be found. He looked at the woman in front of him, rubbing her head. "Kerin?"

When the pangs of pain filtered through, he looked down at his broken arm, grunting as he adjusted his hand.

Kerin was crying.

"What's wrong?"

"Dillon." She pointed to the boy on the ground in front of him. "Snake bite."

David jumped to his legs, too fast for his body, then dropped to his knees again, fighting hard to stay awake. He was tired, spent. He couldn't focus on a single thought, his mind all over the place. He was unable to do anything pertinent. Megan and Kerin were looking at him with expectant eyes, wet cheeks glistening. Looking at Dillon's clammy face, he noticed how much it resembled the faces of his own boys.

He got to his feet, slower this time, cautious not to fall over again. His arm, firmly tucked into the opening of his shirt, hung so that it limited movement of the limb. Whenever it did move, an intense ripple of pain shot through his body, making him cringe. He kneeled down beside Dillon.

Kerin lifted the leg, pulling back the material. Even at night, David knew exactly what he was looking at. Snake bites had a certain look about them. Two little dots, red swollen skin that looked like melted plastic, unmistakable. The bite was recent. Dillon's ankle was nearly twice it's normal size. Even his socks were stretched across the bloated flesh.

All his first-aid and survival training seemed so far removed from his memory. Acting on instincts, he unfastened his leather belt and pulled it free in one motion.

"Here, loop it around his leg underneath the knee. It's not swollen there yet."

Kerin lifted the leg, which brought about a fresh burst of screams. She looped the belt, hooked it through the buckle and fastened it.

"Tighter. As tight as you can. Like that. Yes."

Using some of his own blood he painted a red T on Dillon's forehead. An old army habit, to indicate to field medics that there was a tourniquet that had to be released.

"Now what?" Kerin asked.

"I saw red lights at the house. Ambulance or fire rescue. Either way, they'll have stuff to fight the venom." He rose to his feet, pulled his shirt straight without trying to upset his arm. "Quick, put his arms over my shoulders and his bum on my forearm, like so." He held out his right forearm to illustrate.

"You can hardly walk."

"There's no time. Just do it."

She nodded, complied, placing Dillon's backside into the crook of his arm, leaning the boy forward so that his head rested against David's neck. He felt Dillon's breathing against him, slow and warm.

The weight of the child was surprising at first and took a while to adjust. It brought back memories, like taking his own boys to bed when they fell asleep somewhere.

"Hey, buddy. Can you hear me?" he whispered. Dillon moved his head up and down in his neck. "Hold on tightly, okay? Don't let go." David felt the boy's grip tighten ever so slightly.

They ran in the direction of the house, David setting the pace, Kerin and Megan trying to keep up. He ran towards the billowing smoke, towards the comfort of flashing lights. With every step, the commotion at the house grew nearer and brighter. Once or twice, Dillon's grip weakened and he almost slipped out of the grip, tipping backward in an absent manner. David slowed down, hoisted the boy up, told him to hold on tight, waited for the head to move up and down, then ran on.

They had been running for a while when a glaring flashlight lit up their sights.

"Stop there! Police!" a woman screamed.

David stepped out of the light to reveal Kerin and Megan behind him.

"We need a doctor! The boy is hurt," David called, and as an afterthought, "Snake bite."

Two more officers joined them, a series of light beams playing across the night sky.

"Medic! Where's the Medic? We got a snake bite over here," a deep guttural voice, then softer, "Snakes on site. Repeat, snakes on sites. Use caution."

There was some commotion, all a blur to him in his state, and then he felt someone pulling at the boy. David was far-gone. He didn't even feel Dillon's weight being removed. David couldn't focus his eyes on anything. Whether the sudden introduction of light, or the blood loss, or the exertion, or all of these, didn't really matter. He was swaying from side to side, kept upright by his inability to surrender. His health and his condition no longer mattered.

"Mitchell is ill," he mumbled at the medic, unaware that he had used the wrong name.

"I'm a paramedic, sir. I'm here to help."

Slowly he relented his grip on the child, rocked back and forth, vaguely aware of what was happening.

"Tourniquet, right leg," he said as two men in red jumper suits placed Dillon on a board. He saw one loosening the tourniquet to prevent pooling, and then, the world turned upside down, and an immediate darkness wrapped around him.

CHAPTER 12

His shoes sank into the rich dark earth. Heydenrych didn't care about his shoes. They were just that – shoes. Useful for walking, partially useful for kicking suspects. He moved the tips up and down, rolled his shoulders, shifted his head. There was a lot of tension in his neck. He was due for a back and neck massage.

"Detective!" a uniformed officer called from the other end of the scene, out of breath.

Detective Inspector Tomas Heydenrych flicked his head back at the road and pulled on a second glove, allowing it to slap against his forearm. He loved that sound. Not many detectives used gloves these days, but he trusted the basics of investigating.

"There's a car coming," the man mumbled, resting against a tree, a chubby finger pointing at the main road. "What must I do?"

"Probably Sunday hikers. Send them away. This is a crime scene. And block off the road. Stop all traffic coming in."

"Ja, ja, ja," the officer mumbled in Afrikaans and waddled off, sulking. "Why don't you come play the flipping traffic."

"What was that?" Heydenrych called but the officer was already gone.

Josh Collins rose up from his haunches with youthful ease, scratched his head with a gloved hand, visibly irritated. He was Heydenrych's new partner. Like all rookies he had a lot to learn, and, unfortunately, Heydenrych had to teach him. He disliked newbies, preferred partnering with older cops, men who had experience. However, he was not young anymore. There were no older cops to learn from. He was part of a dying breed. Now he was the experienced old detective to partner newbies with. He still felt young and eager enough to learn things. What could he offer young ambitious detectives? What had he learned in his years as detective? Not much. The only kernel of wisdom he could share was this: CYOA. Cover Your Own Ass! Other than that, pray you catch bad guys, and pray even harder that you make it through the day.

Collins slipped in the mud, but steadied himself against a tree to prevent falling.

"Dammit. Look at my shoes."

"Hey, buddy," Daniel Cupido said. "Mind your step. You messing up the scene."

Cupido was the forensics expert, a genius, the closest thing to Hollywood crime-series material. When he spoke, detectives listened.

"Sorry. Bought these shoes yesterday. It's so muddy here."

"It's Cape Town, mid-winter. What do you expect?" Cupido looked at Heydenrych, rolled his eyes, shook his head.

"He's right you know," Heydenrych said. "This place is a slop."

"You can say that again."

"What do you see that I don't?"

"I see nothing."

251

"Come on, Danny. You always find something."

Cupido snapped off a series of photos, said, "Not this time. The fire was fierce enough to destroy most of it. Rain soaked what the fire didn't burn. Maybe Sheila will have more luck."

Since relocating to Cape Town, he had worked with Cupido and Sheila Mzimba on every case. They had gelled instantly, a strange little team. Now Collins was joining them. Awkward.

"Where is she?"

"She's coming. Forgot something."

"So why didn't the car explode?" Collins interjected.

Heydenrych appreciated interaction. Most new detectives never asked questions; they just stood there looking at you, sometimes taking notes, drinking coffee, smoking. Besides, it was a good question.

"This is not America, *boet*. Cars seldom explode." Cupido being blunt. "I've done forensics twenty years. Only two explosions resulting from burn-outs. One time the fire heated the tank until it blew. Other time the tank was pierced. If the tank is close to empty, no bang. With this one, might be the rain doused the flames."

"And the car is a diesel model. Less flammable than unleaded," Heydenrych added. "The danger here was the battery exploding, but BMW has a safety feature that disconnects both terminals in a crash. At least the bodies are whole."

"Hey, boys!" Mzimba called in a pitched voice as she stepped into view.

The boys greeted in unison.

Sheila, a forensic pathologist, had a hyper demeanour, a bubbly personality that infected listeners. She was short, moved and spoke fast, like a squirrel, with a mixed African-European accent and an extensive well-educated vocabulary. He had yet to see her unhappy.

"What's up, Doc?" he joked.

Mzimba rolled her brown eyes, large and opal, behind those spectacles, like a teenager with a secret, or a small alien on drugs. "Ag, Tommy, man, forget about the PHD. I'll never leave you guys for private practice."

She stepped down the slope, careful not to get mud on her hiking boots. "Not just another car crash hey?"

"Nope. This was intent," Cupido confirmed.

"No tracks coming or going, just the BMW," Heydenrych said in thought. "But there was someone here, and he or she was brought here."

"You seem so sure," Collins remarked.

"Someone started the fire."

"True, but that doesn't mean he was in the car," Cupido said. He stepped closer to the wreck, pointed his pen at the back seat. Collins and Mzimba leaned into the open windows and inspected the inside of the car. The back of the front passenger seat was completely burnt, leaving a firm metal structure clasped around a dead body. There was a heap of ash behind the seat. It looked like material debris. Burn marks and dark soot was heaviest around this section.

"The fire originated here. Fire damage gets gradually less from this side of the car. Still, doesn't mean our fire-starter was a passenger."

"If there was another car, where are the tracks? Not even heavy rains can hide tyre marks." Heydenrych carefully walked around the back of the car toward Mzimba, engaging Collins and Cupido on the opposite side. "That window was open at the time of the crash."

"What do you mean? There are no windows left," Collins said.

"There is less glass on that side, and the chips of glass stuck in the runners don't go all the way up. All the other windows have the approved standard ratings stamp in the corners except that one. The rest of the window is still inside the door panel."

"That doesn't mean someone sat there."

Heydenrych removed a black handkerchief from a pocket, something he had learned over the years. The dead had a smell that didn't go away easily. He leaned closer and peeked over the dead body in the back seat, the nauseating stench of burned flesh creeping into his nostrils through the handkerchief. He smiled knowingly. "Yes it does, and he was armed, too. Look at this guy propped up into the corner." He crouched low, aiming an imaginary pistol at Cupido and Collins on the other side. "It's a defensive stance for cover, or returning fire. He was shot point blank, and so were the others. Sheila, we need to check the bodies for slugs. Probably untraceable, but we can keep them on file."

She nodded, smiling so enthusiastically that she showed her big white teeth.

Heydenrych studied Sheila's features. Her gloved hands moved over the bodies with a perfected finesse, poetry in motion, wide keen eyes searching for clues. It was important for forensics to work through a scene while the detectives were around. The name of the game was information. As much as possible, as soon as possible.

"There are too many what-ifs." Collins frowned.

"There are always question marks. So, try this, take a step back." Heydenrych illustrated, and Collins did as he was told. "Look at the site, Josh. See it from a distance, as a whole. Things should call out to you immediately. You need to take it in fast, as if it was taking place right in front of you. Look at the evidence. It must be a flash."

Collins, frowning, looked at the site. Heydenrych pointed out the deep grooves in the mud. "The tracks indicate the car breaking through the shrubbery, ploughing through the woods there. That means the driver left the gravel at full speed. He was unconscious, or in distress. The front passenger had to be shot at close range before crashing into the tree, not after. The bulk of his body is turned around so he was facing the back seat when he was shot. There is a bullet hole in the windscreen in front of him, either exit trajectory or a miss. The way the crack in the windscreen makes semi-concentric waves like a messed-up cobweb, indicates the bullet travelled from the inside out. In a head-on crash the windscreen normally cracks from the bottom up, where the bonnet folds, and from the outside in."

"You can tell all that by looking at it?"

"Once you've seen it a couple times, it becomes second nature to spot the difference. You just know that's what happened, like tasting the difference between merlot and cab. The devil is in the details, and we spend our days chasing the devil."

Cupido put a little yellow cone beside the passenger door and gestured toward the front section. "Found a weapon."

Heydenrych narrowed his eyes. "The victim's?"

"Unless it fell forward when the car smashed into the tree," Collins offered as he moved closer.

"No, Tom's right," Cupido remarked. "You don't burn evidence and leave your gun behind. Know bad guys are generally dumb, but this guy took time to start a fire, so he cleaned up."

Mzimba grunted softly. "Ha-ah, Tommy. You are not right, hey. That one was shot, but this one, the driver, no entry or exit wound. But there is something. A shoe print. Looks like a heel."

Heydenrych, covering his nose, pushed his head inside to investigate. The driver was slumped over the steering wheel, his head and shoulders visible. The mark was near the base of the head, where spine met skull. When the airbag burst, a cloud of talcum powder had puffed out over the man's body. Talcum powder was non-flammable, thus preserving the scene. The other bodies were partially charred, but the driver was only slightly burned around the legs, his jeans having melted into the flesh in a sickly manner.

He studied the horseshoe-shaped mark closely. Bruises received moments before rigor mortis sets in, turns blue-purple quickly as the blood coagulates, preserving the impact like a carbon copy. The mark was definitely from a shoe. He had seen these prints before and recognized it on sight. Whether in mud, wet cement, a flower bed, on a wooden cabinet, or on a dead body, a shoe print always looked the same.

"Clever girl." He smiled at Mzimba.

"Hey, I'm not here for looks. Ha-ah! I work." And then, that smile.

"I stand corrected. He wasn't shot. But we need an ID ASAP." He studied the driver's face. Though contorted and warped by the shard of plastic protruding from one cheek, he looked vaguely familiar. "Think I know this guy." He stepped back, looked at the three dead bodies, his scrutinizing gaze stopping on the big body in the back seat. "And I'm sure I know who this is, too."

Everyone stopped what they were doing, anxiously waiting for him to do what he did best. Any cop worth their salt, knew that cases were either solved at lightning speed, or else it took years. The first couple hours were crucial.

"I'll bet you my Sunday overtime this is Roelf Lassen. And the two in front are his goons."

"Why do you say that?"

"I arrested this guy in January. He was our prime suspect for the Gerald Moksoena killing. Moksoena had to testify against Lassen. There was no evidence, of course, so he walked." Heydenrych rounded the car, wiped at the partially blackened licence plate. "The licence says WULF. On the streets Lassen is known as the German Wolf."

"Gang killing?" Collins asked, stepping back a few paces, then began shaking his head. "I mean, this is still Cape Town after all."

"No, not a gang killing. You think the fire starter acted out of self-defence? Maybe they brought him here to kill him?"

Heydenrych liked Collins but didn't know what to make of his detective skills yet. The big shades hanging from his collar, the shiny new shoes, all gave the wrong impression. There was

KING OF SORROW | James Fouché

probably a detective inside dying to come out, and Heydenrych would be the one to set that detective free.

"Sounds plausible. But whoever he was, he didn't make a quick getaway. He took time to cover his tracks, slip into the woods. We need to check all traffic fines coming and going. Hopefully someone was in a rush. Collins, find out if taxis or busses were running a route that time. Check the nearest stops and filling stations, and have someone question staff on duty. Danny, we need some photos of the shoeprint." He turned to Mzimba. "Let us know when you do the autopsy. The trajectories might show if he was tall or not." Back to Collins. "There's nothing more to do here. Let's bag what we need and hit the streets. The media will be all over this when they hear we lost another beloved kingpin."

Before they reached the Focus, Heydenrych had already informed the captain, who called the SAPS media and public liaison officer. The press was either a valuable ally or a splinter. The liaison officer was the go-between, the one who sugar-coated facts with a delicate diplomacy when dealing with journalists or reporters. He had to be slick, smooth-talking and able to lie with a straight face.

Collins drove while Heydenrych scanned through his own notes, replaying events, analysing. When they reached the base, Collins went to make them both Ricoffy, the policeman's breakfast. Because it was Sunday, there were only a few people moving around the department.

Heydenrych had barely reached his desk, when his phone began vibrating. He answered, listened. He never had a chance to say a thing. He only listened, and then the line went dead. When the call had finished, he sat looking at Collins for a long time. His partner was sipping at his coffee, eating an old muffin.

"What?" he asked, spewing out bits of muffin across the desk.

Heydenrych was unsure what to make of the phone call. People seldom called in with information about a murder, even less seldom before it hit the media. And why call his direct number?

"Hey, what's wrong with you," Collins asked with a hint of concern.

"We have a problem. We got an anonymous lead."

"What, a tip-off? Something coming or something gone?"

"Guy said whoever killed Lassen, paid the German to arrange the George attack."

Collins shook his head. "What George attack?"

"Exactly. Let me make a call to find out."

Collins, using youthful initiative jumped to his feet and shouted, "Anybody know about an attack in George?"

It was Ben Ndlovu who leaned back in his chair and looked at Collins, a tired, irritated expression on his face. "Don't you watch the news?"

"I was working."

"So turn on the TV. George is front page news."

The Antagonist sat looking at the images on the television. His mind was blank. He hadn't imagined things would turn into a public spectacle.

On the screen he made out a number of police officers in uniforms, forensic investigators, yellow tape strung around trees, white sheets with bloodied patches over bodies, a lone photographer flashing away from behind a police van. At the bottom it read: FARM ATTACK IN GEORGE.

He'd been following the news since it broke that morning. He watched, he sighed, he sank deep into his living room couch. It was Sunday morning, and he was feeling very confused.

The other fascinating Sunday headline had a startling contrast: GANG KILLING IN TOKAI. The media had such a blunt way of announcing news. The news had reported Lassen's demise with a pinch of salt, making it out to be a divine form of street justice which had claimed the life of a notorious villain. In contrast he was staring at a public display of victimisation in George. The poor little millionaire who had been attacked on his private estate. He wondered why Lassen was seen as a mercy killing by vigilantes while Harlem was showcased as another terrible farm attack.

Then the media accidentally disclosed that none of the gunmen had been black, so that ruled out racial implications. One reporter caught wind of the Harlem Properties sale, hinting at all types of corporate corruption. It was a fiasco.

Shit! The last thing he wanted was for the link between Lassen and Harlem to be discovered. He jumped onto the couch, pressed the power button, then flung the remote across the room. He couldn't watch anymore of it. It was too depressing. He felt like hurting a small animal.

South America it is! Yes, South America, then by boat to an island somewhere, or some other godless country where no one would come looking for him, where SA Rands could be converted into a life of luxury, and where governments could be bought. He had purchased the tickets yesterday. It cost a bloody fortune but at least he had the tickets. It was now a waiting game.

He certainly didn't need this shit. He'd given the matter some thought. If he collected his foreign accounts and left a scattered paper trail, he could disappear. This was real life. Bad guys get away with crimes every day.

And there, standing on the couch in his white bathrobe, The Antagonist began to realize that he had become the antagonist. He was the criminal, the bad guy, the object behind the headline. He was rather nonplussed by this revelation. It felt more as though his life made sense for once, as though he had been living a lie his whole life and was only now discovering himself. In a flash, he re-evaluated his life and found it to be a house of cards, neatly plastered together with lies. Could it be that one was born evil and never know about it? Had his pride, his intrinsic view of self, prejudiced the truth hiding in the darkness of his soul? Had he been lying to himself more than to others?

One thing was sure, lies or no lies, life was about to get difficult. The truth always hurt. Already he was considering what to do about his girlfriend and her daughter. There was no easy conclusion. He had no clear thought about that, and he didn't really care about it either. It was as though his callousness had been validated. Cutting them off and never giving them another thought seemed like such an easy thing to do.

This mess with Harlem was more of a distraction. The only link between him and Harlem was Sendiwe. That was his one obstacle. He had promised to deliver Harlem Properties on a platter. That was no longer an option. The company was damaged goods now. The sale would still go through, pending an investigation, but that was a long-term effect of a tragic incident. Right now, the company was a high risk for everyone involved. Media was all over it, waiting for filth to surface. It was a public affair and he had to distance himself. Luckily Sendiwe was as corruptible as a Johannesburg traffic officer, so The Antagonist only had to make it worth his while.

As if summoned, Sendiwe's name began flashing on the display of his cell phone. He let the phone vibrate for a while before answering, thinking before doing for once.

"What a lovely mess you made."

The Antagonist hated that smug voice, that condescending tone of someone who knew he had the upper hand, the bargaining chip.

"Hey, I didn't make anything. This is not *my* doing," he said through clenched teeth.

"Of course, not. You're the victim here."

There was a long pause. The Antagonist was reluctant to say anything.

"This little oops changes everything." Sendiwe spoke in a playful, yet demanding, tone.

"What do you want?"

"Well you can't give me what I asked for anymore, can you? Who wants Harlem Properties now? I wouldn't touch it with a dead hooker's hand." Sendiwe coughed on the other end. The Antagonist hoped he was choking on something. Then Sendiwe's mocking voice resumed. "I don't need that publicity. There's no time."

"So, what do you want?" he repeated.

"What do you think? I want money. That's one thing you have plenty of, so you can buy my silence."

The Antagonist clenched his fist until his nails cut into the soft tissue of his palm. It always came down to money, the root of all evil, even his own.

"You have more money than Kenya. Why do you need more?"

"I don't need more, I want more. And my money is not your business."

"How much?"

"Hundred million. That is reasonable."

"Fifty."

"This is not a negotiation. I'm going below seventy five."

He felt like smashing the television screen to bits. He closed his eyes and bit his fist to alleviate some pressure. What could he do, but agree to the terms.

"I need time to get it."

"I don't have time. Your flight to Brazil leaves Tuesday morning, doesn't it?"

He unclenched his fist, flabbergasted. How did Sendiwe know about his ticket to South America.

"How did ..." He restrained himself. It didn't really matter how Sendiwe knew. He had booked it with his SA identity for a reason. He wanted a trail to South America. He wanted authorities to get lost in the maze of deception of the corrupt South American judicial system.

"Never mind how. I don't care where you go or what you. I care about my money."

"I'll need a bank account number for the transfer."

"We can meet tomorrow at eleven to do the transfer."

"Monday night? Same place?"

"Yes."

"Alone?"

"I'll bring my driver as a witness, in case you have other plans."

"I'd rather you come alone."

"Either I bring my driver, or the police."

Again, The Antagonist considered his response. Technically the money was not an issue. He had enough money saved away. Most of it wasn't really tied up. He could have money available in hours. Everything was done electronically, even bribes and corruption. Hiding money was no longer difficult.

"Tomorrow. Eleven," he agreed.

Paying Sendiwe for his silence was not a problem, but he had no intention of paying. He had other plans.

Twice in one week was a new low. She hadn't been to a hospital in years, partly because it reminded her of the beatings, the buried past. Now she had a whole mess of memories to replace that one with. Waking up in hospital with a hangover, now here in George.

She sat beside the bed, trying to replay events leading up to the attack. She couldn't. When she closed her eyes she saw gun flashes, masked men, blood, and Margie's face. There was no logical way to digest everything all at once. It would take time, a very long time indeed.

"I'm so sorry," David said again in a husky voice.

He looked battered, bruised, humiliated. A section of his hair had been trimmed back, revealing a bubbled piece of flesh where stitching had been done. His arm was in a sling and he had a black eye. One leg had a thick bandage, covering a wound. She noticed a faded tattoo on his shoulder, an eagle in flight, quaint. Probably an army thing.

Looking at his injuries, Kerin felt cheated. She had a small cut on her arm, some minor aches, pains, and bruises. She had survived the ordeal, but had very little to show for it. It was a blessing, and Dillon's encounter with the snake even more so. They had administered anti-venom in time. He was fine. Random muscle spasms but no long-lasting tissue damage. Her children were safe now. To assess the nature of things, police officials had advised Kerin to place them in protective custody, just until police had a chance to investigate. She was so utterly perplexed by events that she agreed willingly. She had consoled the children, but now she needed time on her own.

"Sorry for what?"

"For all this, for everything."

"Why? It was not your fault?" Even if she wanted to blame him, she couldn't.

"If I hadn't invited you to George ..."

She shook her head, stopped him short. "I wanted to come. It's not like you forced me."

She almost expected him to start crying. It looked as though he was fighting back tears. He seemed like a sure, strong man, confident about the way of the world. Yet, here she was, the strong one, pushing him up, accepting and forgiving.

"But your mother."

"Don't, please. Not yet."

"I just don't know why."

She took hold of his hand. His fingers were clammy, but not as weak as she thought. He closed his fingers around hers, stared at her.

"It's okay. We're here now, so let's just get through it."

They spoke for a while before an officer interrupted. He explained that they needed to answer some questions and make a statement. He told David that a detective would be with him shortly, then guided Kerin to a small coffee shop. There she met with Detective Tomas Heydenrych. He was a tall man, touch of gray, a detectable heaviness to his soul, no wedding ring. She instantly felt at ease, as she had felt with David. They were alike in many ways, not just physical.

The detective greeted her, smiled and pulled out a chair. Over coffee, the detective began asking some light probing questions in a polite manner, mindful not to turn an innocent questionnaire into an interrogation. He had clever, sincere eyes which peered into her, searching for signs of deception. They talked about the incident for an hour.

"Why did this happen?" she asked when they were done.

The detective considered the question, pushed the edge of a piece of paper back into the folder, closed the notepad.

"Mr. Harlem is a wealthy man, and wealthy men have enemies. Comes with the package, I guess. We will investigate the incident."

The detective arranged police escort to a guest house where she would stay the night. A woman named Jocelynne had made all the reservations. Apparently David and the kids would join her there later.

Two photographers were camped outside the hospital entrance. Police kept them at bay when they left. Soon she was booked into a guest house in Wilderness, sitting on a big bed looking at the news. The photo they showed of her was the one from her waiter card. It was a terrible photo: no make-up, no smile. She looked like a criminal. She turned the television off and rested for a bit, listening to the sound of the sea outside. The waves were lapping at the long stretch of beach, fighting with the sand, pushing it this way and that.

And that was the end of it all. She had expected more of a fuss. It was an anti-climax. When she removed the trauma from the ordeal, it was no longer an ordeal. It became a mundane occurrence, a statistic and a stack of papers on some detective's desk. It was hard to accept that not much more could be done. It felt inconclusive. She wanted to know why, but what would that benefit her? Knowing why would not bring Margie back.

David was about to drift away again, when a man entered. He wore black pants, purple button-up shirt, no tie, and a bulky black jacket that accentuated his broad shoulders. He had a two-day beard stubble, intense eyes.

"Evening Mr. Harlem."

"Please, the name's David."

"Very well. David, I'm Detective Tomas Heydenrych, Organized Crimes Unit, Cape Town. You mind if I have a seat?"

David nodded. The detective pulled the chair close to the bed, sat down slowly.

"Cape Town? What are you doing here?

Heydenrych flipped open a file, put it on the bed so that he could reference it. "Flew in last night, on special request."

"Special request? What does that mean?"

"That's what I'm here to find out."

"I don't follow."

Heydenrych removed a pen from his pocket, sighed. "I'm not the most diplomatic person around. I've become a bit blunt over the years, so I'll be direct. You are not being detained at the moment. You are still the victim, but there are some hard questions that needs answering. That clear enough?" David nodded. "It's your right to have your lawyer present."

"I'm an open book," he said without hesitation. "And I've had my fill of lawyers."

"Great! So I can fire away?" Again he nodded. "David, do you know why someone would send me an anonymous tip-off about a plot to kill you?"

David shook his head, not sure what to make of that statement.

"Okay. Why would Lassen want to have you murdered?"

"Who?"

Heydenrych stared at him for a long time, a penetrating stare. He relented after a while, turned back to his file, paging through the documents until he found something of importance. David felt as though he was strapped to a lie detector.

"Roelf Lassen? Oh, we've got quite a file on him. He's linked to a number of criminal activities. Nothing solid, though. He likes distancing himself from his crimes, you see. Very clever, nice and clean. Seems he arranged the hit on your farm. Any idea why he would do that?"

"I honestly don't. I think that's something you should ask him."

"Oh I would if I could, but someone beat me to it. His car was torched Friday evening, with him in it."

"Not sure what to make of that," David mumbled.

He was feeling queasy all of a sudden. He was a bit dopey from the medication, but the pain was still there. The pain kept him awake. With all the drugs, the confusion and the pain, David was certain he had nothing to hide.

He hadn't heard of Lassen before today. He had no idea how the two incidents could be linked. Had he ticked off the wrong person? Had he been part of something diabolical without even knowing about it? He couldn't imagine any of his business ventures, past or present, meandering into the criminal realm. Yet the detective claims there is a plot to assassinate him. Who would want him dead? Harlem Properties had ruffled some feathers over the years, but that was business. Who would be prepared to kill over a business acquisition? Who would be likely culprits? Linden Sendiwe? Unless the matter had a deeper treachery. Parker was a possible threat. Would he stoop that low for a higher share price? It made no sense at all.

David became more disoriented as his mind rambled on. He shook his head, rubbed at his eyelids.

"If you take something from this conversation, let it be this: someone wants you dead. But at the same time, someone also wants you alive. I'm looking for the who. Or the why."

"I can't say. You believe in being blunt, so I will reciprocate." David shifted his pillows, sat up straight to delay the inevitable dizzy spell beckoning. "The who and the why is baffling me. I can only brief you on my business dealings, rivals and disgruntled ex-employees. It appears I'm more in the dark than you at this point." In as few words as possible, he told Heydenrych about his business ventures and those who might hold grudges, all seemingly innocent enough in the business world.

"You can obtain relevant contractual material from my office. Speak to William Botes. He'll get you whatever you need."

"Thank you. I appreciate that. There anything else you can think of? Cars following you? Strange calls?"

He retold his encounters with Parker and Sendiwe the last week, and how it tied in with the Nigeria sale. He also wanted the matter resolved, and Heydenrych seemed capable enough to find answers.

Minutes after the detective vacated the room, David slipped into a deep sleep. He was confused, exhausted. His dream was a series of short bursts, made up of uncertain thoughts strung together in an elongated spool of film, starring Kerin, only Kerin.

Tom was mulling over his notes. His method of police work was a bit different to others. He had to see something once, then his mind went to work on it. But this was not like having the total recall of a photographic memory. When he reviewed notes or replayed events, certain things illuminated and others became bizarre. The most crucial material almost always sounded too good to be true. His was the gift of discernment, the ability to see the whole picture when still fragmented and incomplete, scattered about the pages in a file. It was like looking at a box of puzzle pieces and seeing the picture come together while everyone else hunted for missing pieces. Logical answers surfaced quickly and lingered there, waiting for the right time. He had learned to restrain himself till the very last moment. This was how he solved cases.

However, looking at David's file, Heydenrych couldn't see the final picture. This type of case consumed a lot of man-hours. Interviews still had to be conducted, suspects identified and interrogated, and pressure applied. That took time. Corporate crime unfolded slowly during investigations, revealing a host of suspects as it progressed. White collar criminals used the system to slow down the case, using fake identities, false permits, stalling the process. It was either resolved within a week, or two years later, or never at all. If rival companies were implicated, it meant court orders, surveillance, interdicts, applications for arrest warrants, and so on. A mountain of paperwork ending in a watered-down jail sentence for a couple elite sniffs with expensive suits and a team of lawyers. During the hoopla, the matter would travel up the chain to another department and he would go back to unsolved cases. And should the case go International, then the Harlem file would be wrapped up in red tape.

The only way to wrap up the farm attack and the Lassen case fast, was to get a lucky clue or an eye-witness. Both crime scenes offered neither. Lassen's scene only had a partial heel print on a dead body. Forensics could give him nothing on the bullets.

The farm attack was even worse. The evidence was inconsequential. A lot of work was being done to avail little. He followed the money trail and it ended with Lassen. The German footed the bill for the Harlem hit. The attackers were nobodies, independently contracted hit men, ex-military or ex-prison, weapons untraceable. There was a never-ending pile of paperwork to be sifted through, not one piece leading anywhere.

Collins called mid-consternation with more bad news. The heel print was a dead end. It was a standard heel design used by foreign companies, nothing unique about it. His partner briefed him on the autopsies, his first live autopsy since joining the police. He pictured Collins' pale face, those desperate eyes betraying his panic.

"I'd never sat in on an autopsy before."

"Don't worry. My first one was a horror show. You'll remember this for the rest of your life."

It was a Sunday evening in George. He sat on his single bed, notes and files spread about the room, television muted. Tom was looking at the pack of cigarettes he had bought, not sure if he should light one. He didn't smoke, but there it was, still wrapped. It seemed like a promising new habit. He didn't drink either, but he had removed a whiskey from the mini-bar just in case. He did very little besides work, but he was alone now, and there was nothing else to do. The receptionist annoyed him because she kept popping gum while she spoke, and the local police irritated him with their machismo. Could it be that he missed Collins, the partner he had only met a couple days ago? Lighting up or downing tots in quick succession wouldn't make it disappear: he was lonely, and it was not a group activity.

It was well after twelve when he decided to hit the pillow.

CHAPTER 13

"You can stay as long as you want," he told Kerin. "It's safe here."

"Safe? What a strange word."

"I know. The word has no meaning now. I'm surprised you haven't jumped on a plane yet. Surprised you're still speaking to me after what happened."

Kerin scoffed, shook her head, stared out the window.

"There are guards outside. The police department is just across the road."

He was resting against a large cabinet opposite the bed, half-seated, half-standing. She sat on the edge of the bed, pushed so far back that her feet dangled in the air. She was avoiding eye contact, shifting her gaze from him to the carpet, then back to him again. Whenever her eyes fell on him, it seemed as though she wanted to say something, do something, then back to the carpet, fighting, forcing up a steely pretence. David could almost see her building a wall around her, one brick at a time, and there was nothing he could do about it. She swayed her feet gently through the air, indicating an advanced state of internal debate. She was planning her next move. He had seen this same indecision in business meetings. He had closed very few deals after it had reached this tumultuous pinnacle.

He stood up and kneeled down in front of her. His arm was still in a sling. When he bent over he had to bite his lip to counter the pain. His medication was a wild cocktail of painkillers and antibiotics. Though it numbed the pain and made him sleep like a baby, it caused severe dizzy spells.

"I can't begin to imagine where this weekend puts us. I never wanted this." He took her hand in his, felt her resisting slightly, then letting go, then resisting, then letting him hold her hand. There were tears in her eyes. It was horrible to see her so torn up. "You're probably thinking about thousand things at once. It must be terrible. There's nothing I can say or do to make this easier. In fact, I want to make it more difficult." She looked up at him. "Wait for me in George until I come back."

She flicked her head sideways as the tears began rolling down her cheeks.

"You're going to miss your flight," she said suddenly, dabbing at her eyes with a hand towel. "We must do this later."

David rose to his feet, a surprisingly difficult feat with just one arm. A white cloud drained his vision, blotting out his sense of up and down. He leaned back and steadied himself against the cabinet to clear his head. When the white gave way, he saw Kerin's hand holding his, keeping him up. There was concern in her eyes, real concern.

David said goodbye, left, made it to the airport and took the flight back to Cape Town. It was Monday morning, and he couldn't reach anyone from Harlem Properties. Only Jocelynne answered when he called. Even she was brief, saying that reporters were terrorising everyone at the company for information, even contacting her husband at home.

David had been in the media before, but never knew it would one day get this bad. The media had alienated him from his own company and all the members. He instructed Jocelynne to wait until the following week to call a meeting, to allow the dust to settle. It was business as usual and business could carry on without him present. The sale was still priority number one. Nothing would stop the sale. He had discussed the matter with Godfrey Benjamin earlier that morning. Though Benjamin showed great concern for David's wellbeing, he had no concern regarding the internal structure of Harlem Properties or the increased media attention. Benjamin had said there was no such thing as negative publicity, that the whole incident only sweetened the deal. But that was business humour at its most inappropriate form.

He spent the duration of the flight replaying all his business activities since his return. Every single action became suspect. He made lists with names, jotting down some suspect dealings that might be linked to the attack. He wrote a detailed account of his many encounters with Ashraf Parker and Linden Sendiwe. But it still made for a very thin argument.

After arriving in Cape Town, he began calling people, attempting to rattle cages wherever he could. Most of the morning he read up on Lassen, reading all articles the Internet had to offer. He cross-referenced Lassen's accomplices with the list of names he had made, but he came up empty-handed. Nothing made sense. After a number of calls to Heydenrych with new names or with more information, the detective finally asked to meet. He was on his way to meet the detective when the call came in. It was his old nemesis, Sendiwe. They spoke briefly about the attack, which concerned David. Sendiwe was not really a chit-chat kind of guy.

"You are probably calling to hear if I changed my mind about selling off to you?" David asked. He was a bit woozy from the medication, but he was still a businessman.

"Not at all," said the deep voice on the other side. "I hear you asking questions and I thought I would offer you an answer."

"What makes you think I'm interested in what you have to answer?"

"Ai, same old David. Always looking for another giant to slay."

"What does that mean?" There was a long silence. "You there?"

"Come alone tonight and you will have your answer."

"Alone? You must be out of your mind. I'll bring the cops with."

"Not necessary. Pick you up at ten?"

David thought about it for some time, reluctant but exceedingly inquisitive.

"Fine. Ten," he said, and the phone went dead.

It was a brief conversation and it changed everything. Not really what he had in mind, but it was still a lead he had to follow up.

Heydenrych had suggested a trendy coffee shop in Buitenkant Street. It was a busy place, attracting an arty crowd, mostly students or young businessmen. The coffee did him a world of good. He was on his second cup when the detective finally joined him.

"How are you doing, Mr Harlem?"

"David. Please call me David."

"Ok, David. How is the arm?"

"Good as can be, I guess. Still sore. You?"

"Been better."

Heydenrych took a deep breath, calming himself. "Thank you for agreeing to meet me. I felt it was important for us to talk a bit."

David leaned forward eagerly. "I agree, after our last conversation I kept thinking about this trip to Nigeria. It occurred to me that this guy's one son might be ambitious enough to try something like this. I'm not sure, but it could be."

"It could be anything, Mr. Harlem," Heydenrych snapped softly.

"David."

"David, look I'm sorry you are in this situation, but you can't run around conducting your own investigation. It doesn't work that way."

"I know, but it's still my company. And it's personal. I need to find out who arranged the attack. It's driving me crazy."

"And that's where it gets dangerous," Heydenrych said. "The last time a civilian became involved with a case it ended badly. And technically, you might still be in danger. You refused police protection. Do you have any idea what that looks like?"

"I understand, but I have nothing left to lose."

"I don't care. You're not doing this."

"Listen, I built this company from nothing. There were hundreds of times where I had an opportunity to screw someone over, or to do something illegal to make more money, and I never sacrificed my ethics, not once. I'm not going to let someone drag my name through the mud days before I sell everything."

"You are playing with fire. This is not a movie."

"I'm under no illusions, Detective. I'm no James Bond, but there's limited time available. Just give me 24 hours."

Heydenrych stared at him, reading him, then smiled. "Someone called you."

"What do you mean?"

"David, I study people for a living. Someone called you. You have something." He looked down at his empty cup, nodded yes. "Withholding evidence. Man, you're playing a dangerous game, you know that?" Again, he nodded. "Who called you?"

"I just need 24 hours. It might be nothing."

"It might be everything." Heydenrych put some money on the table. "Whatever happens, never isolate yourself. Here's my card, my private number." He stood up, looked down at David.

"You know, I kind of like you. But if you interfere with my investigation, I'll arrest you."

Heydenrych left the coffee shop. Once outside he made contact with the driver in the Toyota across the street and gave him a quick nod. The driver, a very casually-dressed Josh Collins nonchalantly returned the nod and continued chewing his gum. Heydenrych put on his sunglasses and walked away.

David left a short while later, robbed of clarity. He couldn't think straight. He headed back to the hotel and took a much needed nap, sprawled out across the double bed as though he was in flight.

In the parking lot, Collins was on the phone, briefing Heydenrych on David's movements.

The Antagonist was looking at her through the windscreen. She wore a floppy yellow shirt that hung loose around her breasts, red bra straps looping over her bare shoulders, loose-fitting jeans, white sandals in the middle of winter. Her feet were pale from lack of sun, toe nail polish as red as fresh blood. A young, perky and innocent-looking brunette. He never fancied brunettes, but this one was different, more sensual. A regular free spirit, girl without a care, ripe for the picking. When she brushed her hair back, her smile called out to those looking at her. She seemed to be playing with the boys, pouting her lips in a coy manner, swinging arms seductively, clasping her miniature handbag as though it carried the secret to eternal youth. Open and inviting. Such a flirt!

He was instantly attracted to her, more attracted than aroused. He wanted to see more of her, touch her. A horde of impure thoughts and images snapped inside his mind. They were of her, and of him, them, together. When he considered the possibilities of the future, his marriage and the accompanying obligations seemed invalid. Life on the run, no longer being attached to one person, was a blissful bonus. He no longer had a partner. She had become expendable, replaceable. He was free to look and engage without remorse. It was so liberating to be the bad guy.

He watched and yearned, waiting for her to see him, to invite him to join her. She scratched her chest, pulling the yellow shirt away to reveal more of her cleavage. He was panting softly, on the verge of climbing out of the car, stepping right up to her, ripping her clothes off.

She was only fifteen, but to him she looked much older. Without realizing it he began massaging himself while his other hand was gripping the steering wheel. His breathing became more intense, but he kept breathing through his nose. He was thinking about what a little slut she was, such a dirty little whore. He perceived her gaze as enticing and her manner as exotic. He misconstrued the entire scenario to fit his growing insanity. This feeling was new to him. Never before had he experienced this unbridled need to have his way with a woman.

His stomach muscles tightened as the teenager strolled across the parking lot, along the pavement and through the revolving doors. Although she disappeared into the building, she was not really gone. He could still see her, taste her, feel her. He was panting, pining for her.

However, when he closed his eyes, in a brief moment of sanity, there was a sudden flash, an image he had almost forgotten. It was his girlfriend's little brat he saw, her sweet and innocent face, smiling with delight, eyes shut, dark curls floating on the wind. He pictured her moving through the air, giggling loudly, utter joy and innocence. She was playing on the swing he had erected in their back yard.

The Antagonist opened his eyes in disgust. All the arousal was gone, replaced by revulsion. The girl he had been staring at, had evaporated as if she had never existed. The girl he had been looking at was someone's daughter. She could've been his own daughter. Then it occurred to him. He was undergoing a bizarre transformation which represented the death of his former life. He had grown from caterpillar to moth, and the rebirth was a stark contrast to previous beliefs. Had his relationship been a metaphorical stage of denial? And the fathering of her kid, a pupaic bargaining with normalcy? However it had transpired, he was finally staring acceptance in the eyes.

He drove around for a long time after that, aimlessly travelling from place to place. He had no idea what he was doing. He had a tog bag in the trunk, containing a change of clothing. Once in Brazil he could get appropriate attire and disguises to blend in. There was a laptop on the back seat, which he would toss after concluding business with Sendiwe, if business couldn't be avoided. He had transferred a million Rands to a South American account, some spending money until he got to an Asian country. The rest of his money was being reallocated to untraceable accounts. At this stage he no longer worried about the money. Screw it. Even if he lost it all, he would start again.

First step to freedom was meeting Sendiwe. He had no intention of paying. Why fight it? He had nothing left to lose. Things had spiralled out of control, but he was prepared to see it through to the end. No matter of rational thought could be applied to the situation. At this stage, it was act first, think later.

When he hit the freeway there was barely enough time left to make the meeting. He cruised through the southern suburbs, looking at the printout of his plane ticket on the seat every now and then. He parked the car in a blind corner where no lights shone and exited the car. There had been a slight drizzle earlier, only to be replaced by a nearly impenetrable white mist. The tar of the parking lot was dark, wet from the rain, but from his mid-section up the night became a thick hazy blur. His vision was limited, but that just added to the adventure.

When the large limousine finally rolled into the parking lot, he took a couple quick breaths, prepared himself. The limo was low enough to be under the cover of the thick mist. Sendiwe had brought his driver again. That didn't change a thing. The Antagonist was ready, as ready as he had ever been for anything. He noticed he was panting like a dog in heat, so he closed his mouth, forced himself to relax.

Sendiwe climbed out of the long sleek vehicle with noticeable effort. He looked unhealthy, exhausted, probably an act. Sendiwe limped to the driver's side, waited for the window to roll down and said something to the man. He tugged at his pants, propped up his shoulders and slowly approached.

Sendiwe stopped opposite him, spitting distance. He gave off an unpleasant smell, a slight chemical stench.

The Antagonist was stuck in limbo, the joyride between excitement and total calm. He was calm on the outside, but all his muscles were taut. His jaw was clenched, breathing tense. He was curling and straightening his index finger around the trigger.

Sendiwe took a deep breath, said something which would have sounded better had it remained in his mouth. He was mid-sentence when The Antagonist removed the gun. It was one swift, unprompted move. He was close enough for a sure shot. He held the gun's muzzle a few centimetres from Sendiwe's nose, his hand obscuring the bottom half of the face, leaving just the eyes. If Sendiwe was surprised, he did not show it.

David went down to the parking lot just before ten. He was wilfully placid. He had no reason to be concerned. A week ago he wouldn't have imagined being in a similar situation, and here he was. All he wanted was to know who was pulling the strings.

It was cold in the city, unbearably so. He had expected his arm and shoulder to go numb, instead it became inflamed. He felt like ripping the sling off. It caused agony when he shifted his arm.

Minutes later a limo pulled up. The driver, a short man with squinty, searching eyes, came around and opened the door for David, noticing the Toyota at the end of the lot. David climbed in and the car drove off, with Detective Josh Collins following at a comfortable distance.

David sat looking at his oldest rival, but the person on the other end of the limo was not Sendiwe. It was not the Sendiwe he had been in conflict with. This stranger looked at David with dopey eyes, shoulders drooping, shirt unbuttoned. During their meeting on Monday, David had noticed how much weight Sendiwe had lost but now the man was starting to look sickly.

"So here I am," David said after a while.

"And there you will stay until this is done," he mumbled.

"Until what is done?"

"You will have to wait and see."

He was alone and not sure exactly why he was there. He was on drugs, recuperating, but his subconscious nudged him into compliance. He had to know. So there he was, exercising patience, no idea what to expect, waiting to see whatever he was there to see.

Sendiwe said little during the trip. He was vague and shifty when he finally did speak, avoiding direct questions. This was enough to set the alarm bells in his head on the loud setting. They drove through the southern suburbs of Cape Town, occasionally sailing through fog patches.

"Boss, we have a tail," the driver said.

Sendiwe glared at David, shook his head. "Your friends?"

"My friends?! What do you mean?"

"White Toyota. Behind us. Been there for ten minutes," the driver said calmly.

"Doesn't matter," Sendiwe said. "You know what to do."

David looked around but couldn't see a thing in the fog. "How can you see anything in this," he asked the driver.

The man smiled, studying him in the rear view mirror, then closed the panel between him and the passengers. Not the response he was expecting.

The driver made a series of fast turns, first accelerating, then slowing down until there were no headlights following them.

David wondered whether Heydenrych had called for the tail. He was beginning to regret not asking for police protection. There was a certain recklessness about what he was doing, but it was too late now.

Finally the driver turned into an abandoned parking lot in an industrial area and came to a halt. They were surrounded by vacant shops and deserted factory buildings.

"I wanted Harlem Properties, still do," Sendiwe began. "Tried everything to get it, but you wouldn't give up, would you? You should've sold it to me. Would have saved yourself a lot of trouble." He leaned forward, glared at David. "This life is not for you. You're a guppy in a shark tank."

David said nothing. His medication was no longer clouding his judgment. He was in a potentially explosive situation. He was considering exit strategies. Earlier David had noticed the strap of the driver's shoulder holster. Alone with his arch nemesis and an armed limo driver. Not a desirable place to be.

David began positioning himself for a strike, shifting to the middle of the backseat. From there he could manage one swing with his good arm and try for the door.

"Stay here," Sendiwe ordered and climbed out. "Enjoy the show."

As the door slammed shut, his phone began vibrating. It was Heydenrych.

"Harlem, is that you?"

"Yes," he whispered, watching as Sendiwe went to the driver's window and exchanged a few mumbled words with the man.

"Where the hell are you?" demanded Heydenrych. "My guy lost you in Woodstock."

"In a parking lot somewhere, still looks like Woodstock. Can't talk but stay on the line," he whispered as the driver rolled the dividing window all the way down.

"Boss said you should look out the windscreen."

David put the phone out of sight but close enough for Heydenrych to hear the conversation or to trace the call.

Sendiwe was barely visible through the fog and the poor lighting. He vaguely made out another figure. No face, only legs and one hand, but there was something familiar about the posture, though.

"Who is that? Can't you turn the lights on?"

"No, don't want to spook this guy," the driver whispered. "He's edgy. Never know what he's gonna do. I don't trust him."

David stared at the driver, considered his demeanour, his vernacular. Most South African men his age had served an obligatory military term. But it took a fellow soldier to spot those who had remained in service longer.

"Where did you do your basics?" he asked.

The driver stopped chewing his gum, looked at him in the mirror, then back at Sendiwe. "Middelburg. Operations, PF."

David nodded. He had also been Permanent Force, also stationed at Middelburg. Every soldier had been to Middelburg at some point. Reconnaissance and operations, especially snipers, seldom spoke of their time in the army. This was the extent of a business card exchange between ex-militants.

"Name's Curtis."

"David."

"Listen, David, you looking for a driver?"

"A driver?"

"Yes, things are getting pear-shaped over here, you know? This guy, I don't know anymore."

As though the words had some power in them, the mystery guest took out a weapon and aimed it at Sendiwe. The Antagonist didn't hesitate. He squeezed the trigger. There was a loud echoing bark, ripping through ripping through the silence. The bullet struck Sendiwe between the eyes, a spray of blood and brain matter sailing into the white mist.

Instantly that old memory flashed inside David's mind again. He saw the shape on the other end of the rifle's eyepiece, the head bobbing, the puff of red smoke settling over the body. More death, more murder.

Sendiwe's body was still tipping backward, when The Antagonist took aim at the limo. He fired twice, both slugs slapping loudly against the windscreen, not penetrating the bulletproof glass.

Curtis instinctively ducked, reaching for his weapon

"Your window," David said. "Close the window."

It was too late. The Antagonist stepped around the front end and opened fire. The driver rocked sideways, a fresh burst of blood spraying across the backseat. One bullet tore through the driver's eye socket, another ripped open the back of his head, blond hair flopping like a loose toupee. A stray bullet glanced through the dividing section, just missing David, and ricocheted off the rear doorframe.

David pulled back, lost his balance, and collapsed on the limo floor, landing on his injured arm. Fresh pain surged through his body. When he sat up again, he saw bright stars popping across the limousine's roof. He shook his head, calmed his breathing, closed his eyes, listened. He heard a sticky *drip-drip-drip* sound. Blood was flowing from the driver's dangling head unto the leather upholstery.

"You inside," a familiar voice called. "Come out. Now!" It was a deep voice, and as a scream it boomed into the night.

David looked for a weapon of some sort, something he could throw or hit with, but saw nothing. Then he remembered the driver's shoulder holster. He kneeled down near the cabin partitioning and searched the body with his free arm, peeking over the partitioning every few seconds. He tried not to get too much blood on his hand. He had to get the driver's gun. It was his only hope, his only defence.

After a frenzied search, one finger caught on the sling and he traced the leather strap to the holster. He felt around frantically for the weight and reassurance of a weapon, but the holster was empty. Again he scanned the body, cringing every time his hand dragged through a patch of blood. Nothing. A deep sense of doom came over him. Without a gun he had no sure way of defending himself.

He tried wiping his hand clean on his jeans, but the blood wouldn't come off.

At that point, cornered, broken, and beaten, he saw the gun, a snub-nosed Magnum, nestled in the carpeted compartment beside the driver. Before being shot, the man must have gotten a hand on it. David would never fit through the partitioning. The only way to get the gun was by opening the front passenger door. Even if he burst out the other end of the car and rushed to the door, it would take too long. If he could delay his attacker, he could distance himself. A moving target was a difficult target. There were no other options available to him, and no time to ponder.

"Come out now or I torch the car!" The Antagonist called out.

Then he remembered the phone. The connection was still open. "Heydenrych, you there?" he whispered.

"What happened? Are you alright?" the detective demanded.

"I'm in deep shit here. I'm trapped in the car and they."

"We have reports of gunfire in Woodstock industrial. Do you remember seeing factory buildings nearby?"

"Yes, yes, yes, that's it. Just come dammit."

"We're on our way. Five minutes."

The Antagonist returned with a container. He began pouring petrol over the driver's body, whistling as he emptied the container into the vehicle.

"Shit, man, I don't have five minutes."

"We're coming, just keep the line open, okay?"

David put the phone on the floor within earshot so that Heydenrych could hear. He took a quick breath, opened the door, slowly.

The culprit stepped into view, emerging from the heavy fog. David's breath caught in his throat, taken aback by the revelation. They stared at each other, neither saying anything for a couple of seconds. He tried putting the pieces of the puzzle together, but it made no sense. He couldn't comprehend the deception. He had been blind to this type of betrayal. Had he been so unaware? Had he been so blinded by his own personal issues?

"Evening, David. Glad you could fit me into your schedule."

"You?" David said, very much confused, speaking loud enough for Heydenrych to hear. "William? I don't understand." He looked at Sendiwe's body, spread out over the wet tar. "You shot Sendiwe? You killed Sendiwe!" David formed his words clearly.

William was stroking his leg with his left hand. He seemed jittery with delight.

"William Botes?!" he asked again, louder this time. He had no idea what William and Sendiwe had been up to, but he didn't have the luxury of time to think it over.

"Yes, David. I get it. You have eyes. You are surprised. Bla-bla-bla. Now get out of the car."

David complied as slowly as possible, not moving too far away from the car. He could still jump back into the car to buy some time.

"What is this?"

"You really have no clue, do you?"

William didn't have his usual nervous twitch. He looked excited, but in complete control of himself.

"No clue about what?"

"The property? The one I sold to your company for more than 200 times its value?"

A stampede of property details charged through his mind. David was trying to catch up, but he was more preoccupied with his plan to retrieve the driver's gun. If William had indeed overvalued a property prior to purchase, how did he convince the board? Company rules prohibited purchases where members had shares or co-owned the optioned properties.

"Which property?

"The Opus," William said, weapon still aimed at David's chest. "The jewel of Malmesbury. A twelve-phase monstrosity. Your next big money cow. It's all fake."

David was brought up to speed all at once. He replayed the stacks of paperwork flowing across his desk, approvals, valuation reports, insurance policy quotations, enquiries. It happened in a flash. The funnel had been unblocked and information was streaming through.

"The Swartland Opus? Parker negotiated The Opus deal. It was viable on paper, a sound investment. I remember the paperwork."

Botes's smile broadened, a cold, menacing smile that gave David chills. Absentmindedly, revelling in the surprise, William lowered his weapon.

"The paperwork? Bet you didn't look at that ROD?"

"You faked the Rights of Development? Why?"

"Come now, don't be ignorant. Government would never allow a shopping mall in Malmesbury. You should've seen that."

"I wasn't there to see it," David said loudly. "You pushed it through the system when I was away."

"Oh, that's right. You were on vacation."

"Vacation?! I was in mourning, you twit. My family just died."

"Stop with the drama already. Families come and go."

"You know, the sale would go through even if the ROD was fraudulent?" David changed the subject back to the crime.

"Maybe. But I couldn't chance it."

"So you tried to have me killed. Why?"

"For crying out loud. The money, David. The money. If you die, insurance pays out. All asset loans are settled, member shares go up and I'm home-free."

"All for money? Didn't I pay you enough?" David shuffled backward in mock surprise.

"Don't you understand? It will never be enough. Never! Something inside of me wants more. I *needed* more. I was burning to have it all."

David never cared about money, so it was difficult for him to understand William's motivation. Blatant thievery right under his nose, months after the accident. He had had so many things to worry about that he had never noticed the corruption within the company.

"Greed," William said absentmindedly, staring blankly at the gun in his hand. "Greed is a terrible thing."

"If you want money, then take it. I never wanted this, the money, the hype. You can't take it with you, man."

"Now that, right there, that pisses me off. You have what I want and you don't want it nearly as much as I do. You don't deserve to have it."

"And you do?"

"You have no idea," he said, then jumped into a fit of rage. It was a transformation of sorts. His eyes became wild, and his face began to twitch. The veins in his neck popped and the muscles in his forearms bulged. He forced the gun into David's face, screaming at him. "You have no bloody idea! Try having a sadistic old bastard breathing down your neck, looking at you like you were the putty in the toilet, telling you you'd never amount to anything. I was blamed for everything. It was always me. Even when mother died, it was my fault. I've been working every angle to get to the top, and it took too long, so I had to make a shortcut."

"I didn't have to take shortcuts to get here," David said defiantly. "It took years of hard work. Nothing in life is easy."

"You fought for what you have, yet you're prepared to give it all away in the blink of an eye. And that makes you the weak link, not me. Sorry, David, you're forcing my hand here."

William had been building himself up to a point of no return. His finger formed around the trigger, going for a kill shot. Time up. This was it.

David immediately crouched low, ducking behind the limousine's boot. There were two loud blasts. The first zipped over his head, smacking into the brick wall behind him, the other punching into the car's metal body.

He ran for the front passenger door.

William, anticipating this, lunged into the car from the opposite side, his gun in hand, and opened the rear door from inside as David rounded the back end of the limo.

The rear door flew open just as David passed it, with such force that it knocked him off his feet. He stammered sideways, tripped over the curb, and fell backward onto the pavement, sliding over the cement and crashing into the wall headfirst. On impact with the wall there was a sudden blinding flash of light, lasting only a millisecond. Pain ensnared his entire body, from his arm and head, pulsing through him, running down to his toes, his fingertips.

Instinctively his mind was slowing every action down for him, like a coping mechanism. He looked up at the limousine. The rear door, which had been used to knock him off his feet, opened further. Slowly William's gun barrel drifted into view, then William's vengeful face.

By sheer virtue of instincts, David kicked at the rear door. It swung back into place and slammed shut, forcing William back into the car. There was a loud bang in the confines of the car as William's gun went off, a yellow flash behind the tinted windows.

William screamed loudly, a scream of sheer agony, and then there was silence.

David pushed himself up into a seated position. His head felt twice as heavy as before. It rolled forward until his chin rested on his chest. Looking down, he saw blood pouring over the front of his shirt, a steady stream, flowing from the old cut to his head, over his cheeks and onto his chest.

From inside the car there came a vehement guttural growl.

David forced his head up and examined the limousine. There was another loud growl from within. He pressed one leg under his body and forced himself to his feet, using the wall for support. He was dizzy, but he had to get to the driver's gun.

When the door opened again, David half expected something to leap out of the car. Like a predator stalking its prey, William slowly entered the ominous yellow glow of the street lamps, crouched on the floor of the limousine's passenger section, rage in his eyes. But his face seemed warped, as if his jaw-line was askew, one centimetre out of sync on both sides. There was an entry wound, a small round hole, beneath his right cheek, where jaw and neck joined. The exit wound, on the other side, was an absolute mess of flesh and broken teeth where his left cheek had burst apart. His mouth hung open, revealing bloodstained teeth and a swollen tongue. The skin around one bloodshot eye and both wounds had already turned a light purple, a result of contusion and severe haemorrhaging. Testimony that there was no more humiliating a blow than a self-inflicted one.

Wounded or not, William's eyes were still hungry for violence, gun in hand. He spoke, but it came out as a terrifying gargling sound, infecting David with an unfamiliar dread.

David reached into his reserves for adrenaline. He pushed himself away from the wall and managed three quick steps before collapsing to his knees behind the open door. He crawled to the front passenger door, opened it and searched anxiously for the driver's weapon.

William was out of the limousine, stumbling this way and that. He collided with the wall, spewing out blood on impact. Then he saw David, halfway into the opening. His eyes instantly lit up.

Finally David latched onto the weapon. He flipped his body around, took aim and fired, lightning fast, final. He shot William thrice, centre mass. The force flung him back against the bricks. He slid down the wall, bloodied mouth open, eyes lifeless.

David sighed, then began to shiver all over. The gun was shaking and rattling in his hand. His muscles relaxed all at once and he just let go. The fight in him left his body in waves, each wave bringing more peace than its predecessor. He sagged down the inside of the door panel until he lay flat on the tar of the parking lot, face down, one eye staring at William's body.

David could feel himself drifting away. His breathing slowed down. Soon he couldn't even hear his own breathing anymore. All he could see was Kerin, holding that can of pepper spray, make-up running down her cheeks. And then everything went black.

Epilogue

A controlled swarm of gnats hung in the air near one of the trees. They began twirling about as though gaining momentum, then migrated to an old lemon tree. Birds, bees, fragrant blossoms, bright garden colours and all the other wonderful attributes of mid-spring seemed to be accentuated. The contrast between the early morning heat and the fresh breeze cutting inland from the coast, enlivened the senses even more, adding to the delight.

Life almost leapt out at her. And in light of recent events, this virtual rebirth posed a delicate threat. Nature was nudging her on, urging her to forget, but forgetting was such a complex verb.

Dillon was running around on the grass, grabbing at the gnats above his head, then bounding over logs and raising his arms in triumph. His encounter with the snakes had wasted away during the last three months. Megan, on the other hand, still kept a watchful eye over her brother, every now and then pulling him back and giving a suspicious branch a wide berth.

"I'm not sure," she said, staring at the cup of coffee on the table.

David rolled his shoulder over. Two operations later and he still can't use his arm properly. With a series of court cases around the corner, the last thing he wanted was more operations.

"Am I wrong to think there is something between us?" he asked.

"I don't know," she said, then added, "I can't replace her."

"You're right. You're nothing like her, but I'm not looking for someone to replace her."

Both stared out over the restaurant's large colourful garden, following the children as they ran across the lawn. A long, painful silence followed, which was interrupted when the waitress came to clear the table.

This was the third time they had met since the attack in George. The children enjoyed the outings. David always picked places where they could enjoy themselves. But it was getting to that stage where decisions had to be made. Things were either going to get serious, or the outings would occur less frequently. She did not want either option to become a reality. But, in life, decisions are never easy to make.

"I don't know, David. I just started a new job. Things are so hectic at the moment." She shook her head and sighed. "Besides, why me? We come from different worlds. I don't see how this can work."

David got up and moved away from the table. "Come," he said and held out his hand.

She took it without hesitation and walked with him down a series of steps and into the garden. His hand was warm. He held her hand tightly, but did not squeeze it too hard. Even at a distance, and with the breeze playing through her hair, she could smell him. He had a pleasant smell about him, like warm bread and spices.

He plucked off a sprig of lavender and slipped it behind her ear, combing her hair back as he did it. She hadn't felt a man's fingers through her hair in years. As his finger tips slipped through her hair it felt as though he was stroking her soul. A rush of emotions ran through her body like rain. At once she became aware of how neglected she had allowed herself to become.

"I honestly don't know," she said again. "But I'm willing to give it a try."

They stared at each other for a brief moment, smiling hesitantly. He rested his forehead against her forehead and put his arm around her.

ABOUT THE AUTHOR

James lives in the beautiful Garden Route region of South Africa with his wife and their two Jack Russell terriers. He fills life with a vast number of hobbies and interests, from sailing to travelling to hiking, learning different languages and trying his hand at musical instruments. When he is not plotting his next crime novel, James writes about wine, food and travel on his personal blog.

Follow or contact James here:

www.jamesfouche.com

@james_fouche

http://jamesfouche.wordpress.com/

www.ingramcontent.com/pod-product-compliance
Lightning Source LLC
Chambersburg PA
CBHW061944170626
46813CB00006B/2530